Becoming Mrs. Right

by

Sherri L. Lewis

In loving memory of Davidae "Dee" Stewart, one of the original write-or-die chicks. Thanks for your love as a sistawriterfriend and publicist. Miss you much!

In loving memory of my friend, James Riley. Thanks for all you taught me and so many other single, Christian women about becoming Mrs. Right. ☺

And in loving memory of my sweet "baby cousin," Shanita Diane Leverett. You are loved and missed. May you rest in the arms of Jesus.

Acknowledgments

As always, so thankful to God for the gift of writing. I love it when you take over and I just sit there and take dictation. You're my favorite and I love writing with you!

Thanks to my family for all their love and support. Mommy, Daddy, Joy, Kelli, Michael and the boys: I love you always! To my dear niece, Jordan Elise Lewis-Kelly: Aunty is soooo sorry for leaving you out of the acknowledgments for the last book. Thanks for being my inspiration for Brianna and Morgan. One day you'll grow up and be able to read all of Aunty's books, but until then, you can read this part. I LOVE YOU! ☺

Thanks to my faithful besties Yvette Broughton and Kathleen Soto. Thanks for always being there for me even though my wanderlust has taken us far apart. Thanks to my write-or-die chicks Rhonda McKnight and Tia McCollors. Let's keep doing destiny and writing together!

To Felicia Murrell: thanks for all you've taught and shown me about the Father Heart of God! Thanks for being a true friend and always challenging me to see life from heaven's perspective.

To Madre Yaya: thanks for reading this while I was writing and giving me feedback that helped me keep going. And thanks for enduring all those days when I *was* Shauntae and got on your last nerves talking ghettofabulously.

To the best roomies in the world, Bessie "Nchengelita" Nchenge and Susan "Susu" Enjema: thanks for filling my life with sooooo much love and laughter. You are absolutely priceless and I'm looking forward to us taking NATIONS together!

Thanks to my Bethel Atlanta family for all your love and support and to my Bethel Cameroon family for helping me to live out my purpose and destiny. I love you all so much!

Thanks to all my readers and book clubs for your continual support. Thanks for all your emails telling me how my books affect you. You truly keep me writing!!!!

Thanks to all my Facebook friends for all your help with my "research." Instead of having to use the horribly slow Internet here in Cameroon to Google facts, all I had to do was post a question and you guys would give me more information than I needed within minutes. You make it easier to write US-based fiction while living in Africa.

One

Shauntae slammed down the phone. She hated, absolutely *hated* Devon Wright. He had ruined her life in so many ways and this was the worst yet. First, he had kicked her out of his house when the child they had together was only six months old. Then he hadn't married her like he had promised. But putting out an arrest warrant on her so she had to leave Atlanta? That was too much.

She had called to beg him to lift the warrant, but he wouldn't even listen. He just said no without giving her a chance.

Shauntae's door creaked open and her mother slid into her room. "So that's what you been keeping from me, huh?"

"Why you sneaking around listening to my phone calls?" Shauntae sat up on the bed and folded her arms. She stared straight in her mama's face.

Mama folded her arms and stared back. Funny that she wasn't a very big woman, but something about the way she talked to and treated people always made her seem a foot taller than she really was.

The bedroom felt too small for the both of them. It looked like the many rooms Shauntae had grown up in, moving from housing project to housing project with her mother, sister, and brother. How in the world did she end up back under her mother's roof? She swore when she left that she would never, ever, come back. But here she was. Sleeping in a twin bed like she was a child.

Not only was she not a child, she was gonna have a child in about five months.

After a few minutes of staring each other down, Shauntae finally looked at the floor. Her mother sat in the chair opposite the bed. "You been here three months with a warrant out on you and ain't said nothing?"

"It's a Georgia warrant, Mama. Can't nothing happen out here in California."

"What you do?"

Shauntae knew she wasn't showing no motherly concern. She was just nosy and liked drama.

"It ain't important."

"It is important. If I been harborin' a fugitive, I got a right to know what she did. I needs to know if my life is in danger." Mama chuckled. "And here I thought you was coming home because you missed me and wanted me to help you raise your child."

"Whatever, Mama."

They sat there in silence for a few moments. Shauntae knew her mother wouldn't leave without knowing what happened. And the next thing out of her mouth would be how Shauntae had stayed there rent-free for three months and had been fed and provided for. She didn't feel like having all that thrown up in her face, so she started trying to figure out how to tell the story.

"Me and Devon started having problems—"

"Started having problems? Y'all been having problems since before your child was born."

Shauntae glared at her mother. "He got a girlfriend and things got worse."

Mama laughed. "Ain't that always the case? Another woman comes along and they get all tight in the pockets."

"Yeah, and I lost any chance of ever making Devon marry me."

"Shauntae, please. That man was never gon' marry you. You shot too high with that one. Ain't he a computer person or something like that? How you thank you was gon' keep a educated man with that empty head of yours?"

Shauntae pressed her lips together. The last time she had cussed her mother out, things hadn't ended well. She had found herself on the street at age seventeen, left to pick up the same habits she had grown up hating her mother for. Shauntae had sworn her life would never get so low that she had to hustle men to pay rent and eat. But she had ended up doing exactly that.

Her mother kept fussing. "I done told you don't be looking for no smart, rich man to marry you. Give 'em some good sex that keeps their pockets loose for as long as you can. If you do get pregnant by one, let it be a married one you can blackmail for money because he don't want his wife to know. That's how you get set for life. But this dream you got of marrying somebody rich and smart to take care of you, you need to let that go. Like I been telling you for years . . ."

Shauntae zoned out from the sermon her mother had preached too many times. Mama was right, though. She should've never thought she could hold on to Devon Wright. When she first met him, she had planned to do him exactly like her mother had taught her.

She had seen Devon a few times in one of the many upscale bars where she went looking for sponsors. He was always drunk and she could tell he was dealing with some serious mess. Some woman had probably broken his heart and so he needed some sexual healing, which she was all too ready to give.

After the first time they hooked up, he was drunk every time she went to his house, half naked under a long trench coat. He invited her into his bed without much conversation. She didn't have to fake being smart or having some culture like she usually did.

The day she realized she was pregnant, she knew she had struck gold. Devon was a good man. He wouldn't be like the many other guys who slid her money for an abortion. Plus, she had waited to tell Devon she was pregnant when it was too late to get an abortion legally. She showed up after disappearing for a few months and gave him the news. She didn't make the usual threats she made when she told a guy she was pregnant. Even though he had bent over sucking air like she had punched him in the stomach, she knew Devon would do the right thing.

And he did. She left that day victorious, making plans to move in his house and start counting the days to her wedding.

Her mother stopped her sermon and interrupted Shauntae's thoughts. "Wait a minute. Devon got a girlfriend? So y'all wasn't messin' around anymore?"

Shauntae sucked her teeth. "Devon hadn't messed with me since I told him I was pregnant."

Mama frowned. "But you was living with him for a while. Y'all wasn't . . ."

Shauntae shook her head. When she'd moved into Devon's house, she figured they'd still have good sex on a regular, but he didn't touch her. She hadn't had the good sense to know that was a sign of how things would end up.

"How a man gon' live in the house with a woman and not have sex?" Mama asked.

"Like you said, he was educated." Shauntae never told her mother that she "caught" Devon while he was drunk. Things changed after he was sober. "When I moved in, he wanted to talk all the time. Always wanted to know what I was thinking, what I thought about stuff that happened on the news and in politics and all sorts of stuff. And he was smart. And it didn't take him long to realize that I wasn't." Shauntae had known after their first conversation at the dinner table that she was in way over her head.

It wasn't long before he would hardly speak to her. He would come home from work and watch TV or read or be on his computer. Which was fine with her. As long as she had a roof over her head and food to eat, it didn't matter if he talked to her. In fact, it was easier not to have to try to sound intelligent or understand what in the world he was talking about.

He took her to her prenatal appointments and bought whatever she wanted for the baby. He bought some things for her, too, but she didn't push him too far. When she asked for too much, he would get salty with her.

The only time he was really nice to her was when she went into labor with Brianna. So nice, it surprised her. The whole time she was in the hospital, Shauntae pretended in her mind that Devon was always nice to her, paid attention to her, and really cared about her.

"After a while, it got to the point where he couldn't stand me, so he put me out."

Shauntae didn't tell the whole story. When they brought Brianna home from the hospital, Shauntae knew she wouldn't make it. Brianna cried and wanted to eat every two hours. After a couple of weeks of having to get up and make bottles, Shauntae was mad she let her breasts dry up. It would have been easier to breastfeed in the middle of the night. But she didn't want her titties all floppy. It was clear by then that Devon wasn't going to marry her and she wouldn't be able to catch a new man with saggy titties.

Brianna was always peeing and pooping and needing her diaper changed. Sometimes she cried and Shauntae couldn't figure out what was wrong with her. She couldn't imagine why any woman would trap a man by having a baby because it was too much work. It woulda been easier to get a real job.

And then when Devon's parents had come, she was completely busted. Devon was at work most of the day so he couldn't see how bad she was messing up. But Devon's mama watched everything she did. She never said nothing, but there was this look in her eye that said she knew Shauntae wasn't no good mama.

Shauntae wasn't surprised when Devon's parents said they were moving to Atlanta. She wasn't surprised when Devon told her she had to get her own place when Brianna was six months old.

She was surprised Mama was still sitting in the chair, waiting to hear more of the story. She never listened to or cared about Shauntae. The most she ever did was preach to her about how to catch a man.

"So even after you moved out and he was paying child support, he still wasn't getting none?" Mama stared at her, perplexed. "But wait a minute, if you collecting child support, why you been acting all broke since you been out here? Where your check been going every month?"

Shauntae bit her lip. "I don't get it no more."

Her mother stood up, hands on her hips. "You lost your check? You carried a baby in your belly for nine months and raised it all those years and you ain't got nothing to show for it?" Her mother paced around the tight room. "And you got a arrest warrant on you? Shauntae, what did you do?"

Shauntae sat there, swinging her legs and biting her lip like she was a little girl again. "Well, what had happened was, Brianna got sick—"

"Brianna?"

"My daughter." Shauntae rolled her eyes. "Brianna got real bad sick with diabetes and I couldn't take care of her by myself. The first time she stayed with me after she came home from the hospital, I messed things up and she had to go right back in the hospital. So Devon was scared for her to be with me. So I had to let her go live with him."

"I can understand that," Mama said. "You ain't really mother material and a sick child ain't easy to deal with. Especially with sugar. So that explains how you lost the child and the check, but what about the warrant?"

Shauntae wished she didn't have to tell the rest. "My rent got behind so I needed money bad. Even though Devon said he was taking Brianna full time, the court papers still said I was supposed to get child support."

"Wait a minute. You let the check go without going to court first? How you—"

"If you would stop interrupting me . . ." Shauntae stopped herself. She knew better than to raise her voice at her mama and wondered if, at thirty-two, she was finally too old to get slapped. She didn't want to find out, so she lowered her voice. "That's why I did what I did. I needed some money, so I picked Brianna up from school and told him to get me my check and I would give her back to him."

The next part was so bad Shauntae didn't want to say it out loud. "But I gave Brianna too much insulin and she got bad sick again and caught a seizure. The ambulance came, but right after that, the cops showed up to take me away."

Her mother frowned her question instead of interrupting.

Shauntae explained, "The first time Brianna got sick staying with me, it was because . . . I sorta kinda left her in the house alone and Devon found out about it. So he got me in trouble with this social worker who got me in trouble with the police."

Mama got up and started pacing again.

"It wasn't my fault. I was about to get kicked outta my apartment. I needed a new sponsor. I had to go."

Mama's pace slowed down a little. "Keep going."

"The police came to get me while the ambulance people was working on Brianna and I left. And came here."

"That's real low, Shauntae. Leaving your child sick like that."

"What you expect me to do? Go to jail?"

"I never once lost none of y'all to the system and I never woulda done nothing low like that."

"Oh yeah, you was a real good mama." Shauntae rolled her eyes. "The best."

Even though Mama was older, she still moved like she did when Shauntae was a little girl. Before she could blink, Mama was up in her face with her hand drawn back.

Shauntae stood up fast. "You gon' slap your pregnant daughter?"

They stood facing each other for a few seconds until Mama finally put her arm down and went back to her chair. She gave Shauntae a look that said she was lower than dirt. "So whose baby is this?"

"His name is Gary. Gary Jackson." Shauntae couldn't help but smile thinking about him. Now that was a real man. He was a much better catch than Devon. Shauntae was disappointed the first time she had went to Devon's house. He dressed like he was a serious baller, but his house was small and old and his furniture was cheap looking.

Gary had as much money as he looked like he had. Big, pretty house, fancy Lexus, expensive suits. He was a baller for real. With him, she wouldn't have to worry about nothing for the rest of her life.

"So what's his story?" Mama sat on the edge of her seat like she was watching the latest episode of *Single Ladies*.

Shauntae didn't want to hear all the mean things Mama would say if she told her Gary was waiting for her to come back to Georgia so they could get married.

Her phone rang. She looked down at the caller ID. "It's Gary. I need to take this."

Mama didn't move. "Why he calling you so late?"

"Mama, please get out. I need to take this call. And don't be standing outside my door listening, either."

Shauntae shook off her frustrations with Mama, Devon, and her whole situation so she could focus on her conversation with Gary Jackson. Even though her mama didn't believe she could pull it off, she had to find a way to get this guy to marry her.

Two

"Hey, baby, how you doin'?" Phone conversations with Gary wasn't easy. Shauntae had to try to sound proper and educated. And if she messed up, she couldn't distract him by licking her big, juicy lips or leaning forward to give him a better view of her cleavage like she could in person.

"I'm fine, love. How are you and my baby doing?" His deep voice made her stomach feel funny. Mama had taught her never to make the mistake of falling in love with a sponsor, but hearing Gary's voice made her feel some kinda way.

"We're fine."

"How's your mother? Good, I hope. I need her to hurry up and get better so you and my baby can come home."

"She's better, but I'm not sure I can leave her yet." Shauntae had gone straight to the Greyhound station when the police had come to her apartment to pick her up.

She told Gary she had gotten a call in the middle of the night that her mother was sick and she had jumped on a plane to California. He was upset that she didn't give him a quick call to let him know she was leaving. She'd said her mother was in critical condition and all she could think of was getting there as fast as she could so she could be there, holding her hand if she died. Some old Lifetime junk, but he had believed it.

"Are you sure you don't want me to come out there?"

"No!" she almost yelled. "I mean . . ." Shauntae calmed herself down. "I don't want you to have to leave work and come all the way out here for Mama. She'll pull through this."

"Shauntae, I'm not trying to be selfish but I really want to see you and my baby. Business is good right now. I can take some time off if I need to."

Panic rose up in her chest. She didn't need Gary to fly out to California and find her living in the hood in L.A. rather than in Orange County where she had told him she lived. He would see her ghettofabulous mother smoking cigarettes, talking trash on the front porch, and doing just fine . . . other than being evil.

And then he wouldn't marry her and take care of her and her baby. She couldn't afford that. This might be her last chance. It had taken her a long time to get pregnant—longer than ever before. Maybe it was all the abortions. Or maybe it was payback for what she had done to Brianna.

"They said they needed to do a couple more tests and then maybe Mama could come home. Let me see what happens tomorrow and then I'll let you know." Shauntae knew she wouldn't be able to hold Gary off much longer. Ever since she told him she was pregnant, all he talked about was her coming home.

She had met Gary pretty much the same way she met Devon. She was in desperate need of a new sponsor and so had gone to one of her favorite upscale restaurants in Buckhead.

She had studied all the men in the place. There was the man twisting his wedding ring, probably wanting to have a night in bed with a woman he didn't have to worry about keeping happy. He looked like a man who would go back to his wife quickly, so the payout would be small.

There was the rich-looking player at the end of the bar, tossing back expensive drinks. Players were real tight with they money. Shauntae didn't mind sleeping with somebody, but she had to know there would be some financial gain behind it.

Then there was Gary. He had been nursing the same drink for more than an hour. Not because he was too broke to buy another drink. His suit, shoes, and watch said he wasn't broke at all. He looked like he felt guilty to be drinking. Like drinking wasn't his usual thing, but he was nursing some pain that needed more than a Coke. Which made him a good man with a problem—her specialty. All she had to do was figure out the problem and make him realize that a night in bed with her was the answer.

"Okay, I'll be waiting to hear from you. We have to get married soon, Shauntae. We have to make this thing right with God."

"I know. God knows our hearts. He forgives us." That was the only thing she hated about this whole thing with Gary. Pretending like she gave a crap about what God thought. She had hated God since she was a child. He had never done nothing good for her. In fact, for most of her life, He had proved that even though she was supposed to be His child, He didn't care nothing about what happened to her.

"Let's pray, honey."

Shauntae rolled her eyes. "Of course, baby." She didn't bother to bow her head or close her eyes while Gary droned on about her mother's health and their baby and their future together. She inserted a few "yes, Lord's" and a "thank you, Jesus" every once in a while. She knew Gary being a Christian was her best chance of her and her child being taken care of, but that didn't mean she had to like God. She just had to make Gary think she did.

"In Jesus' name, amen," Gary finally finished.

"Amen, baby. I love it when you pray. Oh, I feel God." Shauntae wished she could fake speaking in tongues to let him know she really felt God, but she didn't want to push it too far. He might be able to tell she was faking.

"Okay, sweetness. Call me tomorrow after you find out about the test results. I'm serious, if your mom isn't out of the hospital in the next two days I'm getting on a plane."

"After your prayer, I'm sure she'll be fine."

"I love you, Shauntae."

"I love you, too, Gary." She said those words easily now. At first it had been difficult for her to choke them out. She had practiced saying them in the mirror over and over until it was as easy as saying, "I want some chicken wings and a Coke."

Shauntae hung up the phone, sat up on the bed, and waited. She knew it wouldn't even be a full minute.

"So I'm sick, huh?" Her mother slid into the room again.

"Yeah, you had a heart attack." Shauntae couldn't hide the evil smirk on her face.

"Well, glad to hear I'm doing better." Mama chuckled. "And you a church girl now?" She busted out laughing like it was too ridiculous to even think about.

"Why you always gotta be jokin' somebody? I'm trying to make this thing work."

"I heard you trying to talk all proper. So he's smart and he's a church man. Shauntae, do you really think you can—"

"Mama, I don't want to hear it. Go away and leave me alone." Shauntae got up off the bed and pulled her suitcase out the closet. She started shoving her clothes into it. She didn't have many. Only the few she'd been able to grab when she saw the police lights outside her patio door.

Her mother stood there for a few minutes, watching her. "Where you going?"

"'Bout to catch the bus back to Atlanta."

"You seriously think that man is gon' marry you?"

"All I can do is try, Mama. When I met him, the first thing out his mouth was how his ex-wife had full custody of they children. He said his children was the most important thing to him and he would die without seeing them. Kids and family are everything to him." Shauntae rubbed her barely noticeable baby bump. "So I got a chance."

Her mother folded the jeans and shirts from Shauntae's dresser and handed them to her to put in the suitcase. "Warrants ain't actually that bad. As long as the cops don't pull you over while you're driving and you lay low and live easy, you shouldn't have no problems. Still, you should see if you can get Devon to lift that warrant." She picked up two pairs of shoes in the closet and put them in the suitcase.

"How am I s'posed to do that?" Shauntae picked up another pair of shoes and put them in the suitcase. "Devon's girlfriend is the problem. Before she came along, I used to could get Devon to do whatever I wanted."

If Shauntae could have figured out a way to get rid of that sassy heifer she would have. Even if she couldn't get Devon back, he was easier to manage without a woman in his life.

Shauntae knew she was in trouble the first time she met Cassandra. She was supposed to be all holy and stuff, but when Shauntae had said something smart to her in Brianna's hospital room, Cassandra had given her a look that let her know she would've cussed her out if Devon's parents weren't there. She was probably one of those Christian hypocrites who pretended to be all saved, but was as evil as Shauntae when she needed to be.

"When I was talking to Devon on the phone, I could tell he thinks I want to come back to Atlanta to get in his pockets. Even though I told him Gary would be taking care of me, he's still scared of what I might do to Brianna."

Mama gave her a look that let Shauntae know she agreed with Devon. "Well, don't worry about it right now. Stay out of trouble and you should be all right. As for getting Gary to marry you, it's gon' take you some serious work to pull that off."

Shauntae started to say something nasty, but then she saw the look on her mama's face. The one she got when she was putting a plan together.

"If he's a church man, he's gon' want to get married quick—maybe even before you really start showing. So getting him to marry you shouldn't be too hard."

Shauntae's face lit up with hope.

Mama didn't let the hope last long. "But you learned from Devon that just because you can catch a man doesn't mean you can keep him, even if you have a baby by him. So you gotta become everything he wants and needs in a woman."

Her mother looked her up and down and then shook her head. "You so durn pretty and you got the perfect body, but . . . you just ain't smart. You shoulda done like your sister and learned how to talk intelligent and have some culture. If you had, you mighta been able to keep somebody like she's kept her husband all these years."

Shauntae didn't mention that her younger sister hadn't been thrown out of the house before she finished high school. Even though Mama had said it was because Shauntae disrespected her, Shauntae knew it was because her stepfather had been messin' with her for years. Shauntae had finally gotten grown and brave enough to fight back, so he made Mama get rid of her.

Mama handed her the last couple of pairs of shoes and looked under the bed for any more of Shauntae's stuff. "Anyway, if you get married, even if you can't keep him, you'll be able to collect child support and alimony, so that should be worth something. Two checks are always better than one."

As nice as that sounded, Shauntae didn't want two checks. She had learned from messin' up with Brianna that it wasn't secure. Something could happen and she could lose her checks and she'd be back in her upscale bars with her girls, Sherice and Candy, looking for a new sponsor.

She was tired of all that. She had to do this right, so she could get married and live in Gary's big, pretty house and drive a nice, new car he would buy her. He would dress her in the finest and she would be set for life. Shauntae got happy thinking about the life she was about to have.

"See, that's what's wrong with you." Mama's voice interrupted her thoughts. "I know that look on your face. Don't be getting caught up in no romantic dream of some good man sweeping you off your feet. You ain't that kinda girl. You ain't smart, you ain't got no class, and ain't nobody gonna be falling in love with you 'cause you a beautiful person inside. Use your face and your butt and get what you need. Forget about that old Hollywood mess. Focus on the checks."

Shauntae resisted the urge to cuss her mama out. She zipped the suitcase, put it on the floor, and sat back down on the bed.

Mama looked like she wasn't sure what to do next. Shauntae wanted to tell her not to trouble herself with trying to be sweet or saying something special. She wasn't exactly mother material either.

Mama said, "Sounds likes he anxious for you to get back."

"He said if I'm not there in two days, he was getting on a plane to come out here."

"For real?" Mama laughed. "He coming to visit you in the projects?"

"Stop playing, Mama. I get tired of you jokin' me."

Mama shrugged and sat quiet for a minute. She finally stood up. "Seems like you need to be headed to the Greyhound station. Let's see when the next bus is."

Three

Shauntae squinted out the bus window. She had fallen asleep a few hours ago so she wasn't quite sure where they were. Even though it was dark, it was looking like the desert, so she figured they must be in Arizona already. She hated long rides across the country, but she needed the three days of travel to get her mind right.

Shauntae still couldn't believe her luck. Pregnant on the first try. When she had met Gary, she had calculated that she'd be most likely to get pregnant about eleven days later. She'd have to be careful with him. He had mentioned God enough in that first conversation that he might think she was loose and trashy if she wanted to have sex with him that soon after meeting him.

She'd played the evening just right—a damsel in distress trick that brought him to the rescue and then she'd ended up in his bed "by accident." He was all guilty and kept apologizing and asking her and God for forgiveness.

But the deed was done and miraculously she was pregnant. Maybe God had finally decided to give her some attention.

Shauntae let out a deep breath and laid her head back against the headrest. She elbowed the guy sleeping in the next seat to get him up off her. When he had sat down, she saw that hungry dog look she had seen on men's faces all her life. One quick look let her know he wasn't worth nothing. First of all, he was riding the bus, so he had to be broke. Second of all, he had on a knockoff Tommy

Hilfiger athletic suit, and had a gold tooth in his mouth. Not to mention his raggedy dreadlocks. Smelled like he hadn't washed his hair in two years.

Nigga, please. Don't even sniff or drool in my direction.

Shauntae didn't write him off completely. Maybe if she smiled at him just right, he would buy her some lunch, so she could hold on to the little bit of money she had left.

She elbowed Gold Toothy in the side harder this time and she shifted his heavy body away from her. She reached up and turned his chin away, too. Nasty breath smelling like he had ate a dead armadillo off the road.

Shauntae pulled out her cell phone and called her girl, Sherice.

Sherice answered the phone cussing. "Girl, you crazy? Do you know what time it is in Atlanta? You betta be glad I just laid down otherwise I'd have to cut you when I see you."

Shauntae laughed. "Whatever, girl. I know it's five in the morning and I know you was in the club all night. You answered the phone, which means you're alone. Must not have caught nobody."

"Shut up, Shauntae. Ain't nobody thinking 'bout you. What you doing?"

"I'm on the bus. I'm on my way back."

"Devon lifted the warrant?"

"Naw, girl. But Gary said if me and his baby don't come home, he coming out here. Couldn't let that happen."

"Yeah, well, don't be thinking you gon' stay here with a warrant. I don' need no trouble."

"Yeah, yeah, yeah, Sherice. I know. I need you to pick me up at the bus station and then take me to the airport."

"What the what? Bus station to the airport?" Sherice laughed. "Aw, yeah. I got you. Text me what time your bus gets in and I'll be there to get you. And, heffa, don't ever call me at five in the morning no mo'." She hung up.

Shauntae put her phone in her purse and settled into her seat. She tried to remember whatever she could about Gary so she could get herself ready for the performance of her life.

She remembered that he had been divorced not even a year when she met him. He had showed her a picture of his two daughters. One looked like she was a few years older than Brianna and the other was about the same age. Brianna had to be what, six or seven? Something like that.

She scribbled a list of all she remembered about Gary: things he wore, things he liked, anything she could think of. It wasn't a long list because she didn't remember much.

It was time to study. Shauntae pulled out a small bag of stuff she had took from her mother's house to help turn her into Gary's perfect wife. She opened the bag and pulled out a stack of movies and her mother's portable DVD player. Mama wouldn't miss them. All she watched was soap operas during the day and reality TV shows at night. Shauntae looked through the movies to figure out which one to watch first.

She had took *Pretty Woman* so she could get an idea of the kinds of clothes she should buy when she went shopping. And for real, that was about to be her story. She had met her rich prince and her life was about to change. Shauntae let herself think about Gary for a moment. Unlike many times when she had to deal with some ugly frog to get a few bills paid, Gary was fine. His face was one she would enjoy looking at for the rest of her life. And he was nice and sweet and made her feel good. She thought about his voice and how it sent shivers up her spine.

She had took *How Stella Got Her Groove Back* and *Jumping the Broom* to study Angela Bassett. Shauntae hated that heifer because she was the perfect example of a high-society, stuck-up black woman who would look down her nose at her and judge her. But if she studied Angela Bassett's ways and, most of all, how she talked, she could become the woman Gary wanted.

Shauntae kicked herself for not learning how to talk proper like Sherice always told her to. Sherice could hold on to a smart, rich guy much longer because she could turn on this saddity heifer speech that always left Shauntae wondering if that was really her girl talking all that fancy talk. Of course, Sherice was nowhere near as fine as Shauntae was and probably nowhere near as good in bed. So Sherice spent a whole bunch of time learning how to talk good and Shauntae used her natural assets.

But not this time. Gary's ex-wife was a lawyer so Shauntae knew she had to be smart and classy like Angela Bassett.

She thumbed through the stack of Tyler Perry movies she had took. *Diary of a Mad Black Woman, Meet the Browns, Madea's Family Reunion,* all that applied to her situation in some way. There was a lot she could learn from *Think Like A Lady, Act Like a Man.* Shauntae knew she needed to learn some things about being all romantic and in love. Gary seemed like a sappy kind of a guy.

Shauntae put *Jumping the Broom* in the DVD player. She wanted to practice talking proper while she was good and awake. As soon as the movie started, the wannabe Rastaman sitting next to her woke up and leaned closer to her.

"Does this look like the IMAX theatre, nigga? This is a private viewing. Get back on your side of the seat."

His lusty grin quickly turned into a frown. "Oh, it's like that?"

"Yeah, it's like that. Leaning all over here. You need to try to be leaning on a tube of toothpaste instead of trying to be all up in my face."

His frown turned into a snarl and Shauntae wondered if he might be somebody who could do her some harm. “What, nigga? Don’t even think of looking at me the wrong way. You clearly don’t know who I am. If my man even knew you was sitting by me, you would be dead before the day is over.” Shauntae looked him up and down with a murderous glare. “Forget about him. I could do you myself.” He needed to believe that she was crazy so he would leave her alone.

He got up and moved to an empty seat a few rows back. Shauntae was glad for the extra room and for the fact that he wouldn’t be sitting there looking at her crazy when she stopped the video to repeat Angela Bassett’s lines over and over until she sounded normal talking like that.

After watching the movie and talking proper for almost three hours straight, Shauntae was tired and her brain hurt. But she felt like she had made some progress learning how to talk like Mrs. Gary Jackson. She pulled out her phone.

Gary answered on the second ring. “Hey, honey love. Give me the good news.”

Honey love? This dude was sappier than she thought. “Mama’s tests all came out good. It’s like a miraculous recovery or something. Baby, your prayers really worked.”

“Praise God. I knew they would. So when are you coming home?”

Shauntae hoped he didn’t hear the hum of the bus. “I’ll be on a plane day after tomorrow. I want to get Mama home and good and settled before I leave.”

“I can’t wait to see you and my baby. “

“Aw, I can’t wait to see you either. I love you.” It was the first time she’d said it first. Looked like the movies was helping.

"I love you too, baby."

Shauntae was about to hang up when Gary said, "Wait a minute. I have some good news of my own. My other prayers have been answered. My lawyer called and said my appeal for partial custody of the kids is going to go through. Everything my ex did to desecrate my character didn't work. Soon I will, or we will, be able to have my kids two days a week. Isn't that great news?"

Shauntae's mouth froze. *Partial custody of the kids?*

"Honey love? Did you hear what I said? We're going to be a family. Not completely the way I wanted, but definitely better than before. And when the new baby comes, there'll be a child in the house all the time. And soon after, we can try for another one."

After hours of studying the right way to talk this man, Shauntae couldn't find one word to say.

"Shauntae?"

She pinched herself. "Oh, Gary. God is so good. God is amazing and great." One of her grandmother's favorite religious phrases popped into her mind. "Wonders to behold." It sounded funny coming out of her mouth.

"I know. I feel like God is working out everything and restoring everything that's been lost. I knew you'd be happy about the kids. I know it will be a lot of work when the new baby gets here, but you're going to be an amazing mother."

After they hung up, Shauntae sat in shock. Two kids? Two days a week? She thought of having to keep Brianna every weekend once Devon put her out of the house. Remembering to feed her, bathe her, change her diapers, and wash her clothes on a regular was too much. And then when Brianna got older, Shauntae had to listen to her talk all day about all sorts of silly kid stuff. She always wanted to go kid places and do kid things. Wanted to watch stupid kid shows on television.

The thought of it gave her a headache. And there would be two of them? And instead of being at her own place where Devon couldn't watch her and judge everything she did, she would be with Gary's kids in Gary's house with Gary. This was a nightmare. A test that there was no way she could pass.

But she wasn't going down without a fight. As soon as she got to Atlanta, she'd have to get all the seasons of *The Cosby Show* and study Clair Huxtable until she *was* her. She'd spend all her free hours watching The Disney Channel and Nickelodeon to learn all she could about kids and family kinda stuff.

Instead of taking a nap like she had planned, Shauntae put in *The Preacher's Wife*. She needed to get this churchy woman thing down. She couldn't be using her grandmother's old-timey phrases. And maybe she would have to learn to do the holy dance. Whatever it took. She was going to do anything and everything she could to become Mrs. Gary Jackson and finally have the life she wanted.

Four

"Come on, Shauntae. I don't know how bad the traffic is gon' be and we need to get to the airport." Sherice was getting on Shauntae's nerves, actin' all nervous and jumpy like she was the one going to meet Gary.

Shauntae checked herself in the mirror one last time. Candy had come over to Sherice's apartment to do her makeup and help her get dressed. It had been three months since Shauntae last saw Gary and she needed to look her best. When Shauntae called ahead to let them know she was coming, Sherice and Candy had gone shopping and picked up some really nice designer clothes and shoes at the Goodwill, Ross, and Marshalls.

Shauntae knew all this wasn't for free. Them heifers would be expecting her to slide them a little something on a regular basis once she got settled in Gary's pockets. And she would. She wouldn't be like their friend Keosha, who, when she married a bench-riding Atlanta Hawks player, forgot they even existed. Keosha's dreams of being a NBA wife had came true and even though nobody even knew her man's name, let alone ever got to see him play, Keosha was living nice.

She had gotten all high and mighty and changed her name to Kayla. The first time they had attended a party at her house, Kayla complained afterward saying they had embarrassed her in front of the other NBA wives by acting all thirsty. Then, she stopped inviting them over for champagne lunches and out for shopping sprees.

Shauntae knew it wouldn't be long before she didn't hang with them no more at all.

But she wasn't gon' be like that. She was gon' take care of her girls as much as possible. Men could come and go, but her girls always had her back.

"I finished packing the bags," Candy called out from Sherice's bedroom. She walked into the bathroom and looked at Shauntae's reflection in the mirror. "Come on, girl, you look nice. We gotta go. How you gon' explain it if your man is waiting for you at the airport and you pull up in Sherice's old, busted car?"

"Girl, shut up," Sherice yelled from the kitchen. "Don't be talking 'bout my car. You don't be talking about it when you need me to pick you up from the grocery store. Next time I'ma leave yo' tail on the bus."

Shauntae was glad to be back in Atlanta. She had missed hanging with her girls. She hated that Gary lived all the way across town from them. Gas prices was high and she wasn't sure how often they would get to visit her. When Gary bought her a car, she would visit them all the time. Maybe she could convince him she needed a nanny to take care of the new baby and the other kids. Sherice could come in talking proper and looking nanny-ish and they'd be able to hang out all day.

"A'ight. I'm ready." Shauntae came out of the bathroom and struck a pose. "Let's do this."

The three of them piled into Sherice's car and headed to the airport. There was no traffic, so they got there almost an hour before she had told Gary her plane would land. They decided to park and have a drink to celebrate Shauntae's new life.

They went to the bar in the Houlihan's in the airport atrium and ordered their favorite drinks. Sherice drank a chocolate martini, Candy a Long Island Iced Tea, and Shauntae a pear mojito. They had learned to order fancy drinks for their rounds at their fancy clubs and bars. They still drank forties when they hung out at the house, though.

When hers came, Shauntae drank it faster than she usually did. If she was paying, she could sip on a drink for hours. If a man was paying, she could drink a whole lot and hold her liquor better than he could.

“You nervous?” Candy asked her.

“A little.” Shauntae looked around for the waitress to order another drink. But then she decided she needed to hold on to her little cash until Gary’s wallet was flowing easy. And since they had already bought her a bunch of clothes and stuff, Shauntae knew better than to ask her girls for some cash. They might have been as low as she was.

Plus, she needed to have all her senses straight. Two drinks too fast on an empty stomach could have her lips loose and she would forget all the fancy Angela Bassett talk she had worked so hard to learn. Sherice had complimented her on it and had only corrected her a few times since picking her up at the bus station.

“Why you nervous, girl? You ’bout to have some homecoming sex. That man ain’t had none in three months. Put it on him and he’ll be saying ‘I do’ before next week,” Sherice said. She and Candy slapped hands.

“Yeah, girl. Do what you do. It’ll be all right.” Candy sipped her drink slowly. She was a lightweight when it came to alcohol, and got real silly, real fast if she didn’t watch herself.

“It’s not the sexing part I’m worried about. I know how to handle myself in that department. But Gary . . . he’s . . . different.”

“Girl, a man is a man,” Sherice said. “At the end of the day, they all like sex and you know how to work it, so it ain’t nothing to be scared about.”

Shauntae looked around at the tables next to them. She loved her girl Sherice, but she always talked too loud in public.

Candy looked at her real hard. “You scared for real, huh? What’s different about this man that got you all scared?”

Shauntae shrugged. She didn’t want her girls seeing her all weak.

Sherice put her hands on her hips. “Stop acting hard. Tell us about the man. We your girls. Ain’t nothing so different about him that the three of us cain’t figure out together.”

Candy elbowed her in the side. “Come on, girl. Wassup with this man that got you freaked out like you ain’t one of the baddest chicks in Atlanta?”

Shauntae could always count on her girls to help her out. “Well, he’s real smart like Devon. Maybe even smarter. I know I’m talking better, but what if I don’t know what to say or if I can’t understand what he’s talking about?”

“Girl, you ain’t that stupid,” Sherice answered. “What could he talk about that you cain’t understand? What he do for a living?”

“I’m not sure. He always talking about business or something like that.”

Sherice and Candy looked at each other and rolled their eyes.

Sherice said, “What I done told you about doing your research? You get so blinded by the dollar signs that you forget to listen. Girl, you betta not mess this up again. You already birthed one child and ain’t got nothing from it.”

Shauntae could remind Sherice that she had four kids by four different dumb, broke men. Sherice was always falling for some roughneck dude and was stupid enough to have they baby when there was no chance of getting paid.

Shauntae bit her tongue 'cause she needed Sherice's help. "I didn't have much time, remember? We went out a few times, did the deed, went out a few more times, and then I had to leave."

"Girl, you supposed to find out that kinda information on the first date. You so . . ." Sherice sucked her teeth. "Anyway, the first thing you do when you get in the car is ask him how business is going. Ask him some smart questions and find out what he does. A'ight?"

Shauntae nodded. She wasn't sure what kind of smart questions to ask but didn't want to let Sherice know that.

"What kind of food does he like?" Candy asked.

Sherice interrupted before Shauntae could answer. "I don't know why you asking that. You know Shauntae can't cook nothing but fried bologna and Kraft Macaroni & Cheese. And let a good show be on and she'll burn that."

They both cracked up laughing. Shauntae didn't know if it was the hormones from the baby or what; normally she would have been laughing with them, but today it wasn't funny. "Forget both of y'all. I'll figure this out myself."

She stood up to grab her bags and leave them sitting there laughing and looking stupid, but she got dizzy and almost fell backward. Candy jumped up and grabbed her before she fell. "What's wrong wit' you?"

"She pregnant, fool," Sherice snapped. "That happens to pregnant women. Oh, I forgot, you don't know nothing 'bout that."

Candy's mouth flew open. Shauntae couldn't believe Sherice had hit that low. Candy had caught a disease when she was young and couldn't get pregnant. Which meant she could only pull short-term games and could never collect child support.

Candy put her hands on her hips and got real loud. "Sherice, you always been an evil—"

"Calm down, girl." Shauntae moved over to stand in front of Candy. The three of them had got banned from two of Atlanta's most exclusive restaurants for getting in fights that had started like this. "We supposed to be talking 'bout me, remember?"

Candy took a deep breath and sat back down. She shot Sherice an evil glare and Shauntae knew they would beef in the car on the way home.

Sherice glared back at Candy while asking Shauntae, "What do he like to do? What do he do for fun or to relax?" She turned to Shauntae and continued firing questions. "What are his work hours like? Does he come straight home after work? What is his mama like? Where is he from? What kind of clothes does he like to see his woman in? What made him break up with his ex-wife?"

Shauntae stared at her blankly, not able to answer even one question.

Sherice shook her head. "See, that's what's wrong with you. If I had your face and your body, I wouldn't be sitting here dumb, broke, and single. I'da been married by now. Or, better still, married, divorced, and then married to someone richer." Sherice rolled her eyes. "Got all the natural assets but don't know what to do with no man. Let me be pretty and be able to grow some long hair. Humph."

Sherice kept preaching, "You got to get in a man's head. Know what he likes, what he wants, what makes him happy and sad and mad and all that kinda stuff. Good sex can only take you so far. As much as men love them some sex, they can get sex anywhere. You want to keep him? You got to make him feel special, like he's the king of the world. Listen to everythang he says. And then be everythang he wants and everythang he needs. If you can make him happy and keep him happy, he'll take care of you for life." Sherice finished off her drink with flourish.

Shauntae and Candy sat mesmerized after listening to Sherice's wisdom. They somehow forgot about the fact that she hadn't successfully caught and kept a man herself.

"Looka here. This what we gon' do." Sherice leaned in close and Candy and Shauntae leaned in to listen to her. "For now, you ask as many questions about him as you can. Act real interested and impressed with all his answers. Write everythang down and then we gon' go over it and figure out how you need to be. A'ight?"

Shauntae nodded, then thought for a second. "What if he asks me something and I don't know how to answer? Or what if I say something stupid?"

Sherice pointed to Shauntae's belly. "You got the best excuse for the next few months. If anything goes wrong, fake sick, fast as you can. Thinking about his baby will make him forget whatever dumb junk you do. Or start crying and blame it on your hormones. You can use that even after the baby is born for a few months."

Candy stared at Sherice. "How you know so much?"

Sherice shrugged with a real arrogant look on her face.

Candy said, "I guess I should ask, how come you know so much but you still broke and single like us?" She busted out laughing.

Sherice's mouth fell open. "You know what, heffa? The reason you cain't catch no man is cause of them ugly buckteeth and them skinny legs of yours. You need to try to date a dentist and a trainer."

Candy stood up, her voice getting all loud again. "Let me tell you about you, skank. You always be busting on the fact that I cain't have no children, but you be popping 'em out and cain't keep 'em. You talking about how Shauntae ain't got nothing to show for Brianna, but you got four children in the system and no child support. In fact, we all know you be puttin' money on your last man's books at the prison. So the next time you wanna—"

"Hey!" Shauntae stood up between them. She looked around the bar at the people staring at them. "Stop all that. Why y'all gotta act crazy in public?" Shauntae could almost understand why Keosha/Kayla had kicked them to the curb.

"Oh, you gon' act all new 'cause you got a fancy man?" Sherice asked. "You be acting crazy in public worse than anybody."

Shauntae looked down at her watch. "Oh. It's time. This is what time my flight was supposed to land."

The argument was instantly forgotten. Sherice said, "Okay, call him and tell him your flight landed and you on your way to baggage claim."

Shauntae couldn't believe her hands were shaking as she pulled out her cell phone and speed dialed his number.

When Gary answered, he said, "Baby?" like it was a question.

Shauntae frowned, hoping he hadn't forgotten that her so-called flight was coming in today.

"Yes, it's me, honey love." Shauntae turned her back to Sherice and Candy who were bug-eyed and laughing at the name she called Gary. "I'm here at the airport in Atlanta. On my way to bag claims."

"I pulled up your flight information online. It said your flight was delayed and wouldn't be here for another four hours. How are you here in Atlanta?"

Shauntae heart started beating fast. "Uh . . . I . . . uh . . . I caught another flight. When they announced there would be a delay, I took another airline." She smiled at how fast she came up with an answer.

"How did you manage that? Didn't that cost you an arm and a leg?"

Shauntae turned back around to look at her girls for help, like they could hear Gary's part of the conversation or something. "Huh?"

"My goodness, a last-minute flight from California must have cost you more than a thousand dollars. Please tell me you didn't spend that much money."

"Of course not. I . . . I . . ." Shauntae started letting out deep breaths into the phone. "Oh . . . ow . . . baby, I . . . oh . . ."

"Shauntae, what's wrong? Are you okay?"

"It's my stomach. It's cramping. I think I did too much today. Walking through the airport, and then being in the air all those hours. I don't feel right."

"Should I send an ambulance?"

"No!" Shauntae made herself calm down. "I mean, it's those regular little cramps you get when you're pregnant. I'll be fine when I can rest and relax." She thought for a minute and realized this was supposed to be her first time being pregnant. "I mean, that's what they said in those classes I started taking while I was in California."

"Okay, I'm on my way, baby. Sit in baggage claim and put your feet up. I'm not far from the airport. I'll be there in fifteen minutes or less."

Shauntae hung up and lay her head down on the table. All that deep breathing had made her dizzy. Or maybe she was realizing that she hadn't even seen Gary yet and she had already messed up and had to play sick.

She felt Candy pat her on the back. "Come on, girl. You can do this."

But when Shauntae picked her head up off the table, she could see the truth in both of her girls' eyes. She couldn't do this. And it was only a matter of time before Gary sent her packing. Just like Devon did.

Five

After Gary called to say he was two minutes from the airport, Sherice and Candy helped Shauntae out to the curb with her bags and left real fast before he got there. Shauntae felt a rush when his champagne-colored Lexus pulled up beside her. Gary jumped out of the car and took two big steps toward her. Her heart rushed again when he scooped her up in his arms and spun her around, then kissed her cheeks and her lips with soft, sweet kisses.

What really got her was when he bent down and spoke to her belly. "My little baby is home," he said, then kissed it. When he stood to hug her again, Shauntae let herself be swallowed up in his arms. She didn't remember him being so tall or his arms being so thick and strong, or him smelling so nice and his hug feeling so good.

She wished for a second that the whole thing was real. That she really loved him. That she didn't have to trick him into loving her. That she was happy about having another baby. She held on to him real tight, hoping that maybe some magic dust would fall on her and her wishes would come true.

"You all right, baby?" Gary asked.

Shauntae nodded into his chest.

"You missed me, huh?"

Shauntae nodded again. If she could stay in his arms and not have to talk right, think right, and act right, maybe everything would be okay. Maybe if they had some really good sex that night she could make him forget any mistakes she was about to make. She would do it every day if she had to. Maybe that would be enough to make him love her and ignore all the bad stuff about her.

"Come on, baby. Let's get you off your feet." Gary opened her car door, settled her in the front seat, and then put her bags in the trunk.

Candy had loaned her the suitcases. They were much nicer than the bags she had, but not Gucci like Sherice's suitcases one of her sponsors had bought her. They didn't want her to look like she had too much money. Sherice was convinced that Gary didn't want a woman who could take care of herself, but that he was a man who needed to be needed by a woman.

He got into the car and fastened his seat belt. He glanced over at her. "Baby, your seat belt?"

"Oh." Shauntae hated seat belts and never used them. As she fastened herself in, she made a mental note to always put on a seat belt when she was in the car with Gary. "There we go."

He smiled at her and leaned over and kissed her. She was a little extra over the top with the kiss, hoping to get him all stirred up. Maybe they could have sex as soon as they got to his house and she wouldn't have to talk that much. When she pulled back from the kiss, she smiled and said, "Mmmmmm . . ."

When she opened her eyes, he was frowning.

"Baby, have you been drinking?"

"Huh?" Shauntae had forgotten to eat the mint that Candy had slipped her. Why was he asking though? She and Gary had shared a drink the first time they met in the bar and then had some expensive wine when they had gone out to dinner at a fancy restaurant. What was the big deal? Had he gotten holier since she left and now drinking was a sin?

He shook his head. “Of course you haven’t been drinking. You would never drink while you’re pregnant.”

“Of course not.” Shauntae took a gulping swallow. “I forgot to take my prenatal vitamins this morning, so I took them while I was waiting for you. I have to take the syrup because I can’t swallow the pills. It smells like alcohol.”

This was gonna be harder than she thought. She had to be Miss Holy and Perfect all day and she couldn’t even drink? Maybe it was for the best, though. Sherice drank and smoked all through her last pregnancy and everybody knew her son, Li’l Ray Ray, wasn’t right in the head.

“Sorry for asking, honey. I know you would never do anything to hurt our baby.”

“No, I would never do anything to hurt our baby.” Shauntae couldn’t believe she had barely got in the car and had already messed up. Was there a movie that would teach her the right way to be pregnant?

A police car pulled up beside them and flashed its lights to make them move. Even though she knew it was just airport patrol, the flashing lights made Shauntae nervous. She covered the side of her face with her hand.

Gary put the car in gear. “Where to?”

Shauntae frowned. “Huh?”

“Where’s your place, baby? I’ve never been there, remember?”

“My place?” Shauntae asked as Gary pulled away from the curb.

“Yeah.” Gary laughed. “Have you forgotten where you live?”

“Um, uh rah . . . baby?”

“Yes, dear?”

“I gave up my apartment while I was gone. I didn’t think I was coming back until I found out I was pregnant. I gave all my stuff away and planned to start over in California.”

"Oh . . ." Gary's silence made her even more nervous.

"I thought I was going home with you." The way he had been begging her to come home had made her think she would be staying at his house.

Gary frowned. "You thought we would live together before we get married?"

"I thought . . ." Shauntae was glad his eyes were on the road and not on her face because she knew she looked confused. "I thought . . ."

It must have been the three days on the bus, the almost fight with her girls, the rush from him hugging and kissing her, riding in the front seat of a Lexus with a man who looked and smelled like money, and her durned hormones from this durned baby. Shauntae started to cry. For real and not because Sherice had told her to.

Now it was Gary's turn to look confused. "Baby, what's wrong?"

"You kept telling me you couldn't wait for me to come home. I thought you wanted me." She sucked in a deep sniffle. "I thought you wanted me."

Gary put one of his large hands on her knee. "Of course I want you, baby. I didn't say anything about not wanting you. I want you. I love you. We're going to get married and be a family." He rubbed up and down her arm.

"Then why cain't . . ." Shauntae calmed herself down so her talking wouldn't go bad. "Why can't I go home with you?"

"Baby, we're not married. Like I've been saying, we have to do this thing right before God. I'm happy about our baby, but you know this isn't God's way. Can you stay with one of your girlfriends until we get married?"

Shauntae thought hard before she answered. If she said no, he would think there was something wrong with her because she didn't have no friends. If she said yes, he'd expect to drop her off at Sherice's or Candy's house and that would mess up everything.

"I can . . . but . . . most of my friends are married, so I would have to give them time to get ready." A quick thought came to her mind. "And plus, my friends don't like it when I stay over their houses. You know with their husbands there . . . I think they might be a little jealous."

A broad grin spread on Gary's face. "I can understand that. My baby is fine. I can see why they wouldn't want you around their man."

Shauntae let out a little breath of relief. She had gotten something right.

"Okay, baby. You can stay at my house until we get you situated somewhere. In the guest room, though."

"Guest room?"

"Don't worry. It's a nice room. Not being able to have sex with your fine self right down the hall will be hard, but we'll make it until we get married."

"No sex?" Shauntae tried to keep herself calm. No sex? How could she keep him distracted from her messing up if they couldn't have sex?

"We have to make sure we do things right before God until the wedding."

"Wedding?" *Did he say wedding?* The whole "no sex" thing was pushed out of Shauntae's mind by thoughts of a wedding. Was she going to have a real wedding? Like with a white dress and everything?

"Of course. You didn't think we were going to the justice of the peace, did you?"

That's exactly what she had thought. She never dreamed she would actually have a wedding. This was too good to be true.

"What kind of wedding do you want to have?" Gary asked. "It might be difficult to get the venue we want on short such notice, but I'll see if I can pull some strings. Nothing but the best for my baby. We'll need something big, because I'm sure you want a huge wedding with all our family and friends."

Shauntae shook away the fantasy of walking down the aisle in a gorgeous white dress to imagine what it would be like if any of her family and friends came to a wedding with his family and friends.

"I'm sure you'd love to be featured on the society page of the *Atlanta Journal-Constitution,*" Gary said.

"The newspaper?" Shauntae tried to keep a calm expression on her face. If Cassandra and Devon read the Sunday paper and saw her face plastered there in a high-society wedding, she'd get arrested the very next day. "I don't want no big wedding or to be in no newspaper. Just something small. In fact, I would have been happy with the justice of the peace."

"Baby, I want the best for you. The best for us. Why would you want to . . ." Gary paused. "I know what it is. You don't want to be pregnant in a wedding dress? Baby, you don't have to be embarrassed. This isn't God's way, but you have nothing to be ashamed of. Like you always say, God knows our hearts."

"I know, but . . ."

"But what? I've never met a woman who didn't want a big, fancy wedding."

Shauntae shook her head. "I would be happy if me and you went off somewhere special and got married. Maybe to an island or something."

"You sure we'd have time to plan that? You can only fly for a few more months, right?"

Shauntae shook herself out of her thoughts of a wedding on the beach in Jamaica. "Oh, yeah. You're right." She had forgot all about the baby in her belly, again. "For real, though, we can go to the justice of the peace. I'm not like most women when it comes to weddings. I just want to be married to you."

"Okay, love. I just want to be married to you too. And this way we can get married sooner. The sooner the better."

"Yeah, the sooner the better."

For real though, it needed to be as soon as possible. Shauntae wasn't sure how long it would be before Gary realized she wasn't good enough to marry him.

Six

Shauntae gasped when they pulled up in the driveway of Gary's house. She had only seen it once late at night—the night she had gotten pregnant. She didn't remember it being so big and pretty. It was all rich and fancy looking.

Shauntae had to get this thing right. This could be her home for the rest of her life. She'd have as many babies as he wanted, as long as she could stay in his house and ride in his Lexus.

He pulled into the garage and came around to her side of the car. When he opened the door and she stood, he leaned in to kiss her. "Welcome home, baby." He opened the door to the house. "Make yourself comfortable while I get your bags."

Shauntae walked through the huge kitchen into the breakfast room. If she were Candy, she would have stopped to admire the fancy kitchen cabinets and the island in the middle of the floor. There was a wood thing over it with expensive-looking pots hanging from it. Shauntae wondered if Gary would be expecting her to cook.

Gary came back downstairs after taking her bags up. "Ready for a tour?"

As they walked through the house, Shauntae wondered if she could ever feel at home there. Everything was so expensive and fancy. His office looked more like a library because of all the books he had. She wondered if he had read them all or if they were just for decoration.

He had a fancy living room that looked like there should have been plastic on the furniture. It had a big piano that he said his daughters used to practice on. The dining room had a big, long table and some fancy high-backed chairs.

The family room had the biggest TV Shauntae had ever seen, with surround sound and everything. She knew she would be hanging out in there most of the time. It was the only place that looked like she could be comfortable.

Gary had a liquor cabinet filled with fancy wine bottles and other expensive drinks. Shauntae couldn't wait for Sherice and Candy to come over. They would have to be careful to only drink a little bit from each bottle so he wouldn't notice anything was missing.

When they got upstairs, he led her down the hall. "Here's your room, baby."

The guest room was painted light blue and there was a queen-sized bed with a fancy blue and gray comforter. There were about twenty pillows on the bed that Shauntae would have to take off every night and put back on every morning because they were just decoration. The room had its own bathroom, which was also decorated in blue and gray. It was kinda boring, but for real, it was nicer than any place Shauntae had ever lived.

Down the hall, there were two bedrooms next to each other that shared a bathroom. One was decorated in bright pink and the other in light purple, both with all kinds of girl stuff.

"My daughters' rooms," Gary said, with a funny look on his face.

Shauntae could tell he was missing his children. For a second, she was happy that he would be getting part custody of them soon. Only for a second. It was gon' be a headache having two girls around Brianna's age living in the same house.

When they got to the master bedroom, Shauntae had to stop herself from screaming out loud. She didn't know a bedroom could be that big. It had two sections, one with a big ol' king-sized bed and another with a couch and a big-screen television and a fireplace.

When they went into the bathroom, Shauntae almost fainted when she saw the Jacuzzi tub. But the best part was the two big closets. Each one was almost the size of a small bedroom. His was full of suits, shirts, ties, and some casual clothes, and the other one was empty, waiting to be filled with all the expensive clothes he would buy her.

"So you like the house?"

"I love it, baby. I ain't never been in no house like this. I cain't wait 'til we get married."

Gary's eyebrows went up.

"What's wrong, honey?" Shauntae asked.

Gary shook his head and smiled.

Shauntae realized she had gotten so excited that she had let her proper talking go out the window. *Focus, Shauntae. Do you see this house?*

She followed Gary back down to the kitchen.

"You hungry?" he asked. "I picked up some sushi last night."

Shauntae made a disgusted face.

"You don't like sushi?"

"Uh, of course I like sushi, usually, but . . ." She rubbed a hand over her belly. "Ever since the baby, my appetite has changed. The thought of it makes me ill." Shauntae said each word very carefully.

"I have some leftovers in the fridge. Roasted duck, asparagus, and couscous."

Shauntae frowned again. She wasn't trying to eat nobody's duck or no vegetable that looked like a tree. And what in the world was couscous?

Gary laughed at the frown on her face. "Okay, what would you like?"

Shauntae thought for a minute. She couldn't ask for no hot wings or pizza or Chinese food or any of the things she was used to eating. "I'm not sure. This baby has my taste buds messed up."

"Take a look in the refrigerator and see if anything catches your eye," Gary said. "If I had known you would be staying here, I would have stocked up on your favorites. Except, I don't even know what your favorites are. Guess I have a lot to learn about you."

Shauntae forced a laugh. "Yeah, we have a lot to learn about each other."

She needed to figure out what her favorites should be. He couldn't find out that she lived on frozen pizza, fish sticks, chicken wings, Cap'n Crunch, Pop-Tarts, and ramen noodles.

She pulled open the refrigerator. He came to stand behind her. "Sit down and rest, honey. I'll tell you what's in here."

Shauntae perched herself on one of the breakfast room chairs.

"I have hummus, baba ghanoush, and pita chips." He turned to see the frown on her face. "I have a nice Brie that you can eat with some water crackers and white grapes."

She shook her head.

"Arugula salad with goat cheese, pecans, and strawberries?"

She frowned and shook her head again. Didn't he have no normal food?

"How about a turkey and Swiss on pumpernickel?"

"Sounds good, baby." She wasn't sure what pumpernickel was, but turkey and cheese was the closest thing to normal and she was starving. If she had known he wouldn't have no real food, I woulda ate something at Sherice's house.

"I have some Grey Poupon or aioli if you'd like."

"Ain't you . . ." Shauntae cleared her throat. "Do you have some sandwich spread?"

"I have Hellmann's. Is that okay?"

"Sounds good."

She sat down at the breakfast table and waited until he fixed her sandwich. He brought over a bag of those fancy chips made from all different kinds of vegetables that cost five dollars in the grocery store. She had always wondered who would pay that much for some chips made out of beets and sweet potatoes.

"I'm gonna turn the TV on, baby. I need to catch up on CNN. You can bring your food in here and sit with me if you want."

Shauntae quietly sat and ate her sandwich as Gary got caught up in some ol' boring news show. Why would anybody be interested in wars and people fighting all over the world? There was enough bad stuff happening here in Atlanta. She hoped he wouldn't want to talk about nothing he was watching.

While Gary was all into the TV, Shauntae looked at the pictures on the walls. There was pictures of his daughters at different ages in ballet outfits, soccer uniforms, at piano recitals, and all sorts of stuff. Shauntae remembered how Devon talked about wanting Brianna to be in Cassandra's art classes so she could be well-rounded and have a "bright future." Looked like Gary felt the same way.

There was one picture of the girls with their mother. When she finished her sandwich and those expensive chips, which actually tasted kinda good, Shauntae got up to look at it. The girls were dressed exactly alike in pink lacy dresses. Gary's ex-wife had on a dress of the same color but it was sharp and classy, like something Angela Bassett would wear.

Shauntae studied her face. She was real pretty. Shauntae could tell she was smart 'cause her eyes looked like she knew a lot. She had her arms around the girls and they both had big, pretty smiles on their faces. Gary's ex-wife was looking at her daughters like . . . like she was proud of them, and happy to be their mother, and like she didn't want nothing bad to happen to them.

Gary switched off the TV. "That was last year at the AKA Mother-Daughter Tea. That was a special day for the girls." Gary came and stood beside her. "Does the picture bother you? I can take it down. I took down all the family pictures with the four of us, and most of the pictures with the girls and their mother, but I decided to leave this one up because the girls love it so much. There's lot of pictures of them and their mother in their rooms."

Gary's voice sounded real sad. Shauntae turned to look at him and his eyes looked sad, too. He stared up at the picture. "I never want the girls to think I hate their mother, but after everything that happened between us, I didn't want her pictures up as a constant reminder of our failure." Gary shook his head. "I never thought things could end up so bad."

He walked back over to the couch and sat down. He picked up a picture of the girls from the coffee table. "The divorce was hard on them. As much as I adore my girls, if I had known things would end up this way, I never would have had them. What parent would ever want to put their child through so much pain?"

Shauntae went and sat back down next to Gary. He was acting the same way he had acted that first day she met him in the bar. She didn't know what to say then and didn't now.

Gary traced his fingers along the girls' faces on the picture. "I love them so much. I wanted them to have a family like the one I grew up in." Gary put down the girls' picture and picked up a much older picture. It took a second for Shauntae to figure out it was Gary about twenty-five years ago. He was sitting next to a boy who looked about two years older. Behind them were his parents. Gary looked exactly like his mother and his brother looked like his daddy.

"God blessed me with a great family. My mother took good care of us and loved us. She cooked family meals almost every day. She read us stories when we were little and then listened to us read when we got older. She was always at the school volunteering. She helped us with our homework and school projects. She took us everywhere—football practice, debate club, class trips—everywhere. She was always there for us. My dad worked hard to provide for us, but he always had time, too. Went to all our games and stuff, and we could always talk to him when we had a problem."

He put down the picture and looked at her. "That's why I'm glad God brought you into my life, baby. My ex-wife didn't have the same value for family. She was more committed to her career and not enough to raising the girls. They saw more of the nanny than they did her. That's why I can't believe she took them from me. It's not like she's spending time with them."

Shauntae looked at the picture of Gary's mama. Was he expecting her to be like that? Cooking and reading and doing homework and being all up at the school and spending all day with the kids? What had she gotten herself into?

She thought back to that first night at the bar. When he was bashing his ex-wife and going on and on about how important family was, she had agreed with everything he said. She had probably said some dumb junk about wanting kids more than anything. She remembered talking about how, ever since she was a little girl, all she wanted was a family and kids and stuff.

Her big mouth, trying to catch a man. She didn't know she was gonna get pregnant by him and have to for real live up to her words.

Gary wrapped his arms around her. "Anyway, baby, that's what I love about God. He always gives us second chances. And this time, I'm gonna get it right. We're gonna get it right. I know we haven't known each other long, but we have God on our side. How can you fail when you have two people committed to God and committed to family? Right?"

Shauntae nodded weakly. "Right, baby. God is gonna help us be the perfect family."

"I only wish I could get full custody of the girls. I'm sure if their mother's career picks up, she'll be happy to turn them over. She only did this to spite me."

Gary planted a kiss on her cheek. "I can't wait for you to meet the girls. You're gonna love them and they're gonna love you. They need a woman like you in their lives. Their mother isn't a bad mother. She's just too ambitious and her priorities are out of order. Unfortunately, you'll have to meet her, too, since you'll be taking care of her daughters. Whatever happens, don't let her get to you. She can be rude and condescending, but try to ignore her."

Shauntae couldn't make herself smile this time. "I'm sure we'll all get along fine." Shauntae knew how to put someone like Sherice or Candy in their place with a good cussing out, but how would she handle Gary's ex-wife? She would have to control her temper, because if that heifer got rude with her, it would be hard not to give her a beat down. Gary's daughters would never accept her as their stepmother if she beat down their mother.

"We'll have to set up a meeting soon. I want the girls' blessing before we get married. Should I set up something for next week?"

"Next week sounds perfect, baby."

Shauntae might as well get on the bus back to California now. What made her think she could pull this off?

She sighed. “Just perfect.”

Seven

Shauntae sat at the kitchen table, bouncing her leg and biting her nails until the doorbell finally rang. She jumped up, ran through the foyer, and threw the door open. "It's about time!"

"Dang, heffa, you living large!" Sherice barely stopped to say hi and pushed her way into the house. She looked around for a second, and then started giving herself a tour.

"Wassup, girl?" Candy gave Shauntae a hug and then walked into the house with her eyes all big. "Wow, you didn't tell us it was like this." She passed Shauntae a big, greasy bag.

"Thanks, girl. I'm starving up in this house." Shauntae closed the front door and led Candy to the kitchen table. "Sherice, where you at?" she yelled.

"I'm upstairs. Girl, this place is serious."

"How you gon' be running through my house like that?" Shauntae tried to sound mad, but she was enjoying her girls being bug-eyed about her new house. They would be giving her mad respect from now on.

Sherice came back down the steps, talking in her saddity, rich-girl tone. "This is the grand ballroom, where you'll see a crystal chandelier. Here in the formal living room we have a grand piano and a chaise lounge from Paris."

"Shut up, girl. You so stupid." Shauntae waved Sherice into the kitchen. "Come sit down."

Sherice's butt barely hit the breakfast room chair when she saw the television. "Dang, girl. How many inches is this?" She went and touched all over it like she was showing it on *The Price Is Right*. "It got surround sound? Aw yeah, movie night just went to a whole new level." She walked over to the liquor cabinet. "And what do we have here?" She looked inside. "Aw, yeah. Where's the key?"

Sherice was making Shauntae nervous wandering everywhere and touching everything. "Don't even think about it. Come over here and sit down. I promise I'ma show y'all everything after I eat."

Shauntae opened the greasy bag, pulled out a Styrofoam carton and flipped it open. "Aw, thank you, Jesus!" A mixture of scents filled the air—the sweet smells of buffalo, lemon-pepper, and teriyaki chicken wings and hot fries.

Shauntae almost cried. It had been stressful the last couple of days with Gary. She was tired of thinking so hard, asking millions of questions, remembering to say the right thing. The house made her feel like she was visiting someplace too expensive and she was afraid to break or spill something. And she was starving.

That morning, she could barely wait until Gary left for work to call the girls to come over. Sherice had cussed her out for calling so early and it had taken them hours to get there. But here they were and Shauntae felt better already. She stuck almost a whole chicken wing in her mouth.

"Dang, girl. Slow down," Candy said. "You act like you ain't ate in days."

"I ain't," Shauntae said through a mouthful of food. "All he got up in here is some ol' nasty rich people's food. Ducks and raw fish and goat cheese and funny-looking salad. Can a sista get some iceberg lettuce and ranch dressing?"

They all laughed.

"Oh, I almost forgot." Sherice pulled a *40oz.* out of her purse. "Can't eat wings without this."

Shauntae shook her head. "Naw, I'm good."

Candy and Sherice stared at each other and then back at Shauntae. "You ain't drankin'?" Candy asked.

Shauntae shook her head and stuffed her mouth with fries.

Sherice stared at Shauntae real hard. "Wassup wit' you? I heard you earlier when you opened your food and was talking 'bout some 'thank you, Jesus.' And now you ain't drankin'? It's only been a week and you changin' up on us already?"

Shauntae licked all her fingers, one by one. "I ain't drinking 'cause I'm pregnant."

Sherice halfway rolled her eyes, but then stopped. Must have thought about Li'l Ray Ray and decided not to say nothing smart.

"The 'thank you, Jesus' is me practicing. Didn't y'all say I needed to be exactly what Gary wants? Well, he's a church man, so I gotta be a church girl. You know they be thanking Jesus for everything."

Candy asked, "You mean, you gotta start going to church every Sunday?"

Shauntae's mouth froze as she was about to bite into a chicken wing.

Candy and Sherice laughed. Sherice reached over and pushed her chin up. "Close your mouth 'fore something fly in there. You a'int think about that? Church people go to church. If you marry a church man, what you thank you gon' be doing every Sunday?"

Shauntae groaned. She'd hated sitting through church when her grandmother used to make her go.

Candy looked around at the kitchen and family room. "It's a good thing he rich and you living in this nice house. That's the only thing make it worth it. I can't stand church. I hate seeing people get so-called filled with the Holy Ghost and jumping and dancing and sweating everywhere. Them the same people who'll cuss you out soon as you get to the parking lot. Can't stand some ol' fake church hypocrites." Candy wrinkled her nose up. She asked Shauntae, "You know how to do a holy dance?"

Sherice laughed. "Course she don't. I'm gon' have to teach her." Sherice jumped up out of her chair and did a perfect jumpy, fast-beat dance like them church girls did, like she could hear the organ and the drums playing some Holy Ghost church music.

Shauntae and Candy sat there with their mouths open.

Sherice wiped her forehead, waved her hand in the air and made that special "holy face" that church girls be having. "Haw-ley-loooyah . . . Glory to Jeeesus!" She broke into another shout and then broke into some fake tongues. Her eyes rolled back in her head and she fell out on the floor.

Candy and Shauntae stared at each other and then at Sherice.

Sherice got up and sat back in her chair like nothing had happened. "Y'all don't know nothing 'bout that there."

"Where did you . . . How did you . . ." Shauntae stuttered.

"Let's just say mega church pastors got deep pockets. . . ."

Candy's and Shauntae's eyes and mouths flew open.

"Girl, you are wrong," Candy said.

"Bet I got paid. And that was temporary. Shauntae got a permanent gig here so she need to be able to do all that and more."

"I can't do that." Shauntae got up from the table, washed her hands, and got herself a glass of water.

Sherice looked her up and down. "Hmmm . . . yeah, you probably cain't cut a step like that. Took me weeks to get it right. But you can do what I did until I got my step right."

Shauntae brought her glass of water back to the table. "What's that?"

"When everybody is shoutin', bend your head down, cover your face, and let your shoulders shake like you crying from deep down inside."

"But what about the tongues?" Shauntae asked.

"Well, depends on what kind of church he goes to. They might not be sanctified so you might not have to worry about it. Where he go to church?"

Shauntae bit her lip and shrugged her shoulders.

Sherice threw her hands in the air and shouted, "What I tell you about doing your research?"

"I have been," Shauntae shouted back. "I got whole lists of stuff about Gary. I just didn't think about that part." She brought her voice back down. She couldn't afford to piss Sherice off, since she held the keys to her becoming a church girl. "I been asking all the questions like you told me and doing everything you said." If she had to go on the humble to get Sherice's help, she would.

"Well, that's the first thing you need to know. Because all churches ain't the same." Sherice looked around at the house. "Seem like Gary the kind of guy who might go to one of them high-society churches where everybody be quiet. All you have to do is give a soft clap and look snooty. You don't even have to say hallelujah out loud. Wave a little hanky and you'll be fine."

Shauntae hoped Gary went to that kind of church.

"So I guess y'all pray together?" Sherice asked.

"He prays. I just say a little something here and there."

"What you gon' do when he asks you to lead prayer?" Sherice asked. "Or family devotions?"

Shauntae bit her lip and shrugged. Even sitting up in her gorgeous new house, Sherice was making her feel stupid.

"That's all right, girl. We'll get you straight." Sherice stood up. "Okay, I'm ready for my tour."

Her girls oohed and ahhed through the whole house. Shauntae had to make Sherice stop touching everything. When they got to the master bedroom, she couldn't stop Candy from running and jumping, arms spread out, onto the bed. Sherice was right behind her. Shauntae finally gave in and joined them.

"Girl, this a big ol' pretty bed," Candy said.

"Ugh, I can't believe we in the bed y'all be doing the nasty in." Sherice sat up. "In fact, I'm getting up. I cain't be lying down where you be having sex."

"You might as well lie back down," Shauntae said. "The guest room I showed you down the hall? That's my room. We can't do it until we get married, because Gary is saved."

"What? For real?" Sherice and Candy said at the same time.

"Aw, this is serious," Sherice said. "So you cain't even use your best stuff?"

Shauntae shook her head.

"This is really serious." Sherice scooted off the bed. "Y'all get up. We ain't got time to play. We gots work to do."

Sherice hustled them all back down to the kitchen table and made Shauntae pull out all the lists of information she had got about Gary over the past few days. They went over every detail—his business, his favorite meals, his work hours, stuff about his ex-wife and his daughters—everything. Shauntae was able to answer almost every question Sherice shot at her.

"A'ight, girl. I gots to give you some props. You been on your game." Sherice gave her a high five.

"You forgettin' one of the biggest things," Candy said.

"What?" Shauntae was tired. They'd been discussing stuff for almost two hours. She wanted to finish her chicken wings, put her girls out, and go take a nap. She got up and put the food container in the microwave. She should have told them to bring her an extra one, but where would she have hid it?

Candy gestured her arms in a big sweep. "Look at this big ol' house. Who's gon' clean it? And who's gon' cook?"

"And especially the kind of food he likes to eat," Sherice agreed.

Cooking and cleaning wasn't stuff Shauntae was good at. They all sat there thinking for a few minutes.

"I could come over and cook for you every day," Candy offered. Shauntae had watched Candy when she was eyeing the fancy stove and touching all the expensive pots and kitchen utensils.

"How you gon' get here every day? You know how many buses that is?" Sherice asked. "And what you know about some fancy food?"

"I be watching *Master Chef* and *Emeril Live* and all them shows on the Cooking Channel and the Food Network. I can cook all that stuff Shauntae been talking about. I can even make filet mignon and sushi."

It was Shauntae and Sherice's turn to look at Candy with respect. "For real, girl?" Shauntae said.

"I may not can talk smart like you, Sherice, or be gorgeous and good in bed like Shauntae, but everybody knows the best way to a man's heart," Candy said.

Sherice snapped her fingers. "A'ight den, girl. You got it." She and Candy high-fived each other.

"What about me?" Shauntae whined. Just when she was starting to feel better, Candy had to go and bring up cooking and cleaning. Her mother had never taught her nothing about no cooking and cleaning. When she was growing up, the house was always nasty and they always ate fast food.

"Hmmm . . . Candy cooking for you could only last for a little while. And that would be a whole lot of gas money." Sherice scrunched her nose up, thinking real hard. She snapped her fingers. "Have you been to the doctor yet?"

Shauntae shook her head.

"You gotta go soon. You needs to get yourself on bed rest."

"Bed rest? I'm only about four months. I'll go crazy with five months of bed rest."

Sherice rolled her eyes. "You won't be on bed rest for real, simple girl. He'll just think you are. You wanna clean this house and cook a gourmet meal every day?"

Shauntae shook her head again.

"A'ight den. Here's what you gotta do." Sherice carefully explained all the symptoms Shauntae needed to complain of. "Don't go overboard or you'll end up having to stay in the hospital. Then you'd be on bed rest for real. Let me write it down so you don't mess it up."

Shauntae got up to get her food out of the microwave while Sherice scribbled out the symptom list. "Humph," Sherice said when she finished writing. "You probably get to go to some nice doctor and get to deliver in one of them nice hospitals."

Shauntae ignored Sherice's jealousy. "I don't like lying to the doctor. I could end up on some medicine or having to take some tests I don't need."

Sherice waved Shauntae's fears away. "Ain't I had four babies? I know what I'm doing."

Candy shrugged and gave Shauntae a doubtful look.

Sherice spread out all Shauntae's lists and the new notes they had made. "Okay, let's go over everything again."

Shauntae put her head down on the table. "Aw, come on. I'm tired. I need a nap."

Sherice pulled her back up. "Girl, it ain't time to sleep. You got church this Sunday and a meeting with the ex-witch and the brats sometime next week. We gots work to do."

Eight

Shauntae turned and looked at herself in the mirror. She and Candy had gone "church shopping" and she had gotten herself a sassy new suit, hat, and high heels. She was going to play the part of a church girl for real.

Shauntae came out of the guest room as Gary came out of his bedroom. He looked her up and down and his eyes got big like they did when she spoke bad English.

Shauntae couldn't understand why he was looking like that when she was looking so good in her classy church outfit. What had she done wrong this time? She looked at his clothes. He had on jeans and a button-down shirt.

"I thought you said we was . . ." Shauntae coughed. "I thought you said we *were* going to church."

"I'm sorry, baby. I forgot to tell you. My church is very casual. You look absolutely beautiful, but I think you'd feel uncomfortable if you wore that to church today. Most people wear jeans and some even athletic wear."

Shauntae wanted to ask what kind of church that was, but instead she turned and walked back to the guest room. "Be down in a minute."

By the time they pulled out of the driveway, Shauntae was still looking sharp, but was dressed down in a pair of cute, boot-cut jeans and a white blouse. Her jewelry and makeup was perfect and she knew she was looking like a model. She wore a black wool coat and some gloves that Sherice had loaned her. After being in California the last three months, Atlanta's February weather seemed extra cold.

The building they pulled up to looked more like a high school than it did a church. It was one of those huge, fancy mega churches. Shauntae wondered if the pastor was some rich dude who wore expensive suits and drove a Bentley. *Ugh*. Not only was she about to spend the morning with a bunch of church hypocrites, they were probably snobby, rich ones. The only good thing was she probably wouldn't have to worry about doing a holy dance.

When they got inside, Gary led her by the elbow up some stairs at the back of the huge lobby. "We're late, so we have to sit in the balcony."

Shauntae preferred the balcony. The farther away she could sit from the crooked pastor, the better. She'd had a few pastors as sponsors over the years. They were supposed to be so holy, but they would meet her for a good time on Saturday night and still be in their pulpit on Sunday morning.

One of Shauntae's best sponsors was a pastor who had got her pregnant. His hush money was sweet. When he threatened to stop paying, she'd shown up at his church looking gorgeous, and had stood up to speak during testimony time. Next thing she knew, a very big, very strong usher was escorting her out of the church. But her payments continued, so she had got her point across. Unfortunately, she had a miscarriage with that baby. Otherwise, she definitely could've been set for life. But no baby, no DNA test.

They had barely gotten into their seats when the music started. Shauntae didn't know church music could sound so good. It sounded more like some smooth jazz she and her girls listened to when they was drinking a nice bottle of Boone's Farm.

And they had these people dancing—not like a bucking, jumping, holy dance, but a real pretty dance. Shauntae remembered when one of her sponsors had taken her to see some modern dancers at the Fox Theatre. She had expected it to be all corny and lame but it was real nice. These church dancers were dancing like that.

The choir sang about how much God loves us no matter what we do; and the people was dancing, but it was like a play. They were acting out scenes of people messing up—one was drinking and stumbling all over the place, another girl was dressed all trashy and then she had a big belly like she had gotten pregnant, another person was stealing and shooting up drugs. But at the end, this big, tall dancer guy hugged them and loved them anyway.

For some reason, the dance made her cry. Shauntae figured it was hormones. Gary kept squeezing her hand. He was so sweet to her. She decided if for no other reason, she was going to like church, just for him.

After they took an offering, the pastor got up. He didn't have no expensive suit on. Just a pair of jeans and a sports coat.

Shauntae had never seen no black church like this. The people were nice. They hugged her and shook her hand during the visitors' welcome. The girl sitting on the other side of her kept talking to her between songs and handed her tissue when she started crying. Funny how coming to church was the first time she didn't feel like she had to be nobody smart or cultured.

The pastor read a few scriptures, then started talking. His voice wasn't all preachy and wheezy like most black pastors. He didn't scream or yell. He talked like he was having a regular conversation with somebody he was cool with.

Shauntae paid attention to most of what he said. A couple of times she got distracted by the big screens behind the pulpit. Most of the time they showed the pastor speaking. But sometimes they had cameras pointed on the people in the audience. Shauntae looked at the women to see if she was finer than them or dressed better. When she looked at the men, she realized Gary was one of the finest men in the building. There were a lot of men with money in this church. She was going to have to tell her girls they needed to come out of the upscale clubs and start coming to church on Sunday mornings.

When the camera went back to the pastor, Shauntae made herself focus on what he was talking about. Gary might want to talk about it over dinner and she didn't want to look stupid.

The pastor talked about how much God loves us, no matter what we do. That even if we'd lied, cheated, stolen, or even killed, Jesus already paid the price for our sin. Shauntae had never heard nobody preach like that before. Most of the time, preachers talked about how you go to hell for sinning and how you better get saved if you don't want to burn forever and ever after you die.

Shauntae had always wondered why people could serve a mean God that could let His so-called children burn forever. What kind of love was that? But this guy was saying that as long as she accepted Jesus as her Savior, He had covered her sins and it was like they had never happened. Shauntae thought about all the evil stuff she had done with men and how she had treated Brianna. God could love her even though she wasn't a good person?

This preacher made God sound all nice and loving, like He really was a good Father that cared about His children. Could that really be true?

At the end, Shauntae found herself crying again. Durned pregnancy hormones, messing up her perfect makeup.

When he was finished preaching, the pastor handed the mic to another guy and sat down. The new guy holding the mic held up his hand. "If you've heard God speaking to you today and you want to invite Him into your heart, please come on down to the altar. Jesus is here waiting for you. He wants to take you in His arms and love you with a love you've never experienced before."

Shauntae had sat through this part of a church service before. Where they begged you to get saved or become a member of the church. But this was different. She didn't know if it was that the message was good, or if it was the pregnancy hormones, but she felt like something was pulling her.

She locked her feet in place. There was no way she was going to that altar. She reminded herself that she hated God. He had never done nothing for her and had let a whole lot of bad things happen to her. Even though He had helped her get pregnant by Gary on the first try, that didn't make up for a whole lifetime of hell. She wasn't about to let no hormones make her do something silly like get saved. She could see Sherice and Candy rolling on the floor laughing if she told them. And plus, Gary thought she was already saved. She couldn't go down there and blow her whole game.

The man with the microphone kept bothering her. "Jesus wants to show you how much He loves you. I don't care what you been through, when you experience this love, it will make it like it never happened. Come and receive His love today."

Maybe she should go. She could say she was joining the church so she could be a member with her future husband. That's what she would tell Gary afterward. She started moving toward the stairs down from the balcony. One little step. And then another and then another. Gary looked at her with a question in his eyes. She didn't want to stop to explain, because then she would lose her nerve and wouldn't go.

Shauntae got all the way from her seat to the first step that led from the balcony to the main floor of the church and then looked up.

There on the big screen behind the pulpit was a face she recognized. The camera that went through the audience had landed on a little girl's face.

Her little girl's face.

Shauntae froze in her tracks. The camera moved slightly to the left and Shauntae gasped. There stood Devon and Cassandra.

Nine

Shauntae half ran, half stumbled from the balcony stairs that led down to the main floor of the sanctuary to the stairs that led down to the lobby. She didn't get a chance to trace the location of the camera to find out where Devon, Cassandra, and Brianna were sitting. She had to get out of there before they saw her. She ran down the back stairs and headed straight for the bathroom.

Of all the churches in Atlanta, Gary had to go to the same one as Devon? For real?

She had almost fallen for the preacher's mess about how much God loved her. Just when she thought she might be okay, that her life was gonna get better, here was everything going wrong all over again. God had proved, once again, how much He hated her.

What if, instead of the camera putting Brianna's face up on the screen, it had put her face on the screen? Devon and Cassandra would have seen her instead of her seeing them and they would have known she was back in Atlanta. That skank Cassandra probably would have dialed 911 right there in the church and the police would have been waiting for her when she walked out of the building with Gary.

Shauntae locked the bathroom stall and tried to catch her breath. Now what was she supposed to do? She couldn't hide in the church bathroom all day. But if she came out and tried to find Gary, she could run smack into the three people who could ruin her new life.

Shauntae's cell phone vibrated inside her purse. Her hands shook as she fished it out. "Hey, honey," she said in a loud whisper. "My stomach got real upset and I had to run to the bathroom. I'll be out in a minute."

"Aww, baby. Sorry you're not feeling well. Which bathroom? I'll come down and get you."

"Gary, you can't come into the ladies' bathroom."

He laughed in that sexy, bass voice. "I know that. But it's a huge church and there are thousands of people swarming around. If I don't know where you are, we could be looking for each other for the next hour."

"Oh, okay. I'm in the lobby. The bathroom directly across from the balcony stairs."

"Be right there, baby. I'll be waiting outside."

Now what? She could go out and explain that she had thrown up and didn't know when she might do it again and rush him to the car. If there were thousands of people in this church, they probably wouldn't run into Devon, Cassandra, and Brianna.

A few minutes later, she heard Gary's voice outside the door. "Excuse me, ma'am. Could you help me out? My wife is in the bathroom sick. She's pregnant. Can you check on her for me?"

"Of course. What's her name?"

Shauntae froze at the sound of the woman's voice. It couldn't be . . .

"Her name is Shauntae. Shauntae Jackson," Gary said.

The outer bathroom door opened with a rusty squeak. "Shauntae Jackson? Are you in here?"

Shauntae had only heard that voice a few times, but each time she had heard it, it made her so mad she would never forget it. Of all the people Gary could have sent into the bathroom to find her, of the thousands of people supposedly walking through the lobby right now, he had to pick Cassandra?

Think fast, girl. Think fast or you going to jail.

Shauntae put on her best Angela Bassett voice and talked as proper and perfect as she could. "I think I'm the only one in here and my name is Angela."

"Okay. Thanks."

The door squeaked open and closed again. Shauntae let out a deep breath. Her forehead was sweating and now she really did feel sick.

She heard Cassandra tell Gary, "Sorry, there's no one in there named Shauntae Jackson. Must be the bathroom on the other end."

Shauntae heard Gary say, "Really? I thought for sure this is where she said she was. Okay, thanks for checking."

Even though she knew he did it because he was embarrassed that they weren't married, Shauntae was glad Gary had told Cassandra to look for his wife, Shauntae Jackson. If he had said her real name, Cassandra might've known it was her.

As she was about to come out of the bathroom stall, Shauntae heard a little girl's voice she recognized. "Miss Cassandra, I gotta pee. Can you take me?"

"Sure, sweetie. Come on."

The rusty door squeaked again and Shauntae heard the clack of a woman's heels followed by the sound of squeaky little girl's shoes. She could almost see Brianna's bouncy walk. Shauntae always used to yell at Brianna to stop running and dancing everywhere she went. It got on her nerves.

"Miss Cassandra, are we going to Gammy and Poppy's house for dinner?"

Shauntae hated the silly names Brianna had for Devon's parents.

"I don't think so, chickadee. Your daddy is taking us to a nice restaurant."

"McDonald's?" Brianna's voice was all high and excited.

Cassandra laughed. "No, silly girl. Not McDonald's. Somewhere nice."

"What's nicer than McDonald's?"

Cassandra laughed again. "Come on out, Bree. Don't forget to flush."

Shauntae's cell phone rang. Gary had probably sent somebody into the other bathroom to find her and they told him she wasn't there. She couldn't answer now.

She heard Brianna skip out of the bathroom stall and turn the water on. "I can't get the soap to work."

"Here you go, sweetie."

"Thanks, Miss Cassandra. Can you come to the house after we eat?"

"What's up?"

"Nothing," Brianna answered. "We didn't get our godmommy time after art class yesterday. I want to show you my new dolly that Gammy bought me."

"Of course, Bree. Dry your hands. Hurry up and let's go. Your daddy is waiting. We need to get you some food soon since church lasted longer than we thought. You feeling okay?"

"I'm fine," Brianna said in that singsong voice of hers that aggravated Shauntae's last nerve. Every move she made was like dancing and she talked like she was singing.

None of it seemed to bother Miss Cassandra. She was laughing and helping Brianna do stuff her grown behind should've been able to do. She wanted to spend time with her. Made Shauntae sick.

It sounded like Brianna didn't even miss her. Miss Cassandra had come in and took her place like she never existed. Looked like Cassandra ate dinner with Brianna and Devon after church on Sundays and sometimes it was at his parents' house. Shauntae had never been there for a family dinner.

That rusty door squeaked one last time and finally Shauntae heard their footsteps blend in with the other people walking through the lobby. They'd be hurrying to get Brianna to a restaurant so her sugar wouldn't drop too low. Shauntae wouldn't be trapped much longer.

So Cassandra had really stepped in and become Brianna's "godmommy" and probably soon-to-be stepmommy and had pushed Shauntae out in the cold.

Shauntae reminded herself that it didn't matter. Now she had Gary and this new baby.

Shauntae's cell phone rang again. This time she answered it. "Hey, baby. I'm feeling better. I'm about to come out in a few minutes."

"Which bathroom are you in? I've been to every bathroom in the lobby."

"The one at the bottom of the balcony stairs."

"I sent someone in there looking for you. You didn't hear someone ask for Shauntae Jackson?"

"No," Shauntae said as innocently as she could. It didn't matter that she was lying in God's house. She didn't care nothing about Him no way.

This was her last Sunday coming to church. She'd have to figure out a way to convince Gary she couldn't come here ever again. No way she was gonna chance running into Devon, Cassandra, and Brianna.

Ten

After the whole church fiasco on Sunday, the last thing Shauntae felt like doing was meeting Gary's ex-wife and his daughters. But he had invited them to come over Friday evening, so she didn't have a choice.

Shauntae changed clothes at least four times before they got there. Sherice and Candy had argued for an hour trying to decide which outfit she should wear. And Shauntae wasn't sure how to fix her hair. Or what jewelry to wear. Or whether to go natural or bold with her makeup. She had even gone downstairs to check out the picture of the ex-wife a few times to study her look.

She finally decided on a pair of jeans and a long, black sweater. She wasn't sure if Gary had told them about the baby yet, so she wanted to wear something that could hide her belly. Luckily, this pregnancy was like her first one. Sherice always said she carried Brianna in her back because nobody could tell she was pregnant until she was about six months.

She put on some gold-colored earrings and a thin, gold chain. She figured dressing casual would show that she was confident that she was Gary's woman. If she dressed up too much, she'd look like she was trying too hard. She decided to go barefoot to show she was relaxed and comfortable in her house. Especially since Sherice had treated her to a French pedicure for the occasion.

She wished she felt as good as she looked. She almost jumped out of her skin when the doorbell rang. She stayed in her room as long as she could.

"Shauntae, they're here. Where are you?"

Shauntae had hoped he'd go ahead and open the door and exchange greetings with his family without her. "Coming, honey."

He opened the door as she was coming down the steps.

"Daddy!" Both of his daughters screamed and jumped all over Gary.

He hugged them. "Look how much you guys have grown. Look at my beautiful girls."

Shauntae stood off to the side and watched him hugging and kissing his daughters. He was so happy to see them it was like he wanted to cry. It made Shauntae feel some kinda way—like she felt when she watched some ol' Hallmark movies when nothing else was on cable.

"Ahem." Gary's ex-wife cleared her throat.

Gary looked up. "Oh, sorry." Gary put an arm around Shauntae's waist. The girls moved to the side. "Shauntae, this is my ex-wife, Darla, and my daughters, Daphne and Morgan. Girls, this is Daddy's new . . . friend I told you about, Miss Shauntae."

Each of the girls stuck out their hand for Shauntae to shake. The younger girl, Morgan, said, "You're very pretty."

"Thank you, dear. You're pretty too. Both of you are really beautiful. I'm very glad to meet you." Shauntae had spent the whole evening before and the whole day studying Angela Bassett and practicing everything she thought she might have to say.

"Darla, this is Shauntae." Gary's voice got tight when he said his ex's name. If Shauntae had any fears about Gary still having feelings for Darla, they all went out the window.

"Shauntae." Darla looked her up and down with some kind of snooty look on her face. "Nice to meet you."

"Likewise." Shauntae put out her hand for Darla to shake.

They stood there looking at each other for a few minutes. Darla was taller than Shauntae had thought and a little bit prettier in the face, but not as pretty as her. And she was thin with no curves at all, built like a stick.

"Should we move into the family room?" Gary seemed nervous. He placed his hand on the small of Shauntae's back and guided her in front of him.

"Daddy, can we play the piano?" the older girl asked. She looked exactly like Gary. She was gon' be real pretty when she grew up.

"Yes, dear. Not too loud because the grown-ups will be talking."

"Yes, Daddy." Both girls walked into the living room. Shauntae was surprised. They didn't run or yell or make a whole bunch of noise.

The three of them sat down in the family room—Shauntae and Gary together on the couch and Darla on the chair across from them. Darla looked at the picture of her and the girls on the wall. "I've been looking all over for that picture. I didn't realize it was still here." She talked through her nose and her mouth was stuck in a snooty frown. "I guess the girls should have some pictures of me here. Seems like the rest have disappeared."

"There are plenty of pictures of you and the girls in their rooms." Gary's body was stiff. Shauntae put her hand on his knee to calm him down. How was she supposed to keep her temper under control when he was wound up all tight?

"So, Shauntae, tell me about yourself," Darla said. "Since we'll be sharing the care of my daughters, we should make an effort to get to know each other."

It was Shauntae's turn to go stiff. "What would you like to know?"

"The normal stuff. Where are you from? What do you do? Where did you go to school?"

"I'm from Orange County. Born and raised there."

"Okay . . ." Darla nodded and waited for her to keep going.

What difference did it make where she went to school? Shauntae's girls had been so worried about what she was going to wear that none of them had even thought about stuff like schools and jobs. Shauntae should have known Darla would ask a whole bunch of questions since she was a lawyer. "Uh, I went to Orange County High School." Shauntae didn't even know if an Orange County High School existed.

"High school?" Darla asked.

"Yes. High school."

"I see." Darla looked at Gary and lifted up her eyebrow. Shauntae looked at Darla and then at Gary. By the look on his face, she knew she had said something wrong.

Darla fired her next question. "And what do you do?"

"Do?" Shauntae asked.

"Yes. Your career? Like I'm a lawyer and you're a . . ." Darla gestured like she was talking to a kindergartner and she was trying to help them get an answer right.

For real? Was this heifer trying to clown her?

Shauntae lifted her chin and forced herself to say, "I was an executive assistant."

"Oh . . . a secretary." Darla's frown got snootier. "I see."

"For now, Shauntae is a homemaker," Gary butted in. "She's settling in to prepare to take care of our child."

Shauntae could almost love Gary for taking up for her. But was he taking up for her or trying to keep her from embarrassing him again?

Darla's face didn't change except for a slight rise in her left eyebrow and a tiny quiver of her top lip. This chick was cold, but the news of the baby had got to her.

"Your child?" She turned from Gary back to Shauntae. "You're pregnant?" She pressed her lips together in a thin line. “Of course. That’s why it was important to meet the girls so soon.” She turned back to Gary. “And that’s why you’re getting married so quickly, to keep your holier-than-thou status in your church and community, huh?”

Gary’s jaw clenched, but he didn’t say anything.

Darla sat there for a second not talking, staring at the wall. It looked like she was in a courtroom, thinking about how to put away a defendant for life. “Gary, I must say this is unexpected. Perhaps it would have been wise for you to have told me about this over the phone so I would have had time to process the information. You know how I feel about being caught off-guard.”

Gary half smiled. “I do.”

Darla smirked. “Yes, of course you do. Perhaps we should meet privately at another time to discuss how this will affect the girls.”

“As we’ve said, Shauntae and I are getting married soon. Anything you have to say to me can be said in front of Shauntae.”

Darla’s smirk turned into a nasty frown. “You sure about that?”

“I’m sure, because I’m certain you wouldn’t want to say anything that would further strain our relationship,” Gary said. “Since we’re about to share custody of the girls, it would behoove us all to get along. Don’t you think?”

“I see your point, but I would like the opportunity to speak freely about my opinion on this whole . . . situation. I don’t think it would be beneficial for me to do so with all parties present. Don’t you think?” Darla looked at Shauntae with that nasty smirk on her face. “Well, apparently not.”

Shauntae looked back and forth between Gary and Darla. They were both using big words and confusing sentences, but she was pretty sure Darla had just dissed her. She was even more sure that her usual way of handling things would only make it worse. Shauntae knew Darla had already decided that she wasn't good enough to be around her daughters. She didn't even know what she had done wrong. "If you'll excuse me, I need to use the restroom."

"Yes, you do that, Shaun*tae*." Darla said her name all slow and ick.

Shauntae knew if she stayed in that room for more than five minutes, Darla was gon' get slapped. She hurried and went upstairs.

Before she got all the way up, she heard Darla say in one of those whispers that's louder than talking, "Is she living here? Please tell me that you don't expect to have partial custody of the girls while you're living with your pregnant girlfriend. You can't possibly expect me to be okay with that. What has happened to you? I know the divorce affected you but this . . . this is totally out of character."

Shauntae grabbed her cell phone off her bed and went and hid in the back of Gary's closet. She didn't know why her hands were shaking, but she could barely work the phone.

Sherice answered on the first ring. "Girl, ain't you supposed to be meeting the ex-witch and the brats? They didn't come?"

"They downstairs."

"Well, where you at?"

"Up in Gary's closet." Shauntae kept her voice low, even though there was no chance of anyone hearing her.

"Uh-oh. What you do?"

"Why it's gotta be me who did something?"

"Who else could it be?"

Shauntae almost hung up the phone. "Look, I called you 'cause I need help. I don't need you raggin' on me right now. I got enough of that from Miss Darla."

"Darla? Are you serious? She black? And her name is Darla?" Sherice busted out laughing.

It made Shauntae feel a little bit better. "I don't even know how to deal with this . . ."

"Chill, girl. Tell me what happened."

Shauntae explained everything up until the part where Darla and Gary started using big words. Then she could only say what she thought they had said.

Sherice let out a string of cuss words. "Girl, you's a better one than me. I woulda clocked that heffa right in her nose. Is she even pretty?'

"She a'ight in the face. But ain't got n'an one curve. Built like a tall, skinny boy. And she high yellow. Look like a number two pencil."

Sherice cackled again.

Shauntae felt a little more better. "What I'm s'posed to do, Sherice?"

"Ain't nothing you can do. This is between her and Gary. Anything she say to hurt you is really to get at him. Ain't nothing you need to say for yourself. It is what it is and you is who you is. Don't let her make you feel 'shamed, a'ight?"

"A'ight." Shauntae nodded like Sherice could see her. "Thanks, girl."

"Go on back downstairs. You got this, girl. Don't worry about that yella heffa. She think she all that, but she lost Gary, right?"

"Right."

"Bam. That's that. Call me later, okay?"

"Yeah, thanks, Sherice. You my girl for life."

"You know it."

Shauntae sat in the closet for a few more minutes, trying to get herself back right. Hopefully, Darla and the girls wouldn't be staying much longer. She wished she could give Gary some good sex later that night to make him feel all right about her. And for real, she needed some to make herself feel better.

She walked back downstairs in time to hear Gary saying, "That's completely unnecessary and I'm offended that you asked. Do you think I would bring anyone into my children's lives who would harm them in any way? Shauntae is a good, Christian woman."

Shauntae's heart flipped. Her man was taking up for her. Even though it was a lie, it felt good for him to be saying something good about her. She sat back down next to Gary on the couch.

"Then it shouldn't be a problem for you to do what I'm asking," Darla said. "We've done it for anyone who's ever been a babysitter for the girls. Why should this be any different?"

"Because it's offensive. It's offensive to me and even more to her. Do you always have to be so difficult about everything?"

Darla looked like she was glad to be getting Gary upset. "You know if this were me in a new relationship, wanting to bring another man into the girls' lives, you would want to do the same thing. Now wouldn't you?"

"No, because I would trust your judgment." Gary's voice was so cold it was hard for Shauntae to believe he had ever loved Darla, let alone had two kids with her.

Darla raised an eyebrow and folded her arms. "Maybe we should go back to court."

"No." Gary let out a tense breath. "No more court." He turned to Shauntae. "Baby, I'm sorry to have to ask this, but Darla is insisting on doing a background check on you since you're going to help raise our girls." Gary turned and gave Darla a nasty look. "She doesn't think I'm a good enough judge of character to know what's best for my children."

Shauntae froze.

Gary nudged her. “Honey?”

Shauntae had to work to make her mouth move. “Background check?”

Darla said, “Children are the most precious thing in the world and it’s a mother’s natural instinct to do everything she can to protect them. When you give birth, I’m sure you’ll understand.”

“You want to do a background check? On me?” Shauntae could barely get the words out.

Gary put an arm around her and pulled her to his side. “Honey, like I said, I’m very sorry. I know it’s offensive to ask you to do this, but . . . you know the . . . issues we’ve had over the custody of the girls. Us getting married introduces a new person into the whole situation. Let’s do this to get it behind us so we can go ahead and be a family.”

“What’s the problem, Shauntae? It’s just a formality. I’m sure you have nothing to hide.” Darla was almost snarling at her. “Right?”

“Right.” Shauntae’s voice sounded weak. “What do I need to do?”

Darla reached into her purse and pulled out a notepad and a pen and held them out to her. “I need your full name and your social security number.”

Shauntae did everything she could to keep her hand steady as she wrote out the information. She handed Darla the pen and pad back.

Darla looked down at the paper and up at Shauntae. “Quartisha?”

Shauntae gritted her teeth. “It’s my first name.” She gave Darla “the look.” Darla might have been all high and mighty, but she was still a sista and would know that look meant that if she said anything else—one word more—she was about to get cut. For real.

Darla stood up and put her pad back in her purse. “Well, then. We’ll get this done first thing Monday morning.” She gave Shauntae a sista-girl look of her own. She could probably roll her neck like only a black girl could.

Darla turned to Gary. “If everything checks out, you can have the girls next weekend. If not, I guess I’ll see you in court.”

Eleven

Shauntae sank back onto the couch as Gary walked Darla to the door. She could barely say anything when Gary sent the girls to say good-bye to her. The little one gave her a hug, but the older girl shook her hand. She might look like her daddy, but she had an attitude like her mother.

Gary stayed in the foyer a long time saying good-bye to his girls. When Shauntae heard the front door close and heard his footsteps coming toward her, she tried to get herself back together.

Gary sat down next to her and stared her straight in the eyes. "Honey, I'm sorry about that. I've seen Darla at her worst but I never even imagined she'd behave that badly. As soon as this background check comes back okay, I'm going to demand that she give you a formal apology, face to face. She needs to know she can't treat you that way."

All Shauntae could do was nod. She knew that apology would never happen and that her game was up. She would enjoy her last two nights in Gary's beautiful house and then Sunday night, while Gary was asleep, she'd disappear.

"You okay, honey?" Gary asked.

Shauntae forced herself to nod.

Gary looked at her like he was trying to figure out what she was thinking. "I know Darla is rude and that your first meeting with her wasn't pleasant. I'm sorry. I promise I will have a serious talk with her. She is going to respect you as my new wife and as the mother of my child." Gary tilted Shauntae's chin up. "I promise, honey. Okay?"

Shauntae could only nod. She didn't deserve him being this nice to her. What would he do when he found out the truth? He would probably be so mad that he would look at her and talk to her the same way he talked to Darla. She couldn't handle that.

He lay back on the couch and pulled her next to him. "Don't worry, baby. We won't let her get to us. And did you hear what she said? We can get the girls next weekend." Gary wrapped both his arms around her. "I'm gonna be so happy for us all to be together."

"Me too, honey," Shauntae said numbly. Gary squeezed her tight. She was gonna miss that feeling, like somebody finally loved her.

She'd get on the last bus on Sunday and head back to her mama's house. No way could she stay in Atlanta, because by Monday afternoon not only would Devon and Cassandra be wanting her in jail, but Darla would too. And maybe even Gary when he realized how she had played him.

"What do you want to do with the girls next weekend? We should do something special to celebrate the beginning of our family coming together."

"I don't know. Whatever you know the girls like to do." Shauntae wiggled her body until she found a comfortable spot in Gary's side. She was going to enjoy this until the very last minute.

"Hmmmm . . . I guess it really doesn't matter. They love being with their daddy. They're both daddy's girls. No matter what she's tried to do, Darla hasn't been able to poison them against me. Those girls know I love them more than anything."

Shauntae had a scary thought. What if she messed things up for Gary? When Darla found out that Gary's new baby mama had a warrant out on her for neglecting her first child, she would try to make it so he never saw his children again.

"Nobody could ever separate me from my girls. I honestly think I'd kill somebody if they did anything that would make me lose my girls."

Shauntae buried her head in Gary's side. Maybe she should warn him. She should've never written her real name on that paper. She should've written a fake name and then been gone before Monday morning. At least that way, Gary wouldn't have lost his girls.

"Sorry, honey," Gary said. "I know that's not a very Christian thing for me to say. I guess I should let God take care of things, huh? 'Vengeance is mine said the Lord,' right?"

"Right." What would God's vengeance be against her for messing up Gary's life?

There had to be something she could do. She had to find a way to block Darla from doing that background check. Shauntae worked her brain but couldn't think of anything. Maybe Mama was right. Maybe she was too stupid to figure something out on her own. "Baby, I gotta go to the bathroom again." Shauntae stood up.

Gary's face looked concerned. "Is everything okay?" He rubbed her stomach.

She put her hand on top of his. "Everything's okay. Just pregnant. I'll be back down soon. Wanna catch up on CNN until I get back?"

He leaned over and kissed her belly. "Okay. Hurry back."

Shauntae heard the TV coming on as she walked up the stairs. She found herself in another closet in the master bathroom, the one that would never be hers. Her hands shook as she called Sherice.

"That was quick. Is the ex-witch gone already?"

"Sherice, I need your help bad."

"Aw, man. What happened?"

Shauntae could barely get the words out as she explained about Darla and the background check.

Sherice was quiet for a long time. She finally said, "You know what you gotta do, right?"

"Yeah. I gotta go."

"What time do he go to sleep? I can be there around midnight to get you."

"Tonight? I was gonna leave late Sunday night while he's sleep."

"Are you crazy? You think the ex-witch is gonna wait until Monday to check you out? As soon as she get home and put her daughters to bed, she going straight to the computer. You gotta roll out tonight. Otherwise, I promise, you'll see those flashing lights before midnight."

Shauntae's heart started beating real fast. "You think she gon'—"

"I know she is. What's your problem? You done got settled in that house and it's gone to your brain? The game . . . is . . . up." Sherice said it all slow like she was trying to make sure her words was sinking in. "It's time to roll out. Pack up your stuff. I'll be there to get you as soon as he fall asleep."

"But— "

"But what? Why you actin' all slow in the head? You wanna go to jail tonight?"

"No . . . but what about Gary?"

"What do you mean, what about Gary?"

Shauntae explained trying to figure out how to keep him from losing his girls because of her. "If you could help me— "

Sherice cussed real loud. "What is wrong with you? You going to jail to try to keep that man from losing his children? It's not your problem."

"But it's my fault."

"You's a fool. You done fell in love with that man. How many times have I told you that if you gonna play, you gotta respect the game? You cain't be falling in love. Now stop being stupid. Get up outta that closet. You need to figure out a way to make that man have sex with you so he can go to sleep early. Pack your stuff and then text me so I can come get yo' tail before I have to get you outta jail." *Click*.

Shauntae looked at the phone. Why couldn't Sherice understand? Shauntae was about to dial her back, but she knew Sherice would probably cuss her out and then she might not be willing to fool with her no more.

And besides, Sherice was right. She did need to leave tonight.

Shauntae pulled herself up off the floor and made herself go downstairs. She put on her saddest face when she got to the family room. She might not know how to fix the problem she had made for Gary and the girls. But there was one thing she knew how to do.

"What's wrong, baby?" Gary asked.

"Nothing. I guess I'm worried. I want us all to be a family, but it seems like Darla is bent on making trouble. You just got custody of the girls back. But what if me being here messes that up? What if she hates me so much that she tries to take your girls again? I couldn't bear for that to happen."

Gary pulled her down onto the couch next to him. "Baby, don't be worried. God's got us. There's nothing Darla can do to separate me from my girls. Like the courts saw through her lies, they'll see through anything else she tries to do."

"I know, but . . . I don't want to make things worse for you. I . . . I don't know why she hates me. What did I do wrong?" Shauntae let a few tears roll down her cheeks.

Gary wiped the tears. "Aww, honey, don't cry. You didn't do anything wrong."

Shauntae let the tears flow in full force. "Then why does she hate me? It's like . . ." Shauntae took a few deep, dramatic breaths. "It's like she thinks I'm not good enough for your children. She made me feel like I'm not good enough for you."

Gary pulled her into his arms. "That's not true, honey love. You're perfect for me. You're everything I want in a woman. You're a good, solid Christian woman. You love family; that's everything I want."

"But you were embarrassed that I didn't go to a fancy college or have a fancy job."

Gary held her at arm's length so he could look her in the face. "Darla went to Princeton and she's a lawyer and look at how we ended up. We can't even be in the same room without arguing. I don't want a fancy university and a fancy job. I want you. I love you." Gary bent to kiss her.

Shauntae kissed him back with everything in her. "You love me?"

"Yes, Shauntae, I love you." He kissed her again. Shauntae felt the wall crumbling that Gary had put up to keep them from "falling into sexual sin." She wrapped her arms around him to pull him closer and deeper into the kiss.

"I love you too, baby," she whispered. Shauntae felt Gary lifting her up onto his lap. The kisses never stopped.

She had him.

Next thing she knew, he was carrying her up the stairs and they were in the bedroom. She looked at Gary's face. It was different from most men's faces when they was doing it. It wasn't about him liking sex. He looked at her like . . . like she was special. Like she mattered to him. Like he really loved her. Shauntae had never seen that look on a man's face in her life.

And so she pretended in her mind that she was an executive secretary and a good Christian girl who loved children and family. She pretended that she loved Gary and was excited to be having his baby. She pretended that when Darla did that background check, she wouldn't find out that there was an arrest warrant out on her for being the worst mother in the world. And she pretended that she and Gary would live happily ever after in this beautiful house with a beautiful life.

It wasn't long before Gary was good and asleep.

Pretend time was over. Shauntae wriggled out from under his arm and quietly slid out of the bed. She tiptoed down the hall as quietly as she could and went into her room and closed the door.

The suitcases were still at the foot of the bed. She hadn't even put them inside the closet. Maybe somewhere deep down she had knew it wouldn't last. She packed as quiet as she could.

When everything except the clothes she had left on Gary's floor was in the suitcases, Shauntae sat down on the bed and looked around the room. She couldn't believe it was over. What she really couldn't believe was that she had thought it would work.

As she was about to text Sherice to come and get her, she heard Gary's cell phone ring. They had left it downstairs, but his ring tone was so loud she was scared it would wake him up. He was in the middle of some big business deal and was always tied to the phone.

Fast as she could, Shauntae opened one of her suitcases and pulled out a big fluffy robe Gary had bought her. She stuffed both suitcases in the closet and pulled the sliding door shut. She ran down the steps to get the phone in case it started ringing again.

She got to the family room and Gary was standing there with the phone to his ear. By the look on his face, something was wrong. Really wrong.

Shauntae froze in her tracks. Was it Darla? Had she already done the background check and was calling Gary to tell on her? Were the police on the way to the house? Shauntae knew it was time to run.

"Okay . . . yes, I'll be right there." Gary reached out and clamped his hand around her wrist. Tight. Shauntae imagined that's what a handcuff would feel like.

Gary dropped the phone and grabbed her other wrist. He held both her arms so tight, she was scared. Was he going to hurt her?

"It's Darla. There was an accident. I have to get to the hospital."

Twelve

Shauntae had been asleep on the couch for a few hours by the time she heard the key turning in the garage door. She got up and rushed to the kitchen to meet Gary. When the door opened, Shauntae was shocked to see that it wasn't Gary that walked through it, but Morgan. Then Daphne. Gary followed close behind with two suitcases in his hands.

"Oh!" Shauntae said. "You brought the girls."

"Of course I brought the girls," Gary said. "You thought I would leave them?

"No, of course not. I . . . I didn't know the accident was that bad. Is Darla . . ." Shauntae followed Gary and the girls through the foyer to the foot of the stairs.

He stared at her. "Shauntae, can you help me get the girls upstairs and into bed? They've had a long, difficult day."

"Oh. Of course. Sorry." Shauntae wasn't sure what he wanted her to do. Couldn't the girls walk up the stairs by themselves and get in the bed? Was she supposed to carry them? She thought for a second. What would Clair Huxtable do?

Shauntae held out a hand to each of the girls. "You poor dears. Let's get you upstairs and into bed."

The older girl rolled her eyes and walked past Shauntae. Shauntae knew Daphne was gonna be a problem. The younger one, Morgan, let Shauntae guide her up the stairs and into her bedroom. Gary followed them with the suitcases. They looked heavy. How long were they gonna stay?

"Their pajamas should be in this suitcase." Gary put the bigger suitcase on Morgan's bed. Daphne stood in the doorway waiting while Shauntae and Morgan had found the pajamas.

"Okay, you girls go ahead and put your pajamas on and get in the bed. You need your rest," Shauntae said.

Daphne frowned in the same rude, snooty way her mother did. "We have to brush our teeth and wash our faces first." She looked at Shauntae like she didn't know anything.

"Of course. Change your clothes, wash your faces and brush your teeth, and then get in the bed."

Morgan looked up at Shauntae and said, "Will you say our prayers with us?"

Shauntae put a hand on Morgan's back and rubbed up and down, like Clair Huxtable would. "Of course, dear."

Daphne gave her another nasty look. "You can say prayers with Morgan and Daddy will say prayers with me."

Shauntae waited in Morgan's bedroom until she came back from the bathroom. "You ready?"

Morgan nodded. She was a pretty little girl, and even though she looked exactly like her mother, Shauntae decided she was gonna try to be nice to her. Daphne, well . . . she was gonna have to work hard to keep from slapping her.

Morgan got down on her knees beside the bed, bowed her head, and folded her hands. Shauntae sat there and waited for her to say her prayers. Finally Morgan opened one eye. "I thought you said you would pray with me."

"Oh, I'm supposed to pray? I thought you were saying your bedtime prayers."

Morgan shook her head. "No, my mother says prayers for me. I don't have to say them myself until I'm eight."

"Oh. Okay. All right, then." Shauntae bowed her head. "Um, dear God." Shauntae tried to think of the things Gary said when they prayed together. "Um, we pray for Morgan's mother, Darla, that you would take care of her and help her get better. Um . . ."

What else was she supposed to pray for?

Morgan opened one eye again. "What's wrong, Miss Shauntae?"

Shauntae's eyes widened. "Huh?"

"You're not praying."

"Oh. Um, I'm just upset about what happened to your mother."

"But you have to pray or I can't go to sleep."

"Oh. Okay. Ummmm . . ." Shauntae couldn't think of anything to pray for.

Morgan called out, "Daddy, can you come say prayers with me when you finish with Daphne?"

Not even an hour with the girls in the house and she was already failing the Clair Huxtable test.

Gary appeared in the doorway a few minutes later. "What's wrong, sweetie?"

Morgan looked at Shauntae suspiciously. "She said she would say bedtime prayers with me, but she won't. You know I can't go to sleep without bedtime prayers."

"Of course, dear." Gary knelt beside Morgan. He prayed in that rich bass voice, "Dear Heavenly Father. We thank you so much for life, health, and strength. We thank you for love and family . . ."

Shauntae knew she should focus on every word he was saying and try to memorize it so she would be able to say it if Morgan ever asked her to pray again, but her mind was spinning. She was supposed to be getting on a bus to California right now and instead she was playing mother to Gary's kids?

"God, we trust you to heal Mommy. We know that you're a healer and that you're watching over her right now. Father, I thank you that you give the girls peace, that they won't fear, but that they will trust in you . . ."

What should she do now? She should've been on that bus before Gary got home. But since Darla was in an accident, she couldn't do a background check. Shauntae had more time.

Her cell phone buzzed in her pocket. She knew who it was. She wanted to figure out a plan before she talked to Sherice, so she wouldn't get cussed out. After a few seconds, it stopped buzzing. Almost as soon as it stopped, it started buzzing again.

"In Jesus' name, amen." Gary finally finished praying. No wonder Morgan said she couldn't fall asleep without bedtime prayers. They was so long and boring it would put anyone to sleep.

"Daddy, would you tuck me in?"

"Of course, baby."

"Is Mommy going to die?"

"Of course not. God is taking good care of her."

"So why couldn't we talk to her on the phone?"

"Mommy is asleep right now. The kind of sleep where she can't wake up to talk to you on the phone."

Shauntae's cell phone continued buzzing as Morgan climbed into the bed and Gary pulled the covers up over her. He sat down on the bed next to her.

Shauntae held up the phone. "It's my mama. I gotta get this."

Gary was all caught up in his little girl, like Shauntae wasn't even in the room.

Shauntae slipped out into the hall and answered the phone. "Hello?"

"Heffa, what is your problem? I'm down the street waiting for you. Come outside and walk down the block to the right. I'm at the corner parked not too far from the stop sign."

"I can't."

"When I drove by, I saw that the house was all lit up. He woke up? You must not have handled your business."

Shauntae went down the steps and into the family room. "Darla was in a accident. Gary went to see her and then brought the girls back here to stay until she gets out the hospital."

"And so you had plenty of time to get out of the house."

"But if Darla was in an accident, she can't do the background check. She in the hospital."

"And?" Sherice said. "Women like her travel with they laptops. And the hospital probably has Internet. She could type in your name at any time, Shauntae. This don't change nothing. You still need to get on that bus and get out of Atlanta."

"I think she in a coma. She can't do no background check in a coma."

"Shauntae, you done gone completely fool? That big house done gone to your head? Or is it the man? You done fell in love? Because what you doing right now is stupid. You wanna be pregnant and have a baby in the county jail?"

"But if she can't do the background check, I won't go to jail. And if she in a coma, she ain't gonna wake up and first thing she think about is a background check. I'll have time to get out of here when I find out she's awake."

"Fine. I'm through with you. When you get locked up, don't call me."

"Sherice, don't be like that. I'm just gonna—"

Click.

Shauntae shoved the phone back in her pocket. It probably was a good thing that Sherice hung up on her because she really didn't know what it was that she was "just gonna" do.

"Shauntae?" Gary's voice called out to her from upstairs. "Everything okay with your mom?"

"Yes, she's fine." Shauntae walked slowly up the steps. Gary took her hand and led her into his bedroom—the part where the couch was. They sat down next to each other.

He rubbed his head. "Darla is in pretty bad shape. She's in the ICU with a bad head injury. She's in a coma right now. And she had some internal injuries with bleeding, too. All we can do is watch and wait."

Gary held his head in his hands like he couldn't believe what was happening. "She had just dropped the girls off at the house with the nanny. I'm glad they weren't in the car. My little girls . . ." He let out a deep breath. "It's all so much for them to handle. First the divorce, and then not being able to see me because of the custody battle, and now this. I don't know how all of this will affect them."

Shauntae wanted to tell him that she had been through stuff a hundred times worse and she had turned out fine. Instead she said, "God will take care of them, baby. They'll be fine."

"You're right. Thanks, honey." Gary kissed her hand and then held it in his lap. "So, you're okay with the girls being here for a while?"

"Of course. It's what we wanted. Not the way we wanted it, but still, we're all here together under one roof and that's all that matters." Shauntae was getting kinda good at saying the right thing at the right time. The movies and television shows she'd been studying was helping.

"You sure you're okay taking care of them? I know you've been a little ill lately with the pregnancy."

"I'll be fine, baby."

"Thank God tomorrow is Saturday, so they won't miss school. Come next week, if their mother is doing okay, I want to keep them in their regular routine as much as possible. They've been through so much . . . they need the normalcy. We'll have to get you a car soon, so you can help getting them to and from school and everywhere else they have to go. Like in the next couple of days."

He was gonna buy her a car in the next couple of days? Shauntae tried to remember that Darla was in a coma and she shouldn't be excited right now. Would he get her a Lexus or a Mercedes?

Shauntae made herself focus on what Gary was saying.

"And I'll have to get copies of their daily schedule so you'll know about homework and what school uniforms they have to wear on what days for chapel and PE. And their weekly schedule so you can help out with their dance rehearsals and soccer practice. And, also, Daphne has a few food allergies that I'll have to tell you about so you don't cook anything that will make her sick. And . . ."

Shauntae's face must have looked some kinda way because Gary stopped. "Sorry. Too much all at once, huh?"

Shauntae nodded.

Gary squeezed her hand. "It's okay. I know this is all new to you, but you're gonna be a great mother. Maybe we'll get the nanny to come help you out for a while."

"That would be good."

"And Darla's mother will be flying in tomorrow. I'm sure she'll want to come spend some time with the girls as well."

Shauntae's eyes flew open.

Gary laughed. "Don't worry. Darla's mother is the sweetest person you ever want to meet. Nothing like Darla."

Shauntae would have to see that to believe it. Nobody could be that evil naturally. It had to come from somewhere.

"We should get some sleep," Shauntae said. "It's been a long day and we don't know what tomorrow will hold.

We need to be well rested so we can be there for the girls. And I'm sure you'll need to go to the hospital to check on Darla." Shauntae leaned over and kissed Gary on the cheek.

"That's why I love you, Shauntae. You are definitely the perfect woman for me." He leaned over and kissed her lips. "I'm sorry about earlier. I shouldn't have let that happen. It's . . . I can't stand to see you cry. It really upset me and I . . . I lost control. I'm sorry that I didn't honor you for the woman of God you are."

Shauntae patted his hand. "It's okay. It's not like I tried to stop you. We're both guilty. But God will forgive us. I already prayed for us."

"Thanks, love. I know you got us covered."

They stood up. Gary said, "I think we're going to have to get married sooner than we planned. I can't have you living here with the girls and we're not married. We'll go to the justice of the peace when everything calms down a little, hopefully in the next couple of weeks. Until then, I don't even know what to tell the girls."

"We'll pray and God will tell us what to do. Don't worry about anything." Shauntae slowly walked down the hall to the guest room. She got in the bed fully dressed because she still didn't know what to do. Should she call Sherice back as soon as Gary fell asleep and get a ride to the bus station? Or should she stay and get her new car and get married . . . all in the next few weeks?

Thirteen

Shauntae didn't know she had fallen asleep until the sun shining through her window woke her up. When she threw her legs over the side of the bed to get up, she realized she still had her clothes on.

What was it gonna be? Shower and put on a fresh set of clothes for all day on the bus, or something to lounge around the house with Gary and the girls all day. Before she could decide, there was a knock at the door.

Gary popped his head in. "Hey, baby. I have to get going. I need to go to the hospital to see what's going on with Darla. Then I need to run by the office to pick up a few files so I can work at home. No telling what the next few days will be like so I want to stay ahead of the game. Then I'll need to go to the airport to pick up Darla's mother and take her back to the hospital. And then I'll be home."

"That sounds like a lot, baby."

Gary shrugged. "I know, but it all has to be done. Can you get the girls some breakfast when they wake up? I haven't heard them stirring yet, but they usually wake up starving. Their favorite thing is pancakes, eggs, and turkey sausage. I think we should have everything downstairs. I promise I'll be back as soon as I can. Okay?"

All Shauntae could do was nod and say, "Okay."

He leaned over, put a quick kiss on her lips, and was gone.

Pancakes, eggs, and turkey sausage? She couldn't cook all that. What was wrong with cereal? Or Pop-Tarts?

Shauntae picked up her phone and speed dialed Candy.

"What?" Candy didn't pick up the phone cussing like Sherice usually did but she didn't sound like she was too far from it.

"I need some help, girl."

"I can't talk to you now, Shauntae."

Had Sherice called her and told her about the situation? Usually, when two of them was fighting, the other one stayed cool with both of them and usually brought them all back together.

"I know I shoulda left, but Sherice didn't tell you the whole story. I— "

"What are you talking about? I got company. I can't talk to you."

"For real, girl? My bad. I'm sorry. But . . ."

"What?" Candy was two seconds from cussin'.

"Can you . . . Real quick, could you tell me how to make pancakes, eggs, and turkey sausage?"

Click.

Shauntae was on her own. She went down to the kitchen to practice before the girls got up. If she messed up the first time, she could throw everything away and start over again.

Shauntae looked in the freezer, hoping to find them frozen pancakes you put in the microwave. Brianna used to beg for them 'cause that's what Devon fed her at his house. Instead, she found a box of pancake mix in the pantry. How hard could it be?

Thirty minutes later, the girls came tearing downstairs because the daggone smoke alarm went off.

"What's that?" Morgan ran up to Shauntae and threw her arms around her waist.

Shauntae's first mind was to peel her off and make her go sit down somewhere. She couldn't stand no child hanging all off her like that. Instead, she pulled a Clair

Huxtable move. "It's okay, sweetie." She wrapped her arms around Morgan and held her close.

Morgan covered her ears. "Make it stop. Please, Miss Shauntae."

Shauntae opened the garage door, picked up the broom, and started fanning near the smoke detector.

Daphne rolled her eyes, walked over to the stove, and pushed a button. A metal thing rose up from behind the burners, and then a vent came on and sucked up all the smoke. Shauntae had wondered why she couldn't find a hood vent over the stove. Durned fancy kitchen.

Within a few minutes, the smoke alarm stopped. Morgan looked up at her, hands still over her ears. "Is it over?"

Shauntae nodded and rubbed her back. "Everything's okay, sweetie. Miss Shauntae had a little problem with the stove, that's all."

"Problem with the stove?" Daphne looked at the skillet filled with grease and burnt pancake batter. She gave Shauntae that snooty look. "Is it the stove that's the problem?"

"I'm not used to cooking with gas. My stove was electric," Shauntae said.

Daphne walked over to the bowl filled with pancake batter and lifted the spoon. It was so thick and lumpy it barely poured. She turned back to look at Shauntae, but didn't say anything. She carried the bowl to the sink and turned it upside down.

"What are you doing? Why did you pour that out?"

Daphne gave her another one of her looks. She pulled a bigger bowl out of the cabinet and poured pancake mix into it. She took a couple of eggs out of the refrigerator and cracked them into the bowl. She looked at Morgan, who was still clinging to Shauntae, and said, "Moogie, how many pancakes would you like?"

Morgan scrunched up her nose and started counting her fingers. She stopped when she got to four. "Four baby ones."

"How about we start with three?"

Morgan nodded.

Daphne glared at Shauntae and then looked back down at her sister. "Moogie, why don't you let Miss Shauntae go? I'm sure she doesn't want you hanging all over her like that."

Morgan held on to Shauntae tighter.

"I don't mind." Shauntae put both arms around Morgan and gave her a squeeze. Not because she didn't mind, but 'cause it seemed to bother Daphne.

Daphne clenched her teeth together. After a second, she put on an excited, happy face. "Moogie, it's Saturday morning. You want to watch cartoons?"

Morgan's face lit up. She let go of Shauntae and ran into the living room. She grabbed the remote, jumped up onto the couch, and turned the TV on. She turned the channel and *The Backyardigans* blasted through the room.

"Moogie, turn it down. You know better."

Daphne stirred the pancake batter until it was smooth. She took a new skillet from the cabinet beneath the stove and moved aside the one Shauntae had been using. After giving Shauntae another one of her looks, she grabbed a rag and wiped the spattered grease off the stove, counter, and tiles behind the stove.

Shauntae took the skillet over to the sink and washed it. It was the least she could do since Daphne had taken over breakfast. "Should I cook the turkey sausage?"

"Mommy doesn't want us eating it anymore. Too much saturated fat."

"Oh." Shauntae stood there watching Daphne. She let the oil get to the right temperature and tested it out with a small drop of batter.

"Where did you learn how to cook?" Shauntae asked. She felt funny standing there watching Daphne cook, but it didn't seem right to leave since she should've been the one doing it.

Daphne poured four small pancakes into the large skillet. "The nanny taught me. She said that since my mother is so busy and works all the time, I needed to learn how to take care of me and Moogie."

"Moogie?"

"I was four when Morgan was born and couldn't say her name." Daphne almost smiled.

"Oh. That's cute." Shauntae couldn't think of anything else to say. Daphne didn't seem interested in keeping the conversation going so she stood there, watching her flip perfect pancakes. After the first ones finished cooking, Daphne poured two large pancakes. Shauntae's stomach rumbled real loud.

"How many pancakes would you like?" Daphne asked.

"Huh? Oh, two is fine for me," Shauntae said. "Thank you."

Daphne nodded.

"Should I cook the eggs? Your dad said you would want eggs with the pancakes."

"Miss Shauntae, can you cook eggs?"

Shauntae bit her lip. "Not really."

Morgan called out from the living room. "Miss Shauntae, can you come watch cartoons with me?"

Shauntae looked at Daphne, almost like she was asking permission. Daphne frowned, shrugged, and flipped the pancakes.

Shauntae went to the living room and sat down on the couch next to Morgan. *The Backyardigans* was one of the shows Brianna watched that got on her last nerve with all that singing and dancing. Shauntae had barely sat down and Morgan was snuggling up next to her.

At first Shauntae was uncomfortable with her being so close. She tried to make herself relax. She thought of what Gary had said about all the stuff the girls had been through lately. Shauntae thought about herself snuggling into Gary's side the night before and figured maybe Morgan felt the same way. Maybe she needed to feel loved. Shauntae put an arm around her.

Her mama had never showed her or her brother or sister no affection. In fact, the only time she really touched them was when she was beating them. Morgan was probably used to a whole lot of hugging and stuff because Gary was that kind of person. Shauntae wondered if Darla was all touchy like that too.

After about fifteen minutes of TV and snuggling, Daphne called out from the kitchen, "Breakfast is ready."

Morgan called back, "Can I bring it in here so I can watch my show?"

"Moogie, you know better. Daddy doesn't let us watch TV while we eat."

"But Mommy does."

"Morgan, come to the table, right now." Daphne sounded like she was the mother instead of the big sister.

Morgan hopped off the couch and turned the TV off. Shauntae followed her to the table. They all sat down together.

Daphne's spread looked good. The pancakes were a perfect golden brown, the eggs were fluffy and Daphne had cut up some oranges and strawberries and arranged them on a plate.

Shauntae picked up her fork and was about to dig in, but Daphne said, "We have to say grace first."

She said it so nasty and rude that Shauntae wanted to smack her in her mouth. But after watching her cook breakfast, she knew she needed the little brat on her side.

After they said grace and fixed their plates, they ate in silence for a while. Finally Morgan asked, "Miss Shauntae, where are you from?"

"California." Shauntae sopped up some syrup on a forkful of pancakes. She shoulda told Daphne to cook me four instead of two.

"How long are you gonna be visiting Daddy? I hope you stay awhile."

"Oh, I don't live in California anymore. That's where I'm from. I live in Atlanta now."

"Why are you visiting Daddy's house if you live in Atlanta?"

Shauntae wasn't sure what to say.

"Moogie, finish your food." Daphne shoved a strawberry in her mouth and kept her eyes on her plate.

Morgan went back to eating, but just like Brianna, she couldn't go too long without asking a question. "Miss Shauntae, do you have any kids?"

"No. Not yet." Shauntae felt bad for saying that. For some reason, it was harder lying to a child than it was lying to Gary.

"When are you gonna have some? I thought all grown-ups your age already had children," Morgan said.

"Stop asking so many questions, Morgan," Daphne said in that mother voice. "You need to finish your food so you can go upstairs and take a bath."

"Are you gonna have kids soon, Miss Shauntae?"

"Yes, Morgan." Shauntae didn't want to tell another lie. "In about five months actually. You can't tell, but there's a baby in my tummy right now. You guys are going to have a baby brother or sister soon."

Daphne dropped her fork. "What?"

Morgan frowned. "What's wrong, Dappy?"

Daphne stared at Shauntae. "You and my dad are going to have a baby?"

Shauntae nodded.

Morgan's little face looked confused. "But how can you and Daddy have a baby if you're not married? You have to be married to have a baby."

Daphne glared at Morgan. "No, you don't, stupid."

Morgan pouted. "Mommy said you're not allowed to call me stupid."

"Well, Mommy's not here, now is she, stupid?"

"Me and your daddy are getting married, Morgan," Shauntae said, hoping her good news would break up their argument. "Very soon."

Morgan and Daphne both turned to Shauntae, mouths wide open. Morgan's lips trembled. "What?"

Daphne jumped up from the table. "You're lying. My daddy is not gonna marry you. Him and Mommy are gonna get married again."

Morgan started to cry. "Dappy?" She put her face in her hands and started crying hard. Shauntae reached out to rub her back.

"Don't touch her," Daphne screamed. She grabbed Morgan's arm and dragged her out of her seat. "Come on, Moogie." She put an arm around her sister and led her into the foyer. As she turned to go up the stairs, Daphne shot Shauntae a look too evil for a girl her age.

Shauntae let out a deep breath and pulled out her cell phone and speed dialed Gary. "Honey, are you coming home any time soon? I think I messed up. Really bad."

Fourteen

It felt like Gary was in Daphne's room with both girls for hours before he finally came out. When Shauntae heard the door shut, she walked out of the guest room and into the hall to meet him. "Are they . . . is everything okay?"

Gary gave her a look. Shauntae couldn't tell if he was mad or sad or what. He marched past her down the stairs. She followed him into the family room. He stopped real fast and she bumped into his back.

He turned around. "What were you thinking, Shauntae? How could you have told them about the baby and about us getting married?" She could tell he was trying real hard not to yell.

"I didn't know I wasn't supposed to tell them."

Gary gave her a look that made her feel stupider than stupid. "How could you not know? How could you have thought it would be okay to tell them with everything that's going on?"

"I thought it would be good news."

"Good news?" Gary stared at her like she was crazy. "A perfect stranger is pregnant by their father and has moved into his house and is planning on marrying him while their mother is lying in a hospital bed in a coma. What's good about that?" His voice was so loud that Shauntae got scared.

She sank down into the couch and put her face in her hands. She tried to make tears come, but they wouldn't.

Her fake tears had never failed her before. She finally looked up at Gary. "I'm sorry. I don't know what I was thinking." She didn't feel like faking sick or faking like her hormones were making her act crazy. She didn't feel like faking anything. "I'm really, really, sorry."

He sat down on the couch next to her. He didn't touch her like he usually did.

"Are they okay?"

Gary shook his head. Him not saying anything was making her nervous.

"Gary?" Shauntae said it all soft. "I said I was sorry."

"Sorry doesn't fix it, Shauntae. Those are my . . . children. You know how important they are to me. They're very upset and very hurt right now. I can't understand why you would do that. I had planned to tell them myself. You didn't even give me a chance to explain it to them the way that I thought was best. I don't . . ." Gary's voice got loud again. "What were you thinking?"

Maybe Gary was realizing she wasn't mother material.

"Did you stop to think about what they're feeling right now? Did you stop to think about the fact that they haven't even recovered from the divorce yet? That they're still hoping me and their mother will get back together? Did you stop to think about the fact that their mother was in an accident last night and they're worried that she might die?"

Shauntae shook her head and put her face back in her hands.

Gary pulled her upright so she would have to look at him—not forceful, but firm. "Did you think about the fact that they might want to hear the news that their father is getting married to someone else from their father? Instead of a woman who's not their mother? Did you think about how any of what you told them would affect them? Did you think at all?"

Now he was calling her stupid. Too stupid to be a mother to his children. Too stupid to be his wife. Mama was right. She was too stupid for a man like Gary. What made her think she could do this? She was even too stupid to know when she was in over her head.

"How do I know that you won't make an error in judgment that hurts the girls again?"

"You can't." Shauntae got up and walked toward the stairs. Good thing her suitcases were still packed. Sherice would probably say "I told you so" all the way to the bus station.

"Where are you going? We're in the middle of a conversation."

Shauntae turned around and came back to the doorway of the family room. "Like I said, I'm sorry about telling the girls. I'm sorry I messed up and didn't know what's best for them." She turned toward the stairs again.

"Where are you going?" Gary sounded upset and confused. He got up to follow her. Shauntae started up the steps, but Gary grabbed her arm and stopped her. "Shauntae?" The confused look on his face confused her.

"I'm going back to my mama's."

"California?" he almost yelled. "What? Why?" He looked up the steps like he was worried about the girls hearing.

Shauntae allowed him to lead her back into the family room before she answered. "I'm not . . . I don't know how to be a mother. I messed up. Like you've been saying, your girls have gone through some bad stuff the past year and they don't need me around making it worse. I think it's best if I go."

"Are you leaving because you're upset that I yelled at you?" He sat her back down on the couch, all gentle and sweet, like he was afraid she was gonna break or something. "You can't leave because you're upset," Gary said, his voice much softer now. "I'm sorry that I yelled at you. I was upset that the girls were upset, but you're right. There was no cause for me to yell at you."

Shauntae's eyes had widened. He was apologizing to *her*? "I'm not leaving because I'm upset. I'm leaving because . . ."

Gary took her hands in his. "Just because we have an argument doesn't mean you leave. That's not how a relationship works. I've been there before with Darla—me leaving, her leaving, us being unable to talk about anything. That's not the way to make this thing work." Gary looked worried. "I have to be able to tell you when something upsets me without worrying that you're going to leave."

This was too confusing for Shauntae. "I'm not . . . I wasn't . . ."

"Love says we stay, Shauntae. When we make a decision to love each other, we decide to stay, no matter what. If I didn't learn anything else from my first marriage, it's that. We choose to love, and we choose to stay."

Shauntae nodded, even though he wasn't making much sense to her. First he was mad and now he was begging her not to leave?

"What?" Gary looked like he was trying to figure out why she was so confused.

"I thought you were mad at me with messing up with the girls. I thought . . ."

"You thought what?"

What was she thinking? "I know you love your girls. And . . . I'm not sure I can be a good mother to them. Especially not the kind of mother you want me to be."

"So you thought that because you made a mistake that our relationship is over?"

Shauntae nodded. "Yeah."

"I wouldn't end our relationship over one mistake, Shauntae." Gary pulled her into his arms. "We're having a child together. That means you can't decide to leave for California because we have an argument. I told you before, I can't leave Atlanta because my girls are here. And I can't have my other child growing up across the country from me. You would leave and take my child?"

Shauntae shook her head.

"So what do you mean you're going back to California? How can you say that when you know that my children and family mean the whole world to me? Over one argument?"

Shauntae remembered that whenever she wanted to get to Devon, she threatened to take Brianna and move to California. No matter how calm he tried to be during the whole argument, whenever she said that, he hit the roof. Not that Shauntae ever planned to leave with Brianna; it was just the best way to get what she wanted from Devon.

"Shauntae, you're carrying my child. That's not something I take lightly. I wouldn't throw you away because you made a mistake. Love doesn't do that. If I love you, I forgive you. We talk through it and we keep going. We keep loving each other. No matter what, okay?"

Shauntae nodded.

"Isn't that how God is? Isn't that the kind of marriage we want to have? Where love is forgiveness and love is commitment?"

Shauntae nodded again.

Gary looked at the picture of Darla and the girls on the wall. "Marriage is hard work. If both people aren't committed to it, it falls apart. What kind of marriage would we have if you're ready to leave me after one argument? I can't . . ." Gary let out a deep breath and shook his head. "I can't have children all over the country by a bunch of different women. In our divorce decree, I made

Darla agree that neither of us can move to a different city without the other's consent. I have to be in my children's lives. You have to promise never to take my child away from me."

Shauntae nodded.

"Say it."

"I promise never to take your child away from you."

"And you have to promise that if we're going to get married, that we're both committed to doing whatever it takes. I'm not trying to have a first, second, and third wife. We have to make this work." It was like he was begging her.

"I promise."

"Good." Gary looked down at his watch. "I have to get ready to go. I'm going to take the girls to the hospital and then I'll take them and their grandmother back to Darla's house. I think it would be good for them to spend some time with her. And it would be good for them to be at their other house. I should be back in a few hours."

Gary gave her a quick hug and a kiss, and then went upstairs to get the girls. She went up to her room and shut the door so she wouldn't have to see them when they left.

Shauntae's head was spinning from her conversation with Gary. Now she really didn't know what to do. She thought about calling Sherice, but didn't feel like getting cussed out. She could call Candy, but what could Candy tell her? Her mother, either. None of them knew nothing about being in a real relationship with a real man. All they knew was hustlin' and playing games to get paid. Shauntae was in way over her head and there was nobody who could help her.

For a split second, she thought about praying, but then she remembered she didn't do that. And God wasn't gonna help her seeing how she got herself into this situation trying to play Gary. And since she was faking being a Christian, God was probably getting ready to strike her any day now. Praying was the last thing she needed to do. Maybe if she kept quiet enough, God wouldn't notice her and would forget to punish her.

Shauntae didn't realize she had drifted off to sleep until the phone rang. It was Sherice.

"Hello?"

"You ready to go to the bus station yet?"

Shauntae didn't want to try to explain nothing to Sherice. "No," was all she said.

Sherice was quiet for a minute and then finally said, "You love this guy, huh?"

"No," Shauntae said. Then she thought for a second. "Well, maybe. Girl, I don't know. All this stuff got my head messed up." She lay back on the bed and stared up at the ceiling.

"Why else would your crazy tail not be on the bus right now? You ain't makin' no sense and the only thing that can make a woman not make sense like this is . . . love." Sherice said the word kinda funny. Shauntae couldn't tell if she was mad or surprised or confused.

"I don't know, Sherice. I ain't never . . . I don't know. Maybe I do love him."

"The ex-witch still in a coma?"

"For now."

"You probably right. When she do wake up, you ain't gon' be the first thing she think about. You got time to run while she still in the hospital. And who knows, you might get lucky and she might die."

"I don't want her to die. That ain't right."

"Yeah, I guess you don't want them kids full time, huh?"

Shauntae had to laugh. "Yeah. Plus, it ain't right to want somebody to die."

"Well, maybe she'll wake up and have that thing, what is it when somebody ain't got no memory? Amnesia. Maybe she'll wake up and not remember nothing and nobody."

"Sherice!" Shauntae was laughing out loud now. "Girl, you so crazy. Why you trying to kill people and give 'em amnesia?"

Sherice sucked her teeth. "Girl, I ain't trying to kill nobody. For real though, I think you crazy but . . ."

"But what?"

"I don't know. This messy life gotta end. I gotta go to family court next week to see about Li'l Ray Ray. They wanna check me out to see if he can come home. Talkin' 'bout how I need to get a job and stuff. And Raheem fussing about needing me to put more money on his books at the prison. Girl, I'm tired of all this drama. Tired of going to the club. Tired of faking this and faking that. Tired of all these different men."

Shauntae listened.

"It would be nice if you could make this work. Life gotta get better for at least one of us."

"Yeah, girl. It does."

"Anyway, I wanted to let you know me and Candy talked. Turns out that heffa got a little money in the bank. If anything go down, we got your back. You know I'm broke, but at least I got a car. You get locked up and we'll come get you out. A'ight?"

Shauntae felt like she was about to cry. "A'ight."

"Until we see what's gon' happen with the ex-witch, you keep doing what you gotta do. Watch your movies, watch some cooking shows, learn to eat some of that ol' fancy food. Whatever it takes. Do what you gotta do to become his Mrs. Right."

Fifteen

For the next few days, Shauntae barely saw Gary at all. They skipped church on Sunday because Gary was at the hospital with Darla's mother and the girls. Shauntae was happy that she didn't have to make up an excuse not to go.

Gary rented Darla's mother a car and they worked out a system for someone to be at the hospital and take care of the girls. After work, he picked up the girls from their afterschool program and took them to the hospital to check on Darla and her mother. Then he took them home to do homework and spent time with them until Darla's mother came home from the hospital to spend the night with them. Darla's mother dropped them off at school in the morning then spent the whole day at the hospital again.

Shauntae couldn't help but notice that their system didn't include her. She knew she had messed up bad, telling the girls about the baby and the marriage. It seemed like Gary didn't trust her around them anymore. That made her nervous.

He came home late at night, tired, stressed, and worried. He would tell her a little about his day at work, the girls, and Darla's progress, but then would be ready to go to bed. That made her even more nervous. All she could think about was when she had moved in with Devon and he started avoiding her when he realized she was stupid. Would Gary end up throwing her out of the house with a baby too?

Since she wasn't helping to take of the girls, Gary had forgotten all about his promise to buy her a car. She was stuck in the house all day with nothing to do but watch movies and television shows, trying to become Mrs. Perfect.

One morning, after Gary came in and kissed her goodbye and rushed off to work, Shauntae got up and wandered down the hall to his bedroom. She climbed into his huge bed and lay down on his pillow. When she took a deep breath and smelled his cologne, she felt that funny feeling in her stomach. She thought about Sherice's question. Did she love him? Was this feeling in her stomach love?

She lay there breathing in his smell and pretending he was there holding her and the feeling in her stomach got stronger. Was that what Michael Jackson meant when he sang about somebody giving him butterflies?

The more she stayed in the bed, the more she felt that butterfly feeling. What if it wasn't love? What if something was wrong with the baby? That thought made Shauntae jump out of the bed. She ran down the hall, grabbed her cell phone, and dialed Sherice.

"Heffa, you and these early morning phone calls. Ain't I told you—"

"Sherice, I think it's something wrong with the baby. I think I'm having a miscarriage."

"Oh no, girl. You can't lose that baby. You bleeding?"

"No." Shauntae sat herself down on the bed and rubbed her belly.

"You cramping? Low belly pain?"

"No." She lay down and put her feet up in the air but the fluttery feeling kept going.

"Well, if you ain't cramping and you ain't bleeding, why you thank you having a miscarriage?"

Shauntae took a deep breath and the butterflies went away for a second. "I got a jumpy feeling in my belly. Like it's some butterflies flying around in there."

Sherice laughed. "Girl, you so durned stupid. I don't know why I fool with yo' stupid tail. That's yo' baby moving, fool! Ain't nothing wrong with you."

"But it doesn't feel like kicking. It's a jumpy feeling. I can't explain it."

"I know what you talking about. I done had four babies. You can't tell me nothin' I don't know. That's what it feel like when the baby is moving before it's actually big enough to kick you."

"Oh," was all Shauntae could say. "Oh. Okay." She let out a deep breath and rubbed her belly again.

"You didn't feel that with Brianna?"

"No. I don't remember feeling nothing with her until she kicked me the first time. And that felt like a real foot. This here . . . it feels different."

"Yeah, I remember with my first baby, I thought it was gas. But it's the baby. As long as you don't feel no pain and see no blood, you should be all right."

"A'ight, girl. Thanks. I was scared."

Sherice laughed. "I know yo' tail was scared. You lose that baby and you lose everything. Your mama might not even take you in without no baby."

Shauntae was about to open her mouth and say, "No, Gary really loves me," but she stopped. Did he? Would he even be fooling with her if she wasn't pregnant with his baby?

Instead Shauntae said, "So I can walk around and do normal stuff? Or do I need to stay in bed?"

"I should hang up this phone on yo' stupid tail. Ain't nothing wrong with you."

"Good, then can you come get me? I'm about to go crazy up in the house. I feel like I'm in jail or something."

"See, you can only say some stupid junk like that 'cause you ain't never been in jail. That house ain't nothing like jail. I thought he was gon' get you a car."

Shauntae hadn't told her about messing up with the girls. She didn't need to give Sherice another reason to call her stupid. "Things have been too busy with Darla and the girls. I'm sure he will soon."

"I cain't today. Still dealing with some family court mess. They might make me take some parenting classes or some junk like that."

"That might not be a bad thing, girl. Them classes might help."

"You been watching too much Clair Huxtable if you think I wanna be sitting up in some durned class on how to be a good parent. Ain't nobody got no time for no corny mess like that."

"I'm just sayin'—"

"You just sayin' what?" Sherice's voice was rising to that point that Shauntae knew the cuss words would be coming soon.

"I'm just sayin', maybe it wouldn't hurt . . . you know."

"Don't be trying to judge me 'cause you sitting up in that fancy house pregnant with that rich man's baby. In case you forgot, you lost your child too."

"I'm not judging you. I'm thinking . . . it's like you said the other day. Something gotta get better for us. I know I lost Brianna. Maybe I need to be taking them classes with you. You could pick me up and we could go together."

Sherice didn't say nothing.

"Maybe that'll help me get Devon to lift the warrant off me. If he sees that I'm married with a new baby and I got a certificate for some parenting classes, maybe I can convince him that I'm not dangerous to Brianna anymore."

Sherice was still silent.

"What you think, girl?"

"I ain't taking no corny, stupid parenting classes. Ain't nobody gon' make me prove I can take care of my children by making me take no class. They can keep 'em."

"But, Sherice— "

"But nothing. I don't feel like talking about my kids no more, Shauntae. They probably better off where they at."

"In a foster home?"

"All foster homes ain't bad. My oldest two is with these real nice, white church people. I've met them before and they take real good care of my children. Lonesha is with a black couple and Li'l Ray Ray is with an ol' grandma. She real sweet and takes real good care of him. So they all doing fine."

"So you don't ever want none of 'em back?"

"Do you want Brianna back?"

"I . . ." Shauntae had never even thought about it. She didn't think there was a chance of her getting Brianna back, so she put it out her mind.

"That's what I thought. I hope you ain't gonna get all high and mighty like Keosha did, because you with Gary. You need to remember who you are."

"I ain't like Keosha. I ain't gon' do that."

"Uh huh . . . we'll see."

"Me and you been girls forever. We always got each other back. I ain't neva gonna change up on you like that."

"A'ight, den. Let me get this court stuff took care of. If I finish soon enough, I'll come get you. We'll swing by and get Candy and go get us some wings, fries, and *40's*. You down?"

"Yeah, girl. I'll be waiting on you. Can't wait to get out of this house and get some good food." Shauntae didn't mention the *40's*. She wasn't gon' drink but she didn't feel like hearing Sherice's mouth about not being down.

After they hung up, Shauntae lay real still on the bed. She rubbed her belly and waited for a few minutes. She felt it again. This time, it felt like little bubbles moving around.

"Hey, li'l baby. Wassup?"

The bubbles flipped and then fluttered like butterflies.

"I'm your mama, Shauntae. Your daddy's name is Gary and you got two sisters, Daphne and Morgan." Shauntae patted her belly. "I hope you a boy. I think your daddy would like that. We got enough girls in the family."

Shauntae thought for a second and then added, "You actually got three sisters. You got another sister named Brianna. I hope you'll get to meet her one day."

Shauntae thought about Sherice asking her if she ever was gonna get Brianna back. She knew Devon would probably never let Brianna stay with her, but would he keep her from meeting her little brother or sister? When she had talked to him, she told him she was pregnant, but he didn't seem to care. It didn't seem right, the baby having a big sister and never getting to meet her.

Shauntae lay on the bed with mixed-up feelings inside. The bubbles and butterflies were a happy feeling, low in her belly. But up high in her stomach, she felt a sicky type of pain. It was kinda like the feeling she got when she ate too many wings, fries, and beer, but worse. She hadn't thrown up in over a month. Hopefully it wasn't morning sickness coming back.

Shauntae patted her belly. "Li'l baby, what you doing in there? You trying to make your mama sick?" She wondered if there was any ginger ale or Sprite downstairs to make her stomach settle down.

The more she lay there, the more she realized it wasn't a throw-up feeling. It was more a feeling like when she did something low or when she knew something was wrong. The worst time she had felt it was on the bus all the way to California when she had left Brianna with the ambulance people. Was that it? She wasn't sick from the pregnancy, but was feeling bad about Brianna?

What could she do to make Devon realize she was trying to change and do things right? Would marriage, a new baby, and some parenting classes help? Devon was all about family like Gary was. If he knew Brianna had a little brother, maybe he would let her meet him and spend time with him.

Shauntae thought back to the pastor's words from church that Sunday. If God could forgive her for anything and everything she had ever done, and if Devon was a Christian, wasn't he supposed to forgive her too?

Shauntae felt the butterflies in her stomach and rubbed her belly. "Li'l baby, I'm gonna make sure you get to meet your big sister Brianna, okay? I don't know how, but I'm gonna make sure."

Sixteen

Shauntae was excited when Gary got home late that evening. He was barely through the door when she pounced on him. "I felt the baby move today!"

She felt like a little girl herself, standing there with a big, goofy smile on her face. She wanted so bad to see him smile and be happy—happy about her and the baby moving inside her.

His face broke out into a huge grin. "You felt the baby?"

Shauntae nodded. "I hadn't ever felt nothing like that before. It was like little butterflies in my belly. At first I thought it was something wrong, but then I called my girlfriend, Sherice, and she explained it was the baby moving and that it didn't have feet big enough to kick so it felt like butterflies instead." Shauntae shut her mouth. In all her excitement, she had forgotten to talk proper.

Gary laughed and put his arms around her. "That's wonderful, baby. I know it has to be exciting to feel that for the first time." He pulled back and kissed her on the nose. "I love that you're so down-to-earth. Whenever you get excited, you talk like . . . I don't know . . . like a homegirl or something. You're so cute." Gary kissed her cheek. He bent down and kissed her belly. "Hey in there. How's my baby doing?"

When he stood back up, he asked her, "When was the last time you went to the doctor? You haven't been at all since you've been here, have you?"

Shauntae shook her head. “I haven’t been since I left California.” She remembered the sick, yucky feeling in her stomach. If lying and doing stuff wrong was gonna make her feel sick, she needed to start telling the truth. “Actually, I haven’t been at all. When I was in California, I was . . . dealing with Mama.” It wasn’t really a lie.

“Baby, I’m sorry. I’ve been neglecting you because of Darla and the girls. You can’t be this far along and not have seen the doctor. We have to get you an appointment as soon as possible.” Gary opened the refrigerator door, looking for something to eat. “Can one of your friends recommend a doctor? What did you say your friend’s name was, Sherice?”

Shauntae shook her head. “She lives southeast. I’d rather find someone closer up here.” She didn’t mention that Sherice didn’t have no prenatal care with her last three children. She just showed up at the hospital when it was time to deliver them.

“I’ll see if I can get a recommendation from some of the women in my office.” Gary closed the refrigerator and went to the pantry. “My goodness, it’s empty in here. Have you eaten anything today?”

“I had some Chinese food delivered earlier.” Shauntae had gotten so hungry that she had gone to the phonebook to find a place that delivered and then had to spend some of her precious cash. Gary hadn’t given her one dime since she’d been there.

Gary closed the pantry and came over and put his arms around her. “Baby, I’m sorry. What am I thinking? I haven’t gotten any groceries and you have no way of getting out to get anything. We need to go get you some food and a car. And I’m sure you want to get out and see some of your friends. I’ve had you cooped up in the house while I’m running around everywhere, taking care of everything and everybody but my future wife and child.” He kissed her on the lips. “I’m sorry.”

"It's okay, honey. I've been fine. It's been good to rest." Okay, that was a lie. Shauntae wondered how many lies she actually told in a day. "But yeah, it would be nice to get out of the house."

"Let me change out of this suit and we'll go pick up some carryout and then stock up on a few things for the refrigerator."

Shauntae followed him up the back stairs in the family room to his bedroom. She sat in the middle of his bed while he went to his closet.

"How's Darla?" she asked.

"The doctors think she's better. She looks the same to me. They said something about the pressure in her head decreasing and that it's a good sign that she might wake up soon. They're not sure what her brain function will be like when she wakes up. All we can do is pray." Gary emerged from the closet in some khaki pants and a polo shirt.

"And how are the girls?"

"They're fine." Gary sat down on the edge of the bed. "I know I haven't brought them back over here since . . . that day. I don't want you to feel bad about it and it's not because I think you're not a good mother." Gary reached out a hand to her and Shauntae scooted from the middle of the bed and sat next to him. "I'm giving them a chance to get used to everything. It's good for them to be in their own house spending time with their grandmother. Since she lives so far, she hardly gets to see them."

"I understand, honey." Shauntae wasn't upset that the girls hadn't been around. That one incident with them was enough for her.

"I don't want you to feel bad." Gary leaned over and kissed her on the cheek.

"I don't. I . . ." Shauntae stopped midsentence. The butterflies were back.

"What's wrong?" Gary looked concerned.

Shauntae sat real still. "The baby's moving again," she said, barely above a whisper, like talking too loud might make the baby stop.

A big smile broke out on Gary's face and he put his hand on her belly.

"You feel it?" she asked him.

Gary chuckled. "It's too early for me to feel it. For the next month or so, you're the only one who gets to feel it."

Shauntae smiled and put her hand on top of Gary's. "I wish you could feel it. It's so . . . I don't know . . . amazing."

Gary chuckled and kissed her. He was in a real affectionate mood tonight. Shauntae kissed him back.

He said, "It's not fair. Mothers get to carry the baby and feel it grow inside. You get to feel it move first, you get to breastfeed. The mother gets to be closer to the child and the dad gets left out."

Shauntae laughed. "Please, if men had to do all that, people woulda gone extinct a long time ago. The earth would be filled with animals."

Gary laughed and kissed her again. He rubbed his hand over her belly. "You're so beautiful, Shauntae." He had that look on his face. The look that made Shauntae know she might not have to sleep in the guest bed tonight. She kissed him, longer and deeper. He got lost in the kiss for a second, but then pulled away from her and stood up.

"Baby, we can't." The look on his face was different from the words coming out of his mouth. "I want to, but you know we can't."

Shauntae stood and walked over to him slowly. She tried to work her body back into his embrace. "I know. It's just . . . I've missed you. I know there's a lot going on, but we haven't had any time together. I'm not trying to be selfish with Darla being in the hospital, but . . ."

Gary pulled her close. "I know. I'm sorry. I promise. Soon. We'll spend time together." He kissed her again, but then pulled away from her. "But not like this."

Shauntae folded her arms together and pouted.

Gary laughed at her. "Come on, woman of God. You'll thank me later." He flicked her bottom lip with his finger and bent to kiss it, but made sure to keep his body away from hers. He rubbed her belly and looked at her with that love-struck look on his face. "You're so beautiful, Shauntae. I love you."

The look in his eyes, Shauntae couldn't describe it. How could this man love her like he did? She wished she deserved it. Maybe she hadn't in the past, but from now on, she was gonna try to be the person he thought she was. The person he wanted her to be and the person she was starting to want to be. "Thanks, baby. I love you too."

He kept staring at her with that look in his eyes and finally bent to kiss her again. They kissed and kissed and next thing she knew, the clothes were coming off. And neither one of them tried to stop it.

Shauntae had never felt nothing like that before. She liked sex a whole lot, but this felt different. It felt . . . real somehow. Like some of her favorite romance movies and stuff. She thought about Sherice telling her that she must be in love with Gary and she was starting to believe she was.

Gary rolled over and groaned. "Baby, I'm so sorry. I didn't mean for us—"

"Please, don't apologize. Not tonight." Shauntae turned her body and snuggled into Gary's side. "I know it's not right and we'll ask God to forgive us, but can't we pretend for one night that everything is okay? That we're married and the girls are happy about it and Darla doesn't hate me and . . ." There were so many other things that Shauntae couldn't mention.

Gary kissed her forehead. "Yeah." He was quiet for a second. "We could pretend that I met you first and that all my children are by you and that I've never been divorced and that we were married before you got pregnant." He let out a deep breath. "We gotta get married soon."

Hope rose up in Shauntae's chest. Gary had been acting so funny since Darla's accident and the incident with her and the girls that she had started to worry that he didn't want to marry her anymore. "We do?"

Gary turned and looked her in the eyes. "Of course we do. Why do you ask that?"

Shauntae looked away. "Well, ever since that day with the girls and all . . . and you've hardly been here . . . and we hardly even talk anymore . . ." Shauntae couldn't say that it was exactly how things had been with her and Devon before he kicked her out.

Gary wrapped his arms around her and pulled her close to him. "You thought I didn't want to marry you anymore?"

Shauntae nodded and buried her head in his chest.

"Of course I still want to marry you." Gary pulled back and placed a finger under Shauntae's chin to lift her head. "Just because I got upset that day and because I've been busy with everything doesn't mean I don't want to marry you anymore. How do I convince you of how much I love you?"

"Like this." Shauntae pulled his head down for a deep kiss.

He pulled back and laughed. "Not again. What's gotten into you?"

Shauntae laughed with him. "I don't know. I think maybe feeling the baby move did something to me."

"Yeah, I imagine it's pretty exciting when it happens for the first time. You'll get to experience so many beautiful things having your first baby. I'm glad I get to enjoy it with you."

Shauntae felt guilty when Gary said "first baby." Even though she had made a commitment to start telling the truth, she wasn't sure what to do about the lies she had already told.

"The first pregnancy is always the most exciting. The second one, you kinda know what to expect, but it's still beautiful." Gary had this smile on his face and Shauntae knew he was thinking about his girls. "I tell you one thing, though. That first time labor is no joke. Darla was in labor for twenty-three hours with Daphne. With Morgan, it wasn't even four hours before she was born. It's much easier the second time."

Shauntae didn't want to say anything. What could she say without lying?

Gary said, "Don't worry. I'll be there with you the whole time, no matter how many hours it takes. And when you have our second one, it'll be easier."

Shauntae had only been in labor with Brianna for six hours. Sherice said it was because Shauntae had wide hips meant for having babies. "Not everybody is in labor long with their first baby," she said. What if she had this baby real quick, since it was her second? Would he get suspicious? "One of my friends was only in labor for a few hours with her first baby. Some women have birthing hips, like my mama used to say."

Gary's hands moved from Shauntae's belly down to her hips. "Well, these are birthing hips if I ever saw some." He squeezed her thick hips.

Shauntae laughed. She rolled up on top of Gary, but he rolled her back onto the bed.

"Shauntae!" He said it sternly, but then busted out laughing. "You keep acting like this and I'm gonna have to get you an apartment until the baby is born."

Shauntae froze. "I'm sorry. I won't mess with you anymore. I promise. Don't put me out."

"Don't get upset." Gary rubbed her arm. "I'm joking. Are you always this sensitive, or is it because you're pregnant?"

"Sensitive?"

"Yeah, thinking I didn't want to marry you. Getting scared that I'm gonna put you out? I love you. Stop being so afraid about us. We're going to get married and live happily ever after. I love you and nothing's gonna change that. Stop worrying so much."

Gary wouldn't be talking like that if he knew the truth about who she was. Shauntae thought of every lie she had told. What would he think if he knew about Brianna and what she had done to her? If he knew that her mama didn't have no heart attack and that she went to California running from the police.

"Shauntae?"

"Huh?" She pulled herself out of her thoughts.

"You know that, right? That I love you and that nothing could make me stop loving you?"

Why couldn't he stop talking? Shauntae was starting to get that sick feeling in her stomach. Why was this happening to her? She had hardly ever felt bad about the low stuff she did in the past.

"Shauntae?"

"But what if I did something bad? I mean, really, really bad?"

Gary laughed. "I'm sure there's nothing that you could do that's bad enough to make me not love you."

"But what if I did? What would you do?"

Gary propped himself up on his elbow and looked down at Shauntae with worried eyes. “Honey, why are you asking me that?”

Shauntae wished the lights were off so Gary couldn’t see her face. She could feel her bottom lip shaking like it used to when she got in trouble with her mama when she was a little girl. “I . . .” Her stomach turned like she was gonna throw up.

What if she told him everything? Then she wouldn’t have to worry about Darla waking up and doing a background check. She wouldn’t have to worry about running into Devon and Cassandra at church. She wouldn’t have to worry about rotting in jail because if Gary knew about everything and forgave her like he said, he would come bail her out.

“Shauntae, what is it?” Gary sat up and put his hand on her belly, like he was trying to make that stomach pain go away.

“I need to tell you something.” She couldn’t make her voice stop shaking. She tried to swallow, but her mouth felt like it was full of a peanut butter sandwich without jelly and no milk to wash it down.

“Okay . . .” Gary sat there patiently.

Before Shauntae knew what was happening, tears were flowing down her cheeks.

“What’s wrong? What is it?”

Shauntae couldn’t stop herself from crying. “It’s so many things I need to tell you.” Shauntae could almost hear Sherice, Candy, and her mama screaming in her ear, telling her not to be so stupid, to shut up and keep lying.

But something in her couldn’t. Maybe it was the way Gary looked at her and told her she was beautiful and that he loved her. Maybe it was the way she was starting to feel when she told him she loved him back, not like she was running game, but like she really meant it. Maybe it was wanting to have this baby and be a real family like Gary was always talking about. Wanting the new baby to be able to know Brianna.

"Baby, please talk to me. Whatever it is, it'll be all right."

Shauntae sat up, ready to tell it all. If Gary wanted to keep his promise of loving her no matter what, then they'd get married and live happily ever after without a bunch of lies keeping her scared all the time. If he didn't, then she'd give him his baby and go back to California.

She scooted to the edge of the bed. "Okay, I don't know where to start. And let me finish before you say anything."

"Shauntae . . ." Gary's voice croaked out. She turned around to see what his problem was. Maybe he didn't want to hear the truth after all. She looked at his face and then followed his panic-filled eyes down to the sheets.

From where Shauntae had been lying to where she was sitting, there was a trail of blood.

Seventeen

It was the first time in her life that Shauntae had ever prayed. The whole way to the hospital all she could say was, "God, please don't let my baby die. God, please save my baby," over and over again.

Gary drove fast but safe and in less than twenty minutes they pulled up at the emergency room at Northside Hospital. Gary was calm and able to answer all the questions the doctors and nurses were asking. Everything was a blur to Shauntae.

All she could think of was that if she lost this baby, her life was over. She wouldn't have nowhere to go and no way to bring money in. She was tired of hustling sponsors. Without a baby, her mother would only let her stay so long. She needed this baby.

When they got her back into the exam room, she calmed down. She wasn't feeling any pain and there hadn't been any more blood after that smear on the sheets. She looked at the pad she had put on while getting dressed to go to the hospital. It was clean.

Shauntae shivered on the exam table. The gown she had on was thin and she was cold. Gary stood and put his jacket around her arms. "You okay?"

Shauntae nodded.

"I'm sure the baby is fine, honey. The bleeding stopped, right?"

Shauntae nodded numbly.

He put his arms around her. "The baby is gonna be fine, okay? God wouldn't let another bad thing happen to us right now."

He kept patting her and rubbing her arm. Shauntae thought he was comforting himself more than he was comforting her.

Finally, a medium-brown woman with a tiny, curly Afro came into the room with a clipboard. She was real pretty in the face and had a nice smile. She looked up from the clipboard at Shauntae. "Ms. Randall, I'm Dr. Murray. How are you?" She shook Shauntae's hand firmly and then looked over at Gary. "And you are?"

Gary stood up and shook her hand. "Gary Jackson, her fiancé and the father of the baby."

"Good to meet you both." She looked down at the clipboard again and then back at Shauntae. "So you started having some bleeding this evening? Any pain or cramping with it?"

Shauntae shook her head.

"How much blood was it? Pouring, heavy like a period, or a little?"

"A little on the sheets. Not much at all. And there hasn't been any since then."

The doctor nodded and jotted on her clipboard. She looked back up. "No other issues so far in the pregnancy? The nurse's note says you haven't had any prenatal care and you're not sure of your due date?" The doctor had a worried frown on her face.

Gary spoke for her. "She just moved back to Atlanta from California. Her mother had a heart attack and so she was focused on her care rather than her own. We plan to find her a doctor as soon as possible."

The doctor nodded and looked down at her clipboard again. "This is your first pregnancy?"

Gary spoke up for her again. "Yes."

Shauntae looked at the doctor. She was scared that maybe if she didn't have all her information, she might not know how to take care of her right. If she was having a miscarriage because of all the abortions and diseases she'd had in the past, the doctor needed to know that.

"No, I've been pregnant before." She turned to Gary as she explained, "I had a miscarriage about eight years ago." Shauntae wanted to tell the doctor about her abortions and Brianna, but she couldn't in front of Gary. She had been ready to tell him everything at the house, but the ER wasn't the time or place for making confessions.

The doctor jotted a note on her clipboard and then asked, "Any other pregnancies? It's really important that I have a good grasp on your obstetrical history."

Shauntae sat there for a few moments.

Gary nudged her. "It's okay, baby. Tell the doctor whatever you need to tell her." He took her hand in his.

"I was pregnant a few other times . . ." she turned toward Gary ". . . before I got saved." Shauntae hung her head. "I've had a few abortions."

Gary's mouth became a thin line. Shauntae was sure he was through with her.

The doctor looked at Gary and then at Shauntae. "Ms. Randall, why don't I go ahead and examine you and then we can get the rest of the history later. We should check on your baby."

Dr. Murray reached into a large pocket at the bottom of her white coat and pulled out an instrument that Shauntae recognized from her pregnancy with Brianna. "Lie back for me and let's see if we can hear the baby's heartbeat." She picked up a bottle and held it over Shauntae's stomach. "This may be cold."

Shauntae flinched as the doctor spread cold jelly on her lower stomach. As Dr. Murray placed the probe on her belly, she prayed, *God, please let my baby be alive.*

Within seconds, her prayer was answered. A loud, rhythmic, squishy-sounding *boom, boom, boom* came through the machine. The doctor smiled. "There's your baby."

Shauntae couldn't tell whose sigh of relief was louder, hers or Gary's. He squeezed her hand and kissed her on the forehead. Tears trickled down her cheeks. "He's okay. My baby's okay."

"He?" the doctor asked. "You've had an ultrasound?"

Gary looked at Shauntae with a surprised smile on his face. "We're having a boy?"

Shauntae shook her head while she wiped her tears. "I don't know. I haven't had an ultrasound but I feel like . . . I think it's a boy."

"Okay, honey." Gary kissed her cheek again.

Dr. Murray wiped off the heart monitor probe and placed it on the counter by the sink. "Okay, now that we've confirmed the baby's alive, I'll need to do a few more things. Mr. Jackson, perhaps you'd like to step out while I perform the vaginal exam? It won't take too long. There's a quieter waiting room at the end of the hall."

Gary stood and gave Shauntae's hand a squeeze before he walked out of the room.

After he was far enough away that he couldn't hear, the doctor sat on the small stool near the exam bed. "So exactly how many pregnancies and how many abortions?"

Shauntae bit her lip and counted in her head. "I've been pregnant seven times altogether." She rubbed her belly. "This one is the seventh. I've had four abortions, one miscarriage, and . . ." It sounded so bad when she said it out loud. She had never actually counted it up before.

"And . . ." The doctor nodded for her to go on.

"One child. A daughter. Six, seven years ago. She's not with me anymore."

The doctor put a hand on top of Shauntae's hand. "She died?"

"No." Shauntae shook her head quickly. "She lives with her father. I'm . . . I'm not a part of her life anymore."

The doctor took her hand off Shauntae's hand to jot more notes on her clipboard. "I'm guessing Mr. Jackson didn't know about any of those pregnancies?"

Shauntae shook her head and looked down at her hands.

The doctor let out a deep sigh, like she was used to Shauntae's kind of case. "I'm a doctor, not a therapist or a relationship counselor, but maybe, don't you think, you should have a talk with him? Relationships work best when both people are completely honest with one another."

Shauntae nodded. There was nothing she could say to explain herself to this woman. Not that she would understand. By the way she looked, Dr. Murray had never had a hard day in her life. She probably never had a stepfather who messed with her, or a mother who beat her and cussed her out for no reason, and she'd probably never been broke enough that she had to depend on a man for money.

Shauntae wanted to be mad at the doctor but she couldn't. The doctor hadn't done nothing but treat her nice since she got there. She didn't say nothing to judge her and she wasn't looking down her nose at her. She was nice enough to send Gary out of the room so she could ask the rest of her questions without Shauntae getting embarrassed. Shauntae couldn't be mad at nobody but herself.

Dr. Murray put a hand on her arm. "Let's go ahead and do your exam, okay?"

Shauntae followed the doctor's instructions and slid down to the end of the table and let her legs fall open. She had hated that cold metal thing the few times she'd been examined during her pregnancy with Brianna and couldn't understand why any woman would want to get a pap smear once a year.

When she was finished, the doctor helped Shauntae to scoot back on the table. "Your cervix is closed and I don't see any bleeding at all. Tell me, when was the last time you had intercourse?"

Shauntae's hung her head. "Before we came in. Right before the bleeding started."

Dr. Murray nodded. "That's what I thought. Everything looks okay and your uterus feels about eighteen to twenty weeks' size. We'll be able to confirm that your baby is fine with some blood work and with an ultrasound. We'll also be able to see exactly how far along you are. You ready to see your baby?"

Shauntae nodded.

The doctor smiled and patted her arm. "Okay, we'll get the ultrasound tech in as soon as we can. And I'll send Mr. Jackson back in. I'm sure he'll want to be here for that." She smiled that real nice smile again and Shauntae could tell she was one of those people with a really nice heart. Before Dr. Murray walked out the door, she turned and said, "Ms. Randall?"

"Yes?"

"You said all these pregnancies and abortions happened before you got saved?"

Shauntae nodded.

"Then remember, they're under the blood. God has forgiven you and you have nothing to be ashamed about. You've given your life to Him and He loves you. Nothing can change that." She patted Shauntae's arm one more time and then disappeared from the room.

Shauntae's mouth fell open. She looked around the room, unable to believe what the doctor had said. Did God have secret agents all over the place that He kept sending her, trying to make her believe that He loved her?

Gary came back in the room. "The doctor said it looks like everything with the baby is okay?"

"Yeah, she thinks the bleeding was because we had sex."

Gary closed his eyes. "This is my fault. I should have—"

"Baby, please don't. It's both our faults."

Gary took both her hands in his. He stood there without saying anything. Shauntae wondered if, since Gary was a Christian, he felt the same way about her past that the doctor did.

Gary squeezed her hands. "So is that what you were going to tell me about tonight? The other pregnancies and the abortions and the miscarriage?"

Shauntae nodded, afraid to say anything out loud.

Gary let go of one of her hands and leaned his tall body next to her against the exam table. "I guess there's a lot we don't know about each other's pasts and who we were before we got saved."

Shauntae's breath caught. Maybe he did agree with the doctor.

"I would be lying if I said it didn't bother me."

Her heart sank.

"I mean, you know how I feel about kids and family. It's hard to think about . . . all those children . . ." Gary closed his eyes and shook his head.

Shauntae's heart sank even further.

"But, like you said, it was before you got saved. Jesus forgives you and . . ." Gary turned to face Shauntae and grabbed both her hands again. "Jesus forgives you and so do I."

Shauntae leaned forward and buried her head in Gary's chest. She couldn't believe her ears. Could this man be this good? Could Jesus be that good?

He pulled her close to him and rubbed his hand up and down her back. "I told you, Shauntae, I love you and there's nothing you can do to change that. You have to believe me."

Shauntae wrapped her arms around Gary's waist and held on tight.

"You believe me?"

Shauntae nodded into Gary's chest. He put one hand on her head and the other on her back.

She wanted to tell him the rest. It was one thing to have had pregnancies and abortions before she so-called got saved. But would he still love her if he knew she actually had a living child? A living child she had almost killed by being a bad mother? Would he still love her then?

Tell him, Shauntae. Get it all out there so you can stop being scared of getting caught all the time.

Gary ran his fingers through her thick hair. "I don't want you to ever feel like there's anything you can't tell me. Okay? You have to trust that I love you no matter what."

Shauntae nodded into his chest again. *This is your chance, girl. Tell him!*

"We have to be completely honest with each other for this relationship to work. No more secrets, okay?" He pulled back from her and looked at her face. "Okay?"

"Okay," Shauntae said. She took a deep breath and got herself ready to tell him about Brianna. But then she thought about all the other things she would have to tell him.

Not only did she have a living child, but she had left that child with the ambulance people not even a year ago. She couldn't go anywhere near that child because of a restraining order and an arrest warrant—an arrest warrant for leaving the child in the house alone while she was out dating him. That she was out dating him because she wanted to get her bills paid. That she didn't leave suddenly because her mother had a heart attack, but because she was running from the police.

What they said about stuff happening before she was saved and being under the blood? She wasn't even saved now. All the reasons he thought he loved her were big, fat lies.

So even though he said he loved her and nothing she ever did or could do could make him stop loving her, the woman he loved was Shauntae, the good Christian girl who loved marriage and family. He loved Angela Bassett and Clair Huxtable and all the female stars in Tyler Perry's movies who had taught her to be the woman he wanted her to be. Not the real her.

He smoothed his hands along her face. "That's all? Is there anything else you need to tell me?"

Shauntae smiled up at him sweetly. "No, baby. That's everything. Except that I love you."

Gary smiled and kissed her on the nose. "I love you too, baby."

Eighteen

Even though everything was fine with the baby, the doctor told Shauntae she needed to rest over the next couple of days. She also said no more sex, but Shauntae already knew Gary wasn't gon' touch her again. He wasn't gonna risk anything happening to the baby.

Shauntae figured that hearing the baby's heartbeat and then seeing the baby on the quick ultrasound had done something to Gary. He was all sweet and paying attention to her. Over the next couple of days, he brought stuff from the office to work at home. He brought her breakfast in her room. Every day, he either cooked dinner or brought her carryout.

He would come sit in her room and talk for a long time, staring at her with love-struck eyes. At first she was nervous about saying dumb stuff or talking bad English, but it didn't matter. If she forgot to talk proper, he laughed and said she was down-to-earth instead of stuck-up like Darla.

The first few times he talked about something she didn't understand, she tried to fake it, but couldn't. When he figured out that she didn't understand, he was patient and sweet and broke stuff down to explain it to her. Not like she was stupid, but like she was a smart person who wasn't familiar with what he was talking about. Shauntae didn't know whether he was being nice, or whether he really thought she was the smart person she was pretending to be.

They talked about his business—which she was finally starting to understand—politics, and church stuff. Shauntae remembered Sherice's advice and asked him lots of questions about himself. Partly to learn more about him and how to make him happy, and partly to keep him from asking questions about her.

It was nice. She had never spent time talking to no man like that. Usually, men only wanted to have sex with her, not talk to her. Lots of times when they was talking, Gary told her how beautiful she was. He would kiss her and tell her how much he loved her. A few times he tried to lie down so they could snuggle, but then he had to leave the room so they wouldn't end up having sex.

The last time it happened, he came back in the room and sat on the bed next to her. "Shauntae, can we talk?"

She sat up and clicked off the television. She was always watching the Cooking Channel and was thinking about trying some dishes when she could get out of the bed.

"I think we need to go ahead and get married."

He had Shauntae's full attention.

"I've been waiting because of the girls and was worried about what it would do to them while their mom is still in the hospital. I've been worried about how it might affect things with the whole custody situation with Darla."

Shauntae almost shuddered when he said Darla's name. She was waiting every day for her to wake up, open her laptop, do the background check, and bust Shauntae's whole game.

Gary kept talking. "But, really, this is what I want. It's what we want. I know it's important for parents to make sacrifices for their children, but I'm not sure there's a best time. The girls don't want me to get married because they think I'm gonna marry their mother again. That's never going to happen. I'm going to marry you and whether we do that now or we do it six months from now, it's still going to hurt them."

Was Gary expecting her to say anything? Shauntae waited until he did what he usually did—talk for a while, and then stop and ask what she thought.

"And, in thinking of Daphne and Morgan, I haven't thought about our new baby. I want this baby to grow up in a normal family with a mother and father. I can't give that to Daphne and Morgan anymore, but I can give it to our new baby. Right?"

"Right, baby." The way Gary thought was so different. Most people she knew just had babies. They didn't care whether they was growing up in a good family. They didn't think about they children when they was making decisions; they just did what they wanted. She could tell he thought about his kids with everything he did and how the stuff he did would affect them.

"Plus, with you not working, you don't have health insurance. When we get married, you'll be able to get on my insurance. Dr. Murray is expecting you back in her office soon for your first prenatal visit. And we have to get that full ultrasound she talked about and find out if you are indeed having a boy."

He looked around at the guest room. "It would be perfect if it's a boy. The room is already blue. We'd only have to get baby stuff. I'm thinking you don't want to use the stuff that we kept from when Morgan was a baby. You wouldn't want to use the crib and stuff that Darla picked out, would you?"

Shauntae hadn't even thought about it. "It's fine with me. No sense in buying all new stuff if you already have it. We need to do some decorating to make it a boy's room. I'm sure all Morgan's stuff is pink. Let's wait and see what we're having first."

Gary smiled. "Yeah, I guess we should wait. If it's a girl, maybe we'll do yellow. We already have a pink room."

Shauntae had to work on herself. Gary couldn't be more excited about all this baby stuff than she was.

"I guess your girlfriends will want to throw you a baby shower. You're welcome to have it here if they like."

Shauntae almost laughed. She could imagine Candy and Sherice and some of their other girls tipping up *40's* to celebrate Shauntae's baby shower. "Thanks, but Sherice will probably have the shower at her place."

"And we need to get you a vehicle. I'm sure that now more than ever you'll be ready to get out of this house when the doctor releases you. What kind of car do you want?"

"Whatever you think is best." Shauntae had learned early in her hustling career that you always let a man pick what he wanted to give you. If you order filet mignon and he's only trying to pay for an appetizer, you could get yourself embarrassed. Always let him decide, so you don't get embarrassed by picking something that costs too much.

"You don't have a certain car you'd prefer?"

"No, it's all about our child. Whatever has the best safety ratings. I'm sure you'll do some research on the Internet and pick out whatever's best."

"Okay. I'll surprise you." Gary thought for a second and then said, "I'm sure you'll want to go shopping for the baby and for yourself; your belly is starting to show. You'll need some maternity clothes. I'll have to order you a credit card."

Shauntae could hardly contain her excitement. If she knew that hearing the heartbeat and seeing the baby on the ultrasound would have done all this, she would have faked bleeding or cramping much sooner. "Baby, you're so sweet. You think of everything."

"There's nothing that's too good for you, Shauntae." He leaned over and kissed her on the lips. He lingered for a few minutes and kissed her deeper. "Yeah, we need to get married. What is it that you do to me?"

Shauntae giggled. She couldn't believe she was acting like a silly teenage girl. Giggling and feeling all romantic and in love and all that dumb junk. She could hear her mother mocking her, telling her how stupid she was for falling in love with a man in the biggest hustle of her life.

Girl, you so dumb. Do you really think you can keep this man? Bad enough you dumb, now you got your head all clouded up with some so-called love and you gon' mess this up. And then you ain't gon' have no man, and no check.

Gary kissed her again and she turned off her mother's voice in her head. She reached up and wrapped her arms around him and pulled him toward her. He grabbed her arms. "Shauntae!" He laughed at her. "You know we can't."

She giggled again. "Yeah, but soon we're gonna get married and then we can as much as possible."

He gave her one last kiss. "I'm going back downstairs. Almost finished with this deal. I'll call Dr. Murray's office and see if it's okay for you to come off bed rest. If she says yes, then we're going to the justice of the peace tomorrow."

Shauntae's eyes got big. "Tomorrow? Are you serious?"

Gary nodded. "I'm ready for us to be Mr. and Mrs. Gary Jackson."

Shauntae waited until she heard Gary's feet hit the downstairs foyer and then she did a little celebratory bed dance. She kicked her feet in the air and waved her hands and sang in a loud whisper, "I'm getting married. I'm getting married."

She tried to calm herself down. It lasted for only a few seconds and then she was kicking and waving her hands again. "Mrs. Gary Jackson. Shauntae Jackson." She hoped Gary couldn't hear her.

She calmed down when she heard him on the phone. *God, please let Dr. Murray release me. Please let me get married tomorrow.*

She couldn't hear exactly what he was saying, but Gary's voice sounded worried. Dr. Murray had told her that everything was fine when she left the emergency room. Had they found something on her blood work later? Shauntae got more concerned when she heard Gary's footsteps coming back up the stairs. She sat up on the bed as he opened the door. She couldn't read the look on his face.

"Shauntae, I just talked to the doctor—"

"Is something wrong with the baby?"

Gary shook his head. "No, I didn't get a chance to call Dr. Murray yet. That was Darla's doctor. She just woke up."

Nineteen

Shauntae's wedding dreams crashed. Gary left for the hospital and all sorts of crazy thoughts went through her head. Darla was gonna wake up and the first thing she was going to do was reach for her laptop. Instead of standing in front of the justice of the peace to get married, Shauntae would be standing before a judge to decide what her bail would be.

What to do? Should she rush to get on a bus, risking a miscarriage? Even if she didn't get married, she could still get a child support check. She wanted to call Sherice, but her only suggestion would be a seat on a Greyhound headed to Cali.

She stood and paced the room for a few minutes and then remembered she wasn't supposed to be out of bed. She sat back down on the bed. *Think, girl, think.*

Shauntae remembered Sherice agreeing with her that Darla's first thought when she came out of the coma wasn't going to be about her. So she at least had a few days. But how could she sleep for the next few days, knowing that the police could show up at any moment? What would happen if she told Gary everything? He said he wanted to know everything and that there was nothing she could do that was bad enough to make him stop loving her. But that was fake Shauntae, not the real Shauntae.

She wondered what Darla had done with the paper with her name and social on it. What if she could get that paper back and make up a fake number? Did they have Internet at the hospital? Was Darla's laptop at the hospital? What if she called somebody at her office to do the background check for her?

For the next couple of hours, Shauntae was a mess. She packed all her clothes, and then unpacked them. She picked up the phone to call Sherice at least twenty times and then put it back down. She paced the room and kept making herself lie back down on the bed. The baby fluttered the whole time, like he was upset right along with her.

Finally, she couldn't stand it anymore. She picked up the phone and called Gary.

He answered on the first ring. "Hey, honey, I was about to call you." It sounded like he was in the car.

"Is everything okay? How's Darla?"

"It's amazing. The doctors are surprised at how well she's doing. She's awake and talking and it seems like her brain function is fine. She recognized her mother and then recognized me when I got there and she asked me to go get the girls. We talked for a while and other than looking banged up and tired, she seems fine."

Shauntae's heart leaped into her throat. She could hardly breathe. "That's great news. God is good. I'm so glad she's okay."

"Yeah, the doctors think she'll make a full recovery. Of course it's still early and we'll have to see how things go, but for now, things look good."

"Wow . . . I don't know what to say. It's a miracle."

"It is, baby. God is good. I'm gonna get the girls and take them to spend some time with her and then I'll take them home. It may be late when I get in. Sorry."

"It's okay. I'm glad we got to spend all that time together over the past few days."

"Me too. The next few days may be a little hectic, but I promise I won't neglect you like before. You're the number one woman in my life now."

"Um, does Darla have her laptop at the hospital with her?"

"Huh? Why would she have her laptop?"

"Like you always say, Darla is so focused on her job and career. I'm sure she'll want to get back to work as soon as possible. Make sure she rests. Rest is important for her to get better."

"She's in no condition to do any work. I'm sure that's the last thing on her mind right now. Thanks for being concerned about her, though. That's real sweet of you after the way she treated you. That's why I love you, Shauntae."

"I love you too, baby. Kiss the girls for me. I'm sure they'll be so happy that their mom is awake."

"Yeah, they will. I'll call you later. I promise."

After they hung up, Shauntae flopped back on the bed. Even though Darla was just waking up and probably wouldn't do the background check in the next few days, how long would it be? Probably the next time she saw Shauntae's face and remembered how she didn't want her anywhere near her daughters. Or the first time Gary did something to piss her off and she wanted to get revenge on him. Whatever the case, Shauntae's days were numbered.

She got up and started packing. This time she didn't unpack. She put the packed suitcases into the closet and left only a couple of outfits out. Last time she had to run from the police, she had left all her cute clothes and shoes behind. This time, she'd be ready. She was taking her stuff with her.

She reached down and rubbed her belly. "Hey, li'l baby. Looks like we gon' be making a trip to California soon."

Twenty

Shauntae tossed around in the bed until she finally fell asleep. When she heard the alarm chime and the garage door open, she bolted up out of bed. She forgot all about her bed rest and ran down the stairs.

She found Gary in the kitchen, putting a carryout container in the refrigerator.

"Baby, how is everything? Were the girls okay?" she asked.

Gary turned around. "What are you doing out of bed?"

Shauntae walked over to him and laid her head on his chest. "I'm tired of that bed and those blue walls."

He put his arms around her. "I know you are, but what about the baby?"

"The baby is fine. He's been turning flips in my belly all day."

Gary reached down to rub her stomach. "I can't wait to feel him kick. We've both convinced ourselves that this is a boy, huh?"

I'm pretty sure of it," Shauntae said.

"You hungry? I brought home some roasted chicken and vegetables."

Shauntae nodded and he put the carryout container in the microwave. Shauntae sat down at the table while he got her a fork, a napkin, and a glass of water. She loved it when he waited on her.

When the food was hot, he brought it over to the table. Shauntae blessed her food and then asked, "How's Darla? How are the girls?"

"The girls are great, now. I didn't realize how scared they were that she was going to die until they saw her sitting up in that bed awake. They cried and kept hugging her." Gary took a sip of her water. "It was good to see them that happy. I haven't seen smiles on their faces like that in a long time."

Shauntae took a big bite of chicken. She hadn't realized how hungry she was. "I'm glad Darla is okay. Is she still talking and acting normal?" Shauntae's hopes of Darla having amnesia had gone out the window, but maybe if she had a little brain damage, it could buy her more time.

"She's still talking, but I wouldn't say she's acting normal," Gary answered. "Or maybe she's acting more normal than she's acted for years." He thought for a moment. "She's like she was when we first got married. Nice, kind, and considerate. Talking to her was like talking to the woman I met eleven years ago. It was strange."

Shauntae took a sip of water to wash down the big hunk of chicken breast she had just swallowed. "Like what? What did she say?"

"She was nice to her mother and thanked her for being such a good mother and for taking good care of her since she was a child. She said she could hear her mother praying over her while she was in the coma and she started praying herself." Gary shook his head in disbelief. "That by itself is a miracle. Except for praying bedtime prayers with the girls, Darla hadn't prayed in years. That was one of the problems with our marriage."

"Maybe almost dying made her realize how important God is."

Gary nodded and kept talking. "She told the girls how much she loved them, and apologized for being busy all the time and not spending time with them and being the mother they needed her to be."

Shauntae ate some of her vegetables. They were barely cooked and were still crunchy. She had learned on one of her cooking shows that it was healthier to lightly steam vegetables rather than cook all the nutrients out of them. It didn't taste as bad as she thought it would.

Gary took another sip of Shauntae's water. "Darla apologized to me for her part in what went wrong in our marriage and for the custody battle. She asked me to apologize to you for the way she treated you. She admitted that she was angry about us and the baby and wanted to hurt me, but she apologized and said she would never do anything like that again."

Shauntae dropped her fork. "What?"

"Yeah, she apologized. She said she should have never asked for a background check because it was an insult to me and to you."

Shauntae wanted to push back from the table, get up, and run around the house dancing.

Gary didn't look as happy as she thought he should with such good news. He might not have had a reason to celebrate as much as she did because he didn't know about the warrant. But, still, he should have been happy that his custody issues were over.

"Baby, what's wrong? You should be happy about this. Sounds like almost dying made Darla into somebody who will be a lot easier for us to get along with."

"It's what she said next that's the problem." Gary put his hand on hers. "I don't want you to get upset or worried about what I'm about to tell you. It doesn't change anything between us."

"What is it?"

Gary let out a deep breath. "Darla apologized for the way our marriage ended. She said it was her fault and that she could have fought harder for us to make it. She said she knew it was terrible to ask with you being in the picture and being pregnant, but . . . she asked me to give her another chance."

"What?" Shauntae sat back hard in her chair.

"Baby, it's nothing for you to worry about."

Shauntae sat there with her mouth open.

"Are you listening to me? I love you and want to marry you. The problem is, she said it in front of the girls. They were jumping around and celebrating because they think their parents are getting married again. After all they've been through with Darla almost dying, I didn't want to tell them anything different, but I will. I'll fix this. I promise."

Shauntae pushed her plate away from her.

"What's wrong?"

"Nothing. It's . . . the baby. I should be in bed."

"Honey, I don't want you to worry about this. Me and Darla—"

"I'm not worried. I shouldn't be up until the doctor says it's okay. I'm gonna go back upstairs."

"You want me to bring your food up? You hardly ate."

"No, I'm good. I'm gonna go to sleep."

"Okay. I'll be up to pray over you and the baby in a few minutes."

"Okay." Shauntae walked up the stairs slowly and closed the door to the guest room.

Don't worry? The woman he was married to for ten years and had two babies by was now awake and acting like she did when he first fell in love with her. Shauntae went into the bathroom to brush her teeth.

She knew where this was going. Darla was smart and pretty and the mother of his two girls. Gary would do whatever he could to make those girls happy. Now her greatest threat wasn't Darla doing the background check. It was Darla stealing her man back. Shauntae knew that between the two of them, Darla was the best choice for Gary.

She took off her jeans and slipped into bed. What if they somehow found out about her past? Not only would Gary have every reason to marry Darla, but the two of them could take her child away and then they'd be a real happy family. Gary would have his perfect wife back, his two daughters and her son. And she'd be left out in the cold.

Shauntae pretended to be asleep when Gary came into her room. Since the bleeding incident, he prayed for her and the baby every night. Tonight, he did it real soft and quiet, like he was trying not to wake her up. She didn't move until he had left the room.

Should she still run? Maybe she could file for child support from California. If they didn't find out about her, Gary would do the right thing and pay. Shauntae reached down to rub her belly. "What we gon' do, li'l baby? What we gon' do?"

Twenty-one

"If she said she was sorry and ain't gon' do the background check, what you worried about?"

Shauntae had hardly slept. She dreamed that Darla had come into the house smiling and being really nice, but then she reached in Shauntae's belly, ripped the baby out, and then pushed her out the front door. Shauntae banged on the door, crying and asking for her baby back. Gary, Darla, and the girls all came to the door, dressed in matching blue, preppy rich people outfits. Darla was holding her baby and he was dressed in the same outfit the whole family had on. Even though they opened the door and were standing there smiling at her, there was an invisible wall and Shauntae couldn't get past it. She banged and screamed and all they did was stand there and smile. They looked like one big happy family and she was stuck on the other side of that glass, unable to get back in the house.

She had woken up in a cold sweat. Shauntae kept her hands on her belly, like she was protecting the baby from being stolen from her.

An hour after she woke up, Gary rushed in her room, said he was going to pick up the girls to take them to the hospital, and left. As soon as she heard the door slam, Shauntae had called Sherice.

"Shauntae, the ex-witch ain't gonna send you to jail. What's the problem?"

"If Gary gets married to her again, what happens to me? What if they try to take my baby?"

"He ain't gon' marry her. Remember you said they can't even talk to each other without arguing."

"She's different after waking up from the coma. He said she's like she was when he fell in love with her."

"That ain't gon' last. She'll be back to her evil witchy self in no time. That be happening to folks all the time in the movies. They wake up all wonderful like they done seen Jesus or something. And then, after a while, they go back to being whoever they was before."

"You think so?"

"Yeah, girl. You worry too much. What kind of car you think he gon' get you?"

"I don't know. I ain't worried about that right now. I want to get off bed rest so we can get to the justice of the peace."

Sherice didn't seem to hear her. "When you get them new wheels and that credit card, make sure you stop by my house before you go to the mall. We gon' tear it up!"

"Sherice, I can't be spending a whole lot of money. I'm broke and Darla got her own money and plenty of it. I can't empty his pockets right now. I gotta make sure he marry me first."

"Yeah, you pro'ly right about that. You need to lock him down before you drain him. Dang! You cain't even have sex because of the bleeding."

"Exactly. So what do I do to lock him down?"

"Sounds like you been doing a good job having some good conversations and asking him good questions. And maybe it's a good thing you been kissing on him and making him go running from the room so he won't have sex with you. Sometimes wanting to have sex but not having it makes a man as crazy as some good sex. So keep taking him to the edge and making him have to run away from you. He'll get to the point that he's craving you and will marry you just to get it."

"Okay, that sounds good." Shauntae thought for a second. "But what if . . ."

"What if what?" Sherice was getting irritated with her. "You worry too much. I'm telling you, Darla waking up different was the best thing. It gets you off the hook with the background check and Gary still gon' marry you."

"Let's imagine the worst possible thing. What if he decides to marry her and they want my baby? He always talking about how he wants his kids all together, being raised in the same family. What if they try to take my baby?"

"That could be the best thing. Tell them you'll let them adopt the baby if they give you a million dollars. No, make it two million dollars. You'll be set for life."

"Girl, you talking crazy. They got money, but they ain't got no two million dollars."

"Well, ask for a million. You can put them on a payment plan."

"Sherice, you done lost your mind. I ain't selling my baby."

"Why not? What you gon' do with a baby, Shauntae? Go back to California and raise it with your mama?"

Shauntae couldn't say nothing.

Sherice said, "Let's say they do get married. He ain't gon' give you full custody and if you try to get child support, Darla the lawyer will dig up some dirt on you. And she won't have to dig too far, now will she? They find out what you did and Gary can sue you for custody and the judge will take your baby before you can blink an eye. If you agree to a friendly adoption for even $100,000, you'll be much better off."

Shauntae lay back on the bed. Sherice was telling the truth, but the thought of selling her baby still didn't feel right.

"You been watching Clair Huxtable so much you done forgot who you are. You don't even like kids. Talking 'bout some 'I can't sell my baby.' You done started believing you the person you pretending to be. What you even know about taking care of a baby? Remember how hard it was trying to take care of Brianna? Even before she got sick, you didn't know nothing 'bout raising no child. Best thing that could happen for your child is for them to get remarried and adopt it from you."

Sherice's words slammed Shauntae right in the middle of her chest. The baby got upset too, because he started jumping around and making some serious butterflies. Shauntae rubbed her belly to calm him down.

"You ain't got nothing to say 'cause you know I'm right." Sherice's tone was a little softer. She must've known Shauntae's feelings were hurt behind what she had said.

Shauntae decided not to answer her. Instead she asked, "Do you ever wonder what we woulda been like if we had been raised in a good family? Like with a mother and father who really loved us and treated us right? That wanted us to get a good education? I mean, for real though, look how smart you are. I don't know too many people as smart as you. Did you ever wonder what you would be like if you had a good mama who pushed you in school instead of selling you for some drugs?"

Now it was Sherice's turn to be quiet.

"Lately I been wondering what I would be like. I mean, I ain't as smart as you. And I can't do nothing really. But what if my mama had thought that school was important? Or if she had signed me up for piano or gymnastics or soccer or something? Who could I be right now?"

Sherice still didn't say nothing. Shauntae knew she had her thinking.

"I bet you woulda been a doctor, Sherice. Or a lawyer. Or maybe even a rich businesswoman. Candy would probably be a gourmet chef at a fancy restaurant somewhere. What you think I would be?"

"Shauntae, I ain't playing no silly pretend games with you. All them movies and living in that house done made you stupid, dreaming about dumb stuff that ain't never gonna happen. You need to focus on what you got right now—a rich man who wants to marry you. A man who wants to buy you a new car and give you your own credit card. Even if none of that happens and he remarries the ex-witch, he still love his child and would pay out some serious cash to be able to keep him. Either way you win. That's all you need to be thinking about right now. A'ight?"

"Yeah, girl. A'ight."

"Now call me when you get the car and the card. We gon' do some shopping."

"A'ight. I'll call you. Bye."

Shauntae lay in the bed after she hung up the phone, thinking about Sherice's crazy plan. She rubbed her belly. "Don't worry, li'l baby. I wouldn't never sell you."

Shauntae thought about what Sherice said about her being a bad mama. Would the baby be better off with Gary and Darla if they got married again? She couldn't raise a baby by herself. Especially with no money. Shauntae shook the thought out of her head. She decided to take one day at a time and see what happened.

She got up, took a shower, and brushed her teeth, ready to spend yet another day in bed. She put on a fresh T-shirt and some sweatpants and sat down on the bed. She clicked on the Cooking Channel. She watched four different shows and learned, at least by watching, how to make some of the fancy kinda foods Gary liked. As the next show started up, the phone rang. It was Gary.

"Hey, honey. How is everything? You picked up the girls?"

"Their grandmother brought them and we met at the hospital."

"How's Darla?"

"Pretty much the same. Still talking about us being a family again. She even invited her mother to come live with us. She has the girls in this fantasyland. I'm going to have to put a stop to it today."

"Okay."

"Are you okay? I hope you're not worried about all of this."

"I'm okay. Just tired of being trapped in this room."

"That's why I was calling you. I talked to Dr. Murray's nurse on the way to the hospital. You're cleared. You can come out of the prison."

"Oh, thank you, Jesus."

"I figured you'd be happy about that."

"I am, baby. Real happy."

"Good. Maybe we'll do something special this weekend to celebrate. We can go to your favorite restaurant. Whatever you want."

"Oh. Okay. That sounds good." Shauntae tried to hide the disappointment in her voice.

"What's wrong, honey?"

"Nothing, Gary. Just hungry. I think I'm gonna go downstairs and find something to eat."

"Okay. I'll call you later."

"Bye." Shauntae hung up the phone. Something special to celebrate? Her favorite restaurant? For real? Before Darla woke up, he said they would go to the justice of the peace as soon as she was off bed rest. Now all he was talking about was dinner. Even though he said Darla wanting to get married again wasn't gon' change nothing, it already had.

Twenty-two

Even though he said she was his number one, Shauntae barely saw Gary over the next few days. He kept telling her not to worry, but she wondered what was going on every day with Darla in that hospital. She was a smart woman who went after what she wanted. She'd probably do anything to get her man back.

If it wasn't Darla, it was the girls. Morgan cried about her parents getting married again. And Daphne had told him that her grades, which got real bad after the divorce, would go back up again if their family could go back to normal. They even said that Miss Shauntae and the new baby could visit anytime she wanted and they would be nice to her.

Gary told Shauntae all of this, but at the same time kept saying she had nothing to worry about. How could he expect her not to worry? All he talked about was having a family and this was his chance of getting it back.

Sherice was wrong. Darla wasn't turning evil again. She decided to cut back on her hours at work to spend more time with the girls. She told Gary that as soon as she got out of the hospital, she wanted to start going back to church with him. She wanted the girls to grow up in church and even if they didn't get married, they could still get along well enough for them all to go to church together. She was saying all the right things that would bring Gary running back to her.

Shauntae didn't know whether she was happy that Gary was telling her so she would know the battle she was fighting, or whether she would rather him not tell her because it was making her more worried.

Almost every day, Gary would call to tell her he was on the way home, but then he would call back to say he couldn't come yet because of some drama with Darla or the girls. One day, Morgan refused to eat until he promised that he would marry their mother. Another day, Daphne locked herself in her room and screamed as loud as she could for over an hour until she got tired and cried herself to sleep.

Another day, Darla fell during therapy and they got scared that she had broken a bone and she had to go for X-rays and stuff. Turned out nothing was wrong, but Gary said he had to stay because Darla's mother broke down and got all emotional because she was afraid Darla had a setback.

Gary came home late at night, apologizing and making all sorts of excuses. Sometimes she stayed up to talk to him, and other days she pretended to be asleep while he prayed over her and the baby. Sherice kept telling her that she needed to stay awake and get him hot and horny, but after a while Shauntae felt like giving up. With Darla, her mother, and Gary's daughters trying to get their family back together, it was four against one. Shauntae was fighting a losing battle.

Gary called one afternoon from the hospital saying that Dr. Murray's office had called and asked when she was coming in for a prenatal appointment. She wondered why they were calling Gary's cell phone, but remembered that she couldn't write, talk, or think when they first got to the emergency room. He must have written his cell number on the clipboard.

"Baby, I'm sorry. I know I said I was going to stop neglecting you and I've actually gotten worse. Please forgive me. We have to get you in for a doctor's appointment."

Shauntae was tired of his apologies. She was tired of him being gone and tired of wondering when he was going to come home one evening and sit her down to tell her that he and Darla were getting married again. "Give me the number. I'll call and make an appointment."

"For when? I'd like to be there and I need to fit it in my schedule."

"You have to be there. How else will I get to the doctor's office? Walk? And don't worry. I'll pay for the visit myself." Of course she couldn't, but Shauntae was tired of feeling like her whole life and future depended on him when it didn't look like he wanted to deliver.

"Shauntae, what is wrong with you?"

"In fact, never mind about going to the appointment with me. I'll get Sherice to take me. That way you can make sure your schedule is free for Darla, Daphne, and Morgan. Wouldn't want to take you away from your precious family."

"What is your problem?"

"Give me the doctor's phone number so I can take me and my baby to the doctor. You stay there with your kids. I'll take care of mine."

"Shauntae!" Gary shouted. "That's my child too."

"Then you need to ack like it!" Shauntae hung up the phone on him. When he called back, she switched her cell phone off. When the house phone rang, she knew it was him, but didn't answer.

She paced around the house for a while, trying to figure out what to do. Should she call him back and apologize? Forget that. She was too mad. She had done everything she could to become everything he wanted and he still was gonna end up dissing her for his ex-wife. She was tired of trying. Tired of talking proper. Tired of pretending to be interested when he talked about politics. Tired of pretending to be a church girl. Forget it. She'd find some other way.

She used to do hair when she was in high school. She hooked up all her friends with the best styles. Maybe she'd borrow some money from Candy to go to beauty school and then work in somebody's shop until she could buy her own shop. Or at least rent a booth in somebody's shop.

All the time she spent hustling men had gotten her nowhere. It was time to do something else.

She turned her cell phone back on and called Sherice. "Girl, I need you to come get me."

"What happened? Did you get found out?"

"No, I'm sick of this mess. I'm ready to be done with it."

"You mean you ain't going to jail, but you want to leave?"

"Yeah. Can you come get me?"

"Shauntae, I don't understand. Did he say he was gonna marry Darla?"

"Not yet, but it's just a matter of time."

"Girl, is you overreacting again?"

Shauntae couldn't take no more. "I ain't overreacting," she screamed into the phone. "Is you my girl or not? You got my back or not? COME . . . GET . . . ME." Shauntae let out a loud scream and hung up the phone.

Twenty-three

Sherice could be an aggravating big mouth some times, and then other times she could catch some sense. She arrived about forty minutes after Shauntae hung up on her. She didn't say a word, just helped Shauntae put her suitcases in the trunk, got back in the car, and they pulled off. She didn't say a word the whole time they were driving, which made Shauntae happy because she needed some quiet to think about what she was gonna do next.

When they got off I-285 and made the left to start heading toward her old neighborhood, Shauntae could feel it. She could feel the difference between the high life she had started to get used to and the low life she had always lived. She had never realized how different the neighborhoods were.

Even though she hadn't been out much in Sandy Springs, she knew she wouldn't see no cheap strip malls, beauty supply stores, cheap, greasy Chinese joints, chicken wing joints, or broken-down gas stations that hadn't been open for years. She wouldn't see no cheap apartment complexes and she sure wouldn't see Pookie 'nem on the corner with they pants sagging and lagging. She had been living at Gary's house one day shy of a month, and already her old stomping grounds felt funny to her.

"Home, sweet home," Sherice said as they were getting closer to her street. "Don't you miss it?"

Shauntae couldn't tell if she was trying to be smart. She sucked her teeth.

"Should I stop and get you some chicken wings and a *40* or do you want some roasted duck and asparagus with some Perrier?"

Shauntae shot Sherice an evil look.

"I'm trying to make you laugh. You look like you 'bout to pop."

Shauntae stared straight ahead and didn't say nothing until they pulled up in front of Sherice's apartment. When she got out of the car, the first person to see her was Tyrel, this dude who was always trying to holla at her when she came to visit Sherice. She would flirt with him for fun, but never gave him any attention past that. He was broker than she was and the last thing she had time for was a broke man.

When she got out of the car, he jumped off the steps and headed to the car. "Well, well. My girl is back in town. Did you miss me?"

Shauntae didn't feel like flirting with him. She let her coat fall open. With the jeans and fitted T-shirt she had on, her bulging belly was obvious.

Tyrel's mouth dropped open. "Girl, you been cheating on me? I can't believe it."

"Stop playing, Tyrel. Help me get these bags in Sherice's house."

"Well, he can't be all that if you bringing your bags to Sherice's place. Guess I still got a chance then, huh? Don't worry, girl. I'll take care of you and the baby. Forget about that dude."

"Whatever, boy. Get these bags."

Tyrel lugged the heavy bags up two flights of steps to Sherice's apartment. Shauntae headed straight back to Sherice's bedroom so she wouldn't have to make no more small talk with him. He didn't have no shame and would keep hitting on her until she hurt his feelings.

Sherice followed her to the bedroom. "I know you don't think you staying in here. I don't care nothing about you being pregnant. You sleeping on the couch, heffa."

Shauntae finally broke down and laughed. "You gon' put your pregnant friend on the couch?"

"My pregnant friend could be sleeping in a king-sized bed in a mansion in Sandy Springs, but she decided to bring her silly tail back to the ghetto. So yeah, she gon' sleep on the couch. Maybe that'll make her catch some sense and take her tail home."

Shauntae settled herself in the middle of Sherice's bed. "Not in a king-sized bed in the master bedroom, but the queen-sized bed in the guest room because he won't marry me because his ex-wife is trying to steal him back." Shauntae ran down everything that had happened over the past few days.

Sherice stood with her hands on her hips for a while and finally she sat down on the edge of the bed. "Humph. Them tricks ain't playing, huh? They trying to take that man back, ain't they?"

"You see what I'm saying?"

Sherice nodded. "Especially them girls. They know they the key to they daddy's heart." She made her thinking face for a while and then turned to Shauntae. "So what you gon' do?"

Shauntae shrugged. "I don't know. I'm tired. I need a break from the whole thing."

"So you mean you gon' walk away from that house and a new car and a credit card and—"

"What new car? Didn't I have to call you to come get me? Ain't the clothes in that suitcase the same ones you and Candy bought me at Goodwill? He said when I got off bed rest we was gon' get married." Shauntae didn't mean to, but she was yelling again. "Do you even see a engagement ring on my finger?"

"A'ight, heffa. Don't be yelling at me. I ain't Gary. Chill."

"I'm tired, Sherice. Tired of this hustling game. Ain't you tired, girl?"

"Humph. What else we gon' do?"

Shauntae lay back on Sherice's bed. It was so lumpy Shauntae decided it might be better to sleep on the couch. "I don't know. Ain't you never thought of doing something different?"

"Shauntae, please don't start all that mess again about what we coulda been. I ain't in the mood for no shoulda, coulda, woulda. You made my head hurt with that mess."

Shauntae knew she had gotten to Sherice. "We ain't got to talk about it now, but you might wanna think about it. I think I'ma do hair. You can braid real good. I could do all the perms and cuts and you could do twists, braids, and locs and all that stuff. You always say it's good money."

Sherice had been doing natural hair in her kitchen for years. Especially when she was between sponsors.

Shauntae continued, "Maybe Candy might want to do nails and stuff. We could be a full-service salon."

"And where you think we gonna get money for all that? You know how much it costs to rent a shop and buy products? You need chairs and dryers and sinks and blow dryers and flat irons and curling irons. You got all these great ideas, but have you thought them through? Ain't nobody got that kind of money. I told you I don't feel like talking all that craziness." Sherice stood up and went out to the living room.

Shauntae stayed on the bed. She kept moving and shifting and turning, but she couldn't find any comfortable spot on the bed. She finally sat up. After being in the bed for the past few days, that was the last place she wanted to be. She wandered into the living room and found Sherice watching DVR episodes of *Real Housewives of Atlanta*. Sherice talked to the characters on television like they could actually hear her. She'd be yelling and pointing and cussing and saying all sorts of stuff to them. It used to make Shauntae laugh, but today it was getting on her nerves.

She went to Sherice's refrigerator to find something to eat. All she saw were some old Chinese containers that looked like they might have been in there for a while, a couple of beers, and a pack of bologna. Shauntae went to the cabinets and found some Ritz crackers. She took them and the bologna back into the living room.

Sherice turned away from the television for a second to say, "Heffa, don't eat up all my food."

Shauntae shot her a look. "Seriously, heffa?"

Sherice went back to yelling at the TV. Sherice's apartment was so small that there wasn't anywhere that Shauntae could go to get away from all that loud cussing. She thought of going back out to sit on the step but didn't feel like being bothered by Tyrel. Plus, this was the time of the day he and his friends would be smoking weed. She rubbed her belly. She didn't want to take her baby around that.

Sherice turned from the television. "What's wrong with you? Why you acting all shifty? Ain't this your favorite show?"

"I need to get my head straight, Sherice. You know I got a lot going on."

"Well, go back in the bedroom. You gettin' on my nerves." Sherice turned back to the television.

Shauntae went back to the bedroom and sat on the floor by the bed. She knew she should get up if she didn't want nothing crawling on her, but she didn't feel like sitting on the lumpy bed.

She kept eating the meat and crackers. After a while, the baby started moving in her belly. The flutters were stronger than they had been and she knew it wouldn't be long before she was feeling real kicks. "Sorry, li'l baby. I been starving you all day." She rubbed her belly. "I got mad at your daddy and forgot to eat. I'm sorry. I gotta get you to the doctor soon so we can see how you doing and when you coming."

Shauntae thought about it for a minute. She would need to go sign up for Medicaid to go to the doctor. She doubted Dr. Murray would take Medicaid and plus, her office was too far from where she was now.

Shauntae looked around Sherice's apartment. She knew she wouldn't be able to stay here long and she was in no position to get her own apartment again. Maybe she should get Sherice to take her to the bus station in the morning. Maybe she could get Gary to take her more seriously from California.

Shauntae's cell phone rang. It was Gary.

She didn't answer it. It rang a couple of more times and went to voicemail, and then a text came through.

> Shauntae, please call me. I came home to check on you and you're not here. I'm worried sick about you and the baby. I'm so sorry for not keeping my word. Please forgive me and come home.

At least he had the good sense to be sorry. Shauntae looked down at the time. It was only 6:30. Which meant he had left his time with the girls to come check on her. *Humph.* If it took her leaving for him to pay her some attention, she shoulda called Sherice to come get her a few days ago.

She thought for a few seconds about whether she should call him or let him sweat for a few hours. She decided to be nice and sent a text.

> I'm at my friend, Sherice's. Spending the night. Me and the baby are fine. Have a nice night.

She went back over the message twice to make sure she hadn't spelled anything wrong. And then she decided not to put Sherice's name in case Gary tried to look for her.

A few minutes later, he texted her back.

> I'm sorry, honey. Please forgive me and come home. Tell me where you are and I'll come get you. Let me make it up to you.

Shauntae shut the phone off. She was pretty sure he would spend the rest of the night calling and texting her like crazy. He needed to be afraid that he had lost her and the baby. Even though she didn't feel like staying the night at Sherice's house, she had to make him suffer at least a little bit.

Shauntae's stomach rumbled real loud. She walked out to the living room and asked Sherice, "Can I borrow your car? I need to get some food."

Sherice looked up from the television. "I got some TV dinners and frozen chicken potpie in the freezer."

"I don't want none of that. I want some real food. Where are the keys?"

"You want me to take you?"

"Naw, girl, I don't want you to stop watching your show." Shauntae spotted the keys on top of the television.

Sherice barely looked up. "A'ight, but be careful. Don't get stopped by the police or they'll impound my car when they take you to jail."

Shauntae had almost forgotten about the warrant, since she no longer had to worry about Darla and the background check. "I'll be careful. You got a EBT card?"

Sherice looked up from the television. "You ain't got no money? I spent mine for this month already."

Shauntae grabbed the keys and walked out the door.

Sherice hollered after her, "Turn your phone on in case I want you to pick me up something."

Shauntae got in the car quick before Sherice decided she wanted to go. She needed some quiet for a while. She turned her phone back on. After a few seconds, a text came through.

> Please, baby. Don't do this. Please come home and let me make it up to you.

Shauntae sucked her teeth. "Whatever, Gary," she said out loud like he could hear her. "Take care of your precious Darla and your daughters and leave me alone."

She didn't feel like fast food or going to the nasty grocery store in their neighborhood. She rode Sherice's raggedy car all the way down to the nice part of Flat Shoals Parkway. She could either go to Zaxby's or get something good out of Publix's deli.

She pulled into the parking lot at the Publix. She opened her wallet and pulled out all her cash—fifty-nine dollars, when she counted the loose change. That was all she had left. Reality slammed her in the face. What would she do when this money ran out? How could she get a new sponsor with a pregnant belly?

She decided to go to Publix and get some fried chicken. If Sherice didn't get too greedy, she could eat off of it for a couple of days rather than spending the same money on one meal at Zaxby's. If they had some kind of special, she could spend a little more and get some sides and Hawaiian rolls with it.

She got out of the car and pulled her coat tighter around her. It was mid-March, so the temperature still dropped when the sun went down.

It was dinnertime and the deli line was longer than Shauntae had patience for. But it wasn't like she was gon' cook and it was cheaper than fast food, so she waited. After fifteen minutes, she finally got her food. She took a big sniff of the chicken and her mouth started watering and her stomach grumbled.

Maybe she would eat in the car so she wouldn't have to share with Sherice. That heffa could eat and Shauntae needed to make her food last as long as possible. But she would have to put the leftovers in the refrigerator, and plus Sherice had spent some serious gas money coming to get her and she was sleeping in her house. The least she could do was share her food.

Even the ten item fast lane had a lot of people in it. Shauntae thought about tearing off a chicken wing and eating it right there in the line. After a few minutes, she moved up in the line and was close enough to reach the candy selection near the register.

Shauntae grabbed a Snickers bar and was about to rip the package open and take a big bite when she heard a voice—a squeaky, little girl voice she couldn't help but recognize.

"Daddy, can I push the basket?"

Another voice she recognized answered, "Yes, Bree, but let me guide it. We don't want to hit anybody or anything. You know you can't drive too well."

Shauntae heard that familiar giggle. "I can drive, Daddy!"

It was Brianna and Devon.

Shauntae dropped the Snickers bar from one hand and the green basket carrying her precious dinner from the other. She ducked behind a magazine rack. She had to get out of there, but Devon and Brianna were still in the entrance of the store where the carts were. If she tried to leave, she'd run right into them.

The dude standing in line behind her picked up the green shopping basket and tried to hand it to her. "You dropped your food."

Shauntae pushed past him and ran. She stopped behind each magazine rack on each aisle until she got far away enough that Devon couldn't possibly see her. She waited until he got over to the produce section and started to run between magazine racks back toward the exit. She thought she was clear until he stopped to answer his cell phone.

"Yeah, we're inside already. Where are you?"

Shauntae dashed out the front door. She ran toward Sherice's car so fast that she didn't see the woman on the cell phone coming toward her.

"You're in the produce section? I'll meet you guys inside." The woman turned off her cell phone and looked up.

Shauntae froze in her tracks. There, standing right in front of her in the Publix parking lot was Devon's girlfriend, Cassandra.

Twenty-four

Shauntae looked Cassandra right in the face. Cassandra frowned like she was trying to figure out why Shauntae looked familiar. Shauntae made a quick dip to the left and ran as fast as she could. She fumbled with the keys for a second, got in Sherice's car, started the engine, and pulled out of the parking lot as fast as she could.

The traffic was too heavy for her to turn left to go back to Sherice's place, so she turned right and sped down Flat Shoals Parkway as fast as she could.

Had Cassandra recognized her? They had only seen each other twice, but Shauntae knew she had shown her tail both times, so Cassandra probably remembered her face. And Brianna had a picture of Shauntae holding her right after she was born. It was a real pretty picture and Devon had got it framed real nice and put it on Brianna's wall. As much time as Cassandra was spending with them, Shauntae was sure she had seen it. Unless Devon had took it down.

If Cassandra recognized her, she had either dialed 911 in the parking lot or she had run inside and told Devon and he was dialing 911. Either way, the police were probably after her.

Shauntae made a quick left on Kelley Chapel and then did a quick U-turn to get back to Flat Shoals. What was she thinking? That was the closest grocery store to Devon's house. It was like she was trying to run into him. She could hear her mother's voice in her head.

Girl, you stupid. You make problems for yourself when there ain't none. Your life ain't never gon' be nothing because you always be making stupid choices. Stupid, stupid, stupid.

"Shut up, Mama! I'm not stupid. And if I make stupid choices it's because it's all I ever saw you do! You coulda raised me right. You coulda taught me right. You coulda gave me a better life than this." Shauntae screamed like her mama was in the car with her.

She pushed down hard on the gas pedal, looking in her rearview mirror, waiting to see those police lights coming after her. She drove as fast as she could but the stoplights kept catching her. And traffic was still heavy and people was driving slow.

She crossed over the freeway and was almost at South Dekalb Mall near the turn to Sherice's apartment when she heard it.

Police sirens.

They had gotten her. Had Cassandra chased her in the parking lot and got Sherice's tag numbers? Or were they catching her for speeding? Shauntae's heart beat faster and faster as the sirens got closer and closer.

"God, please don't let me go to jail. I can't have my baby in jail."

Shauntae started to speed up, but did she really think she could outrun the police in Sherice's old, beat-up car? Everybody else had pulled over and the flashing blue lights were right in her rearview mirror. It was over and she was caught. She and her baby were going to jail.

Tears filled Shauntae's eyes as she pulled over to surrender. "Sorry, li'l baby. Mama's so sorry. I promise as soon as you're born, I'll give you to Gary and Darla and you won't have to worry about growing up with no crazy, bad mama."

Instead of the blue lights pulling behind her like she expected, they sped by. Behind that police car was another police car and behind it was a fire rescue truck. They all sped by her like they didn't know she was Atlanta's Most Wanted.

Shauntae let out a deep breath and more tears flowed. "Oh my God. Thank you, God. Oh my God." For the first time in her life, God had answered one of her prayers.

Shauntae pulled into the Big Lots parking lot and sat in the car for a few minutes, laughing, crying, and talking to the baby. "Li'l baby, we ain't going to jail."

She got herself together for a few minutes and then pulled back out on Candler Road. She got to Sherice's place and sat in the parking lot for a few minutes.

It was like Sherice was always saying. She had overreacted. Cassandra didn't recognize her. It was dark. She wasn't paying attention because she was on the phone. Cassandra had only met her twice and it had been awhile. And for real, Devon had probably taken Shauntae's picture off Brianna's wall years ago.

The police weren't after her. She was safe. Shauntae let out a deep breath. Everything was okay and she wasn't going to jail. Her only problem now was that she was still starving. God had saved her once and she wasn't gonna chance it by trying to go out for food. She would have to eat one of Sherice's TV dinners.

Shauntae was about to get out of the car when she heard her phone buzzing. She wasn't in the mood for Gary's begging and apologizing. Now that she was back at Sherice's, she could turn it off.

Just as she was about to turn the phone off, she saw the name on the caller ID.

It was Devon.

Twenty-five

Shauntae's hand shook as she held the phone. She couldn't answer. It stopped ringing. Cassandra had seen her. She had recognized her. They knew she was back in Atlanta. She was busted.

Seconds later, the phone started ringing again. This time she made herself answer it. "Hello, Devon." She tried to keep her voice from shaking.

"Please tell me that Cassandra just saw somebody who looks like you and not you. Please tell me that you're still in California and not back here in Atlanta. Please, Shauntae."

She couldn't answer.

"Shauntae!"

"Devon, let me explain. Please."

"So it was you? You are back in Atlanta?"

"Please, wait—"

His voice exploded through the phone. "I told you what would happen if you ever came near Brianna again. I told you I wasn't lifting the arrest warrant. I swear if you so much as come near her—"

"Devon, please. I'm begging you. Please listen to me for once." Shauntae started crying. It must have surprised Devon. He was used to her cussing, not crying.

He was silent for a few moments and then when he did speak, his voice was still tight, but not loud. "I'm listening. But this better be good."

Shauntae started talking fast. “It’s like I told you. I’m pregnant. I live with my baby’s father in Sandy Springs. We’re going to get married soon. The only reason I’m on this side of town is because I came to visit Sherice. I haven’t been over here since I got back. Well, once, when I first got back, but not since then. I promise I’m not back here to get in your pockets or to hurt Brianna. I’m trying to get my life right. Please, you have to give me a chance.”

He didn’t say anything, so she kept pleading.

“I’m a different person now. I’m trying to do better and live better and be a better person. I promise, if you and Cassandra will give me a chance, I promise you’ll see. “

Devon let out a deep breath. “What if instead of running into Cassandra, you had run into me and Brianna? We were in the same store. Brianna’s happy and doing really well. What do you think it would do to her if she saw you right now? Do you ever even think about stuff like that?”

“I saw you. And I saw her. And I hid because I didn’t want to do that to her. I do think about stuff like that now. With this new baby, I think about it all the time. I know I was a horrible mother, Devon. I’m sorry for everything I ever did to Brianna. I’m sorry for everything I ever did to you. Please, you have to believe me.” Shauntae was using her best Angela Bassett English. She had to make Devon believe she had changed.

“Why should I believe you? After everything—”

“You shouldn’t believe me. I’ve never given you a reason to. I’m begging you . . .” She added, “I’m begging you in Jesus’ name.”

“In Jesus’ name?” Devon laughed. “Seriously? You’ll try anything won’t you? You think you can get at me by bringing God into it?”

“It’s not like that. I swear. Why can’t you believe that I’m trying to change? If Jesus is willing to give me a second chance, why can’t you?”

Shauntae couldn't believe she had said that. Did she really believe the message from church that Sunday? And Dr. Murray and Gary? Would Jesus really give her a second chance and forget about all the bad junk she had ever done?

When Devon spoke, his voice wasn't as tight. "So you're a Christian now?"

Shauntae wasn't sure how to answer that. "I . . . I don't know. I ain't . . ." She caught herself. "I haven't ever been to the altar and I haven't been baptized. But I talk to God sometimes. And I think about Him. And lately, I think He's been trying to talk to me. I ain't . . . I'm not saying I'm saved or a Christian or that I'm perfect. But I'm trying. That's all I can do. Please give me a chance."

He let out a frustrated breath. She knew he wanted to be mean, but Devon didn't have a mean bone in his body. "How can I trust that you won't come near Brianna or hurt her again? If I give you a chance and you hurt Brianna again, then I'm a bad father. I can't risk you hurting her. She could have died, Shauntae. Do you know that?"

Shauntae started crying again. "I know that. I'm sorry."

"Then how do I know that you won't hurt her again?"

Shauntae sniffed and wiped the tears off her face. "Because I know stuff now. I know that I was a bad mama because my mama was a bad mama. If my mama had been a good person like Cassandra, and my stepfather woulda been a good father like you, I wouldn't be all messed up like I am. And I want Brianna to have that. A good mama and a good daddy and a good life. You can believe that I won't come around Brianna again 'cause I know she needs something better than me. I was a horrible mama and I don't want to mess up her life by being around her."

Devon didn't say nothing so Shauntae kept talking. "Remember that day you came to my house and you asked me what kinda life I wanted for Brianna? I know what you was saying now. She could be anything. Look at the way she always singing and dancing. She could be a big, famous star one day. As smart as she is, she can be anything she want to be. And her best chance is if I stay away." One tear ran down Shauntae's cheek. "I know that now. That's why you can believe me."

It took a few seconds before Devon finally spoke. His voice was quiet. "I don't know. You have to let me think about this. I'm not trying to hurt you. All I want is what's best for Brianna."

"Me too, Devon. Me too."

"I'll call you in a few days and let you know what I decide about lifting the warrant."

"Okay." Shauntae started crying again. "Thank you. Thank you so much."

When they hung up, Shauntae dropped the phone in her purse and laid her head back on the headrest. "God, please. Please let him lift that warrant."

Twenty-six

By the time Shauntae stumbled up Sherice's steps, all she wanted was a chicken potpie and a decent night's sleep on the couch, floor, wherever, whatever. She used Sherice's key to open the door and walked straight to the freezer.

"I thought you went to get something to eat. Why you all up in my freezer?"

Shauntae turned to answer Sherice. "You have no idea what I just went through."

She must have looked a mess from all the crying and stuff. Sherice turned off the TV and came into the kitchen. "What's wrong wit' you?"

Shauntae sat down in the chair Sherice kept in the kitchen to do hair and explained the whole incident up to the last words between her and Devon on the phone.

"You said all that? Girl, you was working it. All you want is what's best for Brianna? You might be a hustler after all."

"I meant everything I said. I wasn't running game. Brianna is better off with him and Cassandra."

"Whatever. Anyway, we got to go." She walked to the front door and yelled out, "Tyrel, come over to my place. I need your help."

He yelled back, "For what?"

"Boy, if you don't get over here . . ." Sherice marched back to the bedroom and came back out lugging one of Shauntae's heavy bags.

"What you doing?"

Sherice gave her a crazy look. "What you think?" She went back into the bedroom and came out with the other bag. As she set it down, Tyrel appeared at the door.

"Take these bags back down to the car for me." She handed him the keys.

He looked at her like she was crazy. "I just brought 'em up here."

Sherice put a hand on her hip. "And now you can take them back."

Shauntae stood up. "Wait a minute. Why you sending my bags back to the car?"

Tyrel stopped and looked at Sherice to see whether he should take them. She gave him a glare and pointed toward the door.

Tyrel mumbled while he picked up the bags. "Y'all act like these bags ain't heavy. Women be trippin'. Can't ever make up they minds." He disappeared through the apartment door.

"We gotta go," Sherice said. "You can't stay here tonight. Devon knows you're at my house and like you said, Cassandra might have seen my license plates. The police could get here any minute."

"But Devon said he was thinking about lifting the warrant."

"Exactly. Thinking about it. What do you think is gonna happen when he gets off the phone and talks to Cassandra? You think she's gonna say, 'Okay, Devon, you should lift the warrant'? No, that trick is coming after you. We gotta go."

Shauntae fell back into the chair and whined, "But I'm so hungry."

"Heffa, I ain't foolin' wit' you." Sherice picked up the phone and dialed a number. A few seconds later she said, "Girl, Shauntae done caught herself some serious trouble.

We on our way over. Heat up some food. This baby got her hungry."

She hung up the phone and grabbed Shauntae's arm. "Let's go."

They pulled up at Candy's house fifteen minutes later. Candy's life was in a much better state than Shauntae's and Sherice's. Her grandmother, who had raised her, had left Candy a house when she died. It was paid for and all Candy had to do was keep up the taxes. It wasn't a mansion or anything, but it was a cute little three-bedroom house in a nicer neighborhood than Sherice's.

As soon as they walked in Candy's house, Shauntae could smell some good spices and what smelled like beef. Her stomach gurgled. "What you done cooked? That smell good. I'm so hungry."

"Y'all got good timing. I made some beef stroganoff."

"I don't know what that is, but I'd eat anything right about now." Shauntae clutched her stomach.

They followed Candy to the table. She dished Shauntae up a plate and Candy and Sherice sat there and watched her shovel food into her mouth for a few minutes.

"Dang, heffa. Slow down. It ain't going nowhere," Sherice said.

Candy asked, "So what happened?"

Sherice ran down the whole story while Shauntae ate mouthful after mouthful of the beef with the best tasting sauce, roasted potatoes, and sautéed vegetables. Candy really can cook like them people on the Cooking Channel.

After Shauntae had eaten a little bit, she started interjecting into Sherice's story. "I didn't tell him I was a Christian. I told him I been thinking about God lately."

"And then she played him by talking this mess about how Brianna would be better off with him and Cassandra as parents. Was talking about how she a bad mama 'cause her mama was a bad mama. I'm telling you, Shauntae played him good. If Cassandra don't see through it, he may even lift that warrant. Our girl finally learned a little sump'n."

Shauntae was too tired to try to make Candy understand that she wasn't running game on Devon. She kept eating her food until her plate was clean.

"So what you gon' do now?" Candy asked.

Sherice didn't give her a chance to answer. "This crazy girl talking some mess about the three of us opening a salon. Like she got the stacks to do that kinda stuff."

Candy looked at Shauntae. "For real? That would be nice."

Sherice rolled her eyes. "Don't be encouraging her with no stupid dreams that ain't ever gonna happen. Y'all don't know nothing about starting a business. It take a lot of money and a lot of smarts. Shauntae need to go back to her mansion in Sandy Springs. Until Gary and the ex-witch actually say 'I do' she need to stay there and milk it as long as she can."

After her crazy day and now with the warm food sitting in her stomach, all Shauntae wanted to do was go to sleep.

Candy asked her, "You really think he's gonna get married to her again? Did he actually say that?"

"No. He's been texting me all day saying he's sorry and begging me to come home and telling me he's worried about me and the baby."

Both Sherice and Candy's eyes bugged out. Sherice said, "You ain't told me all that. So take your tail home, heffa. You done made him beg. What more do you want?"

Candy picked up Shauntae's plate and took it to the sink. She brought Shauntae a thick slice of cheesecake—not the kind made from a box either.

Sherice looked at Shauntae's plate. "Where's mine?"

Candy brought her a slice. "For real, why you at my house when the man is begging you to come home? You welcome to stay a few days, but if it was me, I would be in the mansion." She and Sherice slapped hands.

Sherice took a bit bite of cheesecake and closed her eyes and moaned. "Candy, I don't know why you ain't got no man. You keep cooking like this and I'm gon' marry you myself."

Candy laughed.

Sherice pointed her fork at Shauntae. "You might be right about the way you handling Gary. Maybe you do need to stay here for a couple of days."

"That's crazy," Candy said. "Stay here when he's begging her to come back?"

"Shauntae wants him to do more than beg her to come back. She wants the ring and the marriage and the car and the credit card. And this is how you gon' do it. Candy, get me some paper."

Shauntae laid her head on the table. "I don't feel like it, Sherice. I'm tired and I want to go to bed."

"Heffa, I'm trying to get you set for life." She took the pen Candy brought her and said, "Eat some cheesecake and listen up. I got a plan."

Twenty-seven

Shauntae woke up the next morning feeling better. After all the drama and Sherice's scheming last night, Shauntae had been exhausted. And even though the mattress in Candy's guest room seemed like it was twenty years old, she had found a comfortable enough spot at the bottom and slept.

She woke up to the fluttering in her stomach. "Good morning, li'l baby. How you doin'?" She sat up in bed and stretched. Almost as soon as she got up, the phone started vibrating. She knew it was Gary.

The whole time Sherice was spilling her plan last night, Shauntae's stomach was feeling that sick feeling. At first, she thought it was from eating Candy's food real fast after starving all day. But now she was waking up with that sick feeling. She knew it was because Sherice's plan was full of lies. She didn't want to add a new set of lies to the ones she had already told.

At the same time, she had to do something. After counting her money last night, she realized how serious her situation was. After she spent her last, what could she do? She would run this last hustle and then maybe her life would change to the point where she wouldn't have to do it ever again.

The next time the phone vibrated, Shauntae got up to get it, even though she wasn't ready to answer it. When it stopped ringing, she saw eight missed calls and five text messages. All the messages were pretty much the same—I'm sorry, let me make it up to you, come home.

She had to smile a little bit. Gary was really sweating her.

She sat on the bed and got her mind together while she waited for the phone to ring again. If she was gon' do Sherice's plan, she needed to do it well. She hoped the stomach pain wouldn't kill her before it was all over.

A few minutes later, the phone vibrated. Shauntae took a deep breath and answered it. "Good morning, Gary."

"Shauntae, you answered." His voice sounded raggedy. Shauntae wondered if he had slept.

"I just woke up. Sorry I missed your other calls."

"How are you? How is the baby? Where are you guys?"

"We're fine."

"Tell me where you are so I can come get you."

"I don't think that's a good idea. I've been thinking about everything and . . ."

"What, baby?"

Shauntae cringed. She had forgotten how good it felt when he called her "baby." "I'm not sure it's a good idea for me to come home. I know how important family and the girls are to you. Maybe it would be better for everybody if you and Darla got back together."

"You know that's not what I want."

"Are you sure? Because the past week or so, you've been acting like that's exactly what you want. Sometimes the way we act says more than what we say. If I were to listen to your actions rather than your words, what should I hear?" Shauntae was using her best English. She felt smart and confident like Angela Bassett.

"Shauntae, I know I've been—"

"Maybe this is the answer to your prayers about family. You don't have to worry. I'm not going back to California. I made you a promise that I wouldn't leave Atlanta with your child and I won't. We can talk about arrangements for you being able to spend time with him."

"Arrangements? I don't want to make custody arrangements with you. I want you and the baby here with me."

"And you want Daphne, Morgan, and Darla with you too. You want this big happy family and you want to make everybody happy and it's not going to work. We can't get married because you don't want to upset the girls. I understand that, but what kind of marriage can we have if you live your life to make them happy? You need some time to work this all out in your head."

"I don't need to work things out in my head. You're right. I want something that's not possible. I understand that now."

"How do you think I feel being second? How do you think this child will feel being second? Will you neglect him to make Daphne and Morgan feel better?"

"I would never do that. I will love all my children the same."

"Why should I believe that? You leave me and your son in the house starving when you know we have no way of getting out to get some food. I still haven't been for a prenatal visit. All because Daphne throws a tantrum. Or because Morgan wants you and her mom to get remarried. Or because Darla's mother is emotional. I understand you're a wonderful man and your heart is full of love. But I need to make some moves to take care of me and my child."

"Moves? What kind of moves?"

"I need to make sure me and my child are secure. I'm making plans."

"Plans. Like what?"

"We'll talk later. Right now I need to make some phone calls. Say hello to Darla and the girls for me."

"Shauntae—"

She clicked the phone off. So far, she hadn't told any lies, but the next part of the plan was where the problem was.

Shauntae wandered into Candy's kitchen. Candy was standing at the counter with a bowl in her hand, stirring.

"Girl, what you cooking?"

"Remember that morning when you called me all early talking 'bout 'how do I make pancakes, eggs, and sausage'?"

Shauntae laughed. "Yeah."

"Well, you about to learn. I already started the batter. I make mine from scratch, but you'll probably use pancake mix. It's easy if you follow the instructions on the box. Nobody can mess that up."

Shauntae put her hand over her mouth.

Candy laughed. "You messed up pancake mix? How?"

Shauntae shrugged and laughed with her.

Candy showed her how to pour the pancakes and flip them. The first few looked crazy but after a few tries, Shauntae's pancakes came out perfectly shaped and golden brown.

"Let's do some eggs." Candy pulled a few eggs out the refrigerator. "We'll do scrambled first and then I'll teach you how to make an omelet."

"Can't we eat some pancakes first? I'm starving."

Candy grabbed the syrup and some plates and they sat down to eat. Before Shauntae could even digest good, Candy had her at the counter whisking eggs.

After a few tries, Shauntae's eggs were as fluffy as Candy's. "This cooking stuff ain't so hard. I just never had nobody show me before," Shauntae said.

"Girl, cooking ain't hard and it's a whole bunch of fun. All you have to do is follow a recipe. And then, after a while, you can cook without a recipe. You learn how to add your own special stuff to make things taste better. It's like a art. I can show you a whole bunch of other stuff while you're here if you want me to."

"Yeah," Shauntae said, through a mouthful of scrambled eggs. "That would be fun."

Candy started pulling food out of the refrigerator—good-looking food. Not some old, wilted produce like they had in the grocery stores in the hood but good, fresh stuff. And good cuts of meat, not smelly, gray-looking meat with a bunch of fat.

"Where you get these groceries? Where you get money for all this?"

"My new friend took me shopping last week at Publix. Told me to buy whatever I wanted."

Shauntae noticed she didn't use the word "sponsor" like usual. "Friend?"

Candy got this funny look on her face. "Yeah, he's a real nice guy and he like me. We been hanging out for a month and we ain't even had sex. We just be talking."

Shauntae's eyes went big. "For real? What y'all be talking about?"

"All kinds of stuff. We be talking about our past and all the stuff that happened to us. And he be telling me about his business and stuff. Sometimes he be having problems, but he real smart and he figures them out."

"What kind of business he got?"

Candy was chopping red, yellow, and orange peppers and onions. Her hands were working like the people on the Cooking Channel. "He owns a barbershop in East Atlanta. He been there for years, but the neighborhood changed and upgraded. He been making stuff better and trying to keep up with the businesses around him." Candy had this proud look on her face. "He ain't never been to college. He's naturally smart."

Candy started cutting a large onion. "And then he be talking about what he wants to do with his life and stuff. He got all these dreams. Like he wants to expand to a full-service salon and spa. That's why I was excited when you was talking about doing hair. If things don't work out with Gary, maybe you could work for him."

Shauntae thought about Sherice saying she'd never succeed at the hair business. Maybe it could work if she had help from somebody who was successful. "That's real cool. What else y'all be talking about?"

"He be asking me about my dreams, too."

Shauntae's ears perked up. "You got dreams, Candy?"

Candy handed Shauntae the knife for her to try cutting vegetables. She tried to do it fast and fancy like Candy and ended up cutting off one of her fingernails and almost sliced her finger.

Candy took the knife from her. She showed Shauntae how to do it real slow and handed her the knife back again. Shauntae cut the vegetables better this time. They weren't as neat and perfect as Candy's, but she was proud of her work.

"So, what you be dreaming about?" Shauntae asked.

Candy pressed her lips together and shrugged.

"What? Tell me."

Candy walked over to the cabinet and pulled down some spices. She didn't say nothing.

"Why you don't want to tell me?"

"'Cause you and Sherice always be talking trash about stuff. I don't feel like hearing about my dreams being stupid or me being stupid or nothing like that."

"I ain't gon' say that. I promise."

Candy pulled some chicken out of the refrigerator and took it to the sink and washed it. "You can't tell Sherice nothing."

"I won't. I promise."

Candy brought the chicken over to the cutting board and started chopping it into chunks. "I want to start a catering business. I used to want a restaurant but I think catering would be easier and better."

"Wow, Candy . . . wow. That's wassup. So what you gon' do?"

Candy bit her lip. "You betta not tell Sherice. I swear if you tell her, I'll never tell you nothing again."

"I promise I won't. I know how Sherice's mouth can be."

"I'm taking some online business classes. I ain't got business sense like Bobby—that's my friend's name. He made me realize you gotta be smart to run a business. So I'm getting me some smarts. It's hard, but I'm getting it."

Candy was taking classes and making plans. Shauntae didn't know how to feel about that. It made her happy, but it also made her feel like she should be doing something too. Something different than running game on Gary.

"Bobby bought me all this food so I could practice. He believes in me and he keeps pushing me. He a real good man, Shauntae. I ain't never met nobody like him."

"You trying to get serious about this dude?"

Candy shrugged and held out the knife for Shauntae to cut chicken. Shauntae made a face. She hated touching raw meat. Candy sucked her teeth and put the knife in Shauntae's hand.

"I might be trying to get serious about him. It would be nice to like, I don't know, have a real man and a real business and a real life. I ain't never been good at this game like you and Sherice. You know I ain't pretty like you."

"Where has pretty got me? What you talking about is real. I think you would be awesome with a catering business and I'm real proud of you for trying to do something good with your life."

"For real, girl?"

Shauntae elbowed Candy in the side. "Yeah, girl. For real."

Shauntae's phone buzzed in her pocket. She put down the knife and washed her hands. It stopped ringing, but she knew it would start ringing again soon. When it did, she answered it.

"Yes, Gary?"

"Shauntae, you don't have to make plans to take care of you and the baby. I'm going to take care of you. Come home, honey."

Shauntae walked out of the kitchen. She didn't want to play her next card in front of Candy after they had been talking about doing stuff right.

"Gary, I had dropped everything in Atlanta and planned to start my life over in California. But you asked me to come back here, so I did. I don't like being dependent on a man. I need to take care of myself."

"What exactly are you doing?"

"I've been speaking with someone about possible job opportunities."

"Job opportunities? I thought you didn't want to work. I thought you wanted to stay home with the baby."

"And take care of him how?"

"I keep telling you how. You're not listening to me."

"Like I said this morning, I've been listening to everything you do."

"Shauntae . . ." Gary sounded frustrated.

"I'm in the middle of something. I'll call you back later." Shauntae hung up the phone. She hadn't really lied. Candy did mention the possibility of her working in Bobby's dream salon someday.

She walked back into the kitchen. Candy looked up from her knife and cutting board. "Is he buying it?"

"Yeah, I think so."

"So what's wrong?"

Shauntae shrugged.

"You don't want to do it no more do you?"

Shauntae shrugged again. "I don't wanna talk about it right now. I need to get my head straight."

Candy pulled out a big, round skillet like they used in Chinese restaurants. “Okay, then. We gon’ stir-fry this chicken and vegetables and I’ll show you how to make a perfect pot of rice.”

Twenty-eight

For the next couple of days, Shauntae kept telling Gary about her new plans. She told him she was gonna rent an apartment and offered to pick a neighborhood that wasn't too far away so it would be easy for him to come visit their child. She said her mother was sending her money to get a car. She kept telling him to marry Darla and move her, the girls, and Darla's mother into his house.

He begged and pleaded and insisted that he didn't want Darla, he wanted her. He wanted to marry her and provide for her and their child. He didn't want her to work. He wanted her to stay home with their child and with the other children they would have.

In between conversations with Gary, Shauntae and Candy cooked. Candy taught her how to make beef stroganoff, pot roast, stir-fry, fried chicken, roasted chicken, smothered pork chops, and sautéed vegetables. They baked a few cakes and a couple of pies. Candy could do anything when it came to cooking. Shauntae was surprised at how much she found herself liking it.

Candy showed Shauntae the online courses she was taking. It wasn't for no degree or nothing. It was just for her personal information. There was one class on how to manage your finances, another on writing a business plan, and another on how to run a successful business. Candy let Shauntae borrow the computer that Bobby had bought her so she could browse and see if there was any classes she was interested in.

Shauntae started to say she wasn't smart enough to be taking no online classes, but she knew she was smarter than Candy, and if Candy could do it so could she. There was so many classes on so many different subjects that Shauntae didn't know what to pick. After a while it gave her a headache so she stopped looking. Candy showed her how to find YouTube videos that would show you how to do anything you wanted. That was easier.

The first couple of days it was real cool because it was just them, hanging out, talking, and cooking. On the third day, Bobby came over in the evening, after he finished up at his shop. When she met him, Shauntae decided the reason Bobby didn't care that Candy wasn't pretty was because he wasn't nothing to look at either. In fact, looking at the two of them together, it was probably a good thing that they wasn't gon' be able to have no kids.

It was one of the few times Shauntae had ever met a man who didn't stare her in the face and get all lusty. All her life, that had happened—married men, old men, young men, it didn't matter. Bobby barely even looked at her. But he looked at Candy the same way Gary looked at her—love struck and all messed up in the head. Shauntae was happy for Candy, but she missed feeling that feeling. Only difference was, Bobby was love struck over Candy—the real Candy. She wondered how Gary would look at her if he knew who she really was.

Since it looked like Bobby was staying for a while, Shauntae shut herself up in her little guest room. Candy let her take the laptop and she spent hours on YouTube watching all kinds of videos. At first it was gourmet cooking videos, but then one of the cooking videos led her to "quick meals for moms" videos that led her to "how to be a good mom" videos.

The videos explained all kinds of stuff about children. What they did at different ages. What kinda thoughts was going on in they minds. The way they learned. The things they needed from they parents. What happened to them if they didn't get love. The right way to treat them when they did stuff wrong. There was one lady who had done a whole bunch of videos on a bunch of different subjects. Shauntae liked her best because she broke stuff down and made it simple and interesting.

Shauntae was up watching "good mom" videos until two in the morning. After she closed the computer, she rubbed her belly. "See, li'l baby. I can be a good mama. It's like with cooking. Nobody ever showed me how before." She curled into her comfortable spot at the foot of the bed and fell asleep.

That night she dreamed about Brianna. She was playing with her and talking to her and spending time with her and doing all sorts of "good mom" stuff with her. Shauntae woke up crying. The videos had shown her that she had done everything wrong with Brianna. She wished she could start all over again and do it right. She rubbed her belly. "I guess I get to start all over and do it right with you, li'l baby."

She lay in bed for a while, not able to get back to sleep. The phone started ringing at seven. Gary did his usual begging and pleading.

Shauntae listened for a while and then said, "You know the past few days I've been thinking about going back to college?"

Gary was quiet for a second and then said, "Okay . . ." He let out a deep breath. "What is happening with you, honey love? Every time I talk to you it's something different. It's like you're changing."

"Maybe I am changing. Everything that's been going on has got me thinking. I been thinking about becoming a better person."

"But you're already a wonderful person. That's why I love you so much."

It was Shauntae's turn to let out a deep breath. "Like we said before, there's a lot we don't know about each other. There's a whole lot you don't know about me."

"Then come home so we can talk and get to know all these things that we don't know about each other." Gary's voice sounded desperate. "Shauntae, you and the baby need to go to the doctor. Have you forgotten about that?"

"I couldn't forget my baby. I told you I would take care of that."

"I don't get to be there for the ultrasound? You're going to find out the sex of the baby without me?"

"Gary, I'll call you later, okay?" Shauntae hung up the phone.

Her stomach started rumbling, so she went out in the kitchen. Candy was still asleep. Shauntae heard Bobby's voice when she fell asleep at two, so she knew Candy must have been up late.

She pulled some stuff out of the refrigerator and before she knew it, she had made an omelet, home fries, and turkey sausage. By the time Candy came out of her room, looking all sleepy, Shauntae had cut up some strawberries and had arranged the food all fancy on both of their plates like Candy had shown her.

"Dang, girl. Look at you." Candy had a big smile on her face like a proud teacher. "My girl got some skills."

They sat down to eat. "Y'all was up late last night, huh?" Shauntae asked through a mouthful of home fries.

Candy's eyes went all dreamy. "Yeah. We kept talking and talking. He's a real good man."

"He coming over again tonight?" Shauntae asked.

"He taking me out tonight. But . . ." Candy cut her sausage into small pieces.

"But what?"

"He wants to spend the weekend. I think we're finally gonna, you know, do it." Candy let out a giggle.

"You really gone over him, huh?"

Candy smiled. "Yeah. I think I love him."

"Wow, that's serious. And y'all ain't never had sex?"

"This weekend will be the first time. Which means . . . you think you can go back to Sherice's this weekend? I ain't trying to throw you out, but I don't think it would be cool for you to be here if we . . ."

"Yeah, no, that wouldn't be cool at all."

"And we can't go to his house because his two teenage sons live with him."

"Yeah, I feel you, girl. Okay. Let me see what I'm gon' do." Shauntae knew Sherice wasn't letting her stay at her house as long as there was a warrant. There wasn't nowhere else she could go. She started feeling that desperate, fifty-nine-dollar feeling again. The last couple of days at Candy's had kinda made her forget her situation. There was plenty of food and she was happy hanging out with her girl, cooking, and being on the Internet.

The reality of her situation was she didn't have no money, she didn't have no car, and she didn't have no place to live. Maybe it was time to go back to Gary's. But Sherice had told her to hold out until he broke.

"Anyway, it's not 'til tomorrow night. We get to cook all day today again. Bobby's coming in a little while to take me to the grocery store. Anything special you want to cook?"

Shauntae's excitement was lower than it had been the last couple of days. "Whatever you want to cook is fine with me."

They ate in silence for a few minutes and then Candy asked, "Can I ask you a question?"

"Sure. What?"

Candy's face turned red and she pushed the strawberries on her plate around.

"What, Candy?"

"How you learn how to have sex real good? Like is it something special you do to make them enjoy being with you? What if Bobby don't like being with me?" Candy looked like she was about to cry. "What if I can't do it right?"

Shauntae put down her fork. "Girl, please. Don't be worried about that. You gon' be fine. Ain't no sex tips I need to give you."

"But you and Sherice always talking about how the better you are in bed, the longer you can keep a man."

"That's different. It's one thing when you having sex just to be having sex. It's another thing when you actually making love with somebody." Shauntae thought of the look on Gary's face the last time they had been together. "Bobby loves you. I can see it in his eyes. Y'all ain't gon' be having some sex for fun. Y'all gon' be making love. And because he love you, it's gonna be good no matter what."

"You think so?"

"I know so."

"How you know about sex being different when you in love? You in love with Gary?"

Shauntae shrugged. "I'm still trying to figure out this love stuff. I don't think you can love somebody if you can't really be real with them."

"So what you gon' do?"

"Girl, I don't know."

Shauntae took a nap until Candy came back from the grocery store and then they spent the whole rest of the day cooking. In the evening, Shauntae helped Candy get dressed and made up for her date with Bobby.

After Candy left, Shauntae settled onto the couch with the laptop and started watching videos. She watched mom videos for a few hours and then the mom videos led her to healthy relationship/good marriage videos. She watched for an hour and then switched back to cooking videos.

She couldn't stand watching, knowing that everything she was doing was wrong. All the secrets and lies, pretending to be something she wasn't, acting a certain way to get Gary to do what she wanted was all wrong. She didn't want that sicky feeling in her stomach to come back, so it was easier to watch "Ten Different Ways to Make Slammin' Chicken."

She had ignored Gary's phone calls the whole day, at first because she was cooking, then because she was watching videos. And now because she was afraid if she talked to him, she might tell him the truth about everything.

The next morning, she woke up late after watching cooking videos all night. She had barely sat up when the phone rang.

She answered the phone, "Good morning, Gary."

"You didn't call me back like you said yesterday and you didn't answer my calls."

"I was taking care of important things for me and the baby's future."

"Shauntae, you don't have to do that anymore."

"Why are we having the same conversation every day? I keep telling you—"

"Wait, please listen. When I took the girls to Darla's rehab yesterday, we all sat down and talked. I told them Darla and I wouldn't be getting remarried and that I was going to marry you. I told them I knew they were upset about it, but it was my decision. The girls cried and Darla wasn't happy, but I put my foot down."

Shauntae didn't say anything.

"Now will you come home, baby?"

Shauntae felt bad. What if this man was supposed to get back with his family, but because of her games and lies, she had broken it all up? "I wish you hadn't done that. What if God was answering your prayers by putting your family back together?"

"You're my family, Shauntae. You and the baby. Me and Darla tried. We failed. Even if you don't come home, I'm not willing to try with her again."

"But what if we fail? What if I can't be the wife and mother you want me to be?"

"We can do this, baby. Let's give it a chance. Come home."

Shauntae bit her bottom lip. "I'll think about it and I'll call you tonight. I promise."

"Shauntae, please."

"I'll call you. I promise." Shauntae hung up.

She should have been real happy right now. He had broke like Sherice said he would. In time for her not to be homeless for the weekend.

She picked up the phone again and dialed.

Even though it was almost ten, Sherice sounded like she was still asleep. "What, heffa?"

"Can you come get me today? I'm ready to go back home."

Twenty-nine

Sherice got to Candy's house almost three hours later. As soon as she got there, Shauntae rushed her and Candy to the car with her bags and then they all piled in to take her home. Shauntae wanted to be dropped off before Gary got home from work. She couldn't chance him meeting the girls or seeing Sherice's car.

The whole way there, Sherice talked about how her brilliant plan had broke Gary down and how Shauntae needed to remember that when she got her credit card. Shauntae's nerves was aggravated by the time they got to Sandy Springs.

When they got to the house, Sherice and Candy took her bags inside and then Shauntae led them to the front door so they would go on home.

Candy gave her a hug. "I'm glad you came and stayed with me. It was fun."

"Yeah, girl. Thanks for everything. Now I'ma be cooking for my man."

"Yeah, in that gourmet kitchen. I should come visit you so we can cook here."

"That would be cool. And I'll come visit you too. Keep doing all the stuff you doing. I'm real proud of you."

Candy hugged her again. "You gon' be all right?"

"I'ma figure something out. If not, you gon' keep my room ready, right?"

Sherice stared at the both of them. "Wassup wit' y'all? Acting like Celie and Nettie from *The Color Purple.*" She clapped her hands together and sang, "'You and me, us never part, makidada.'"

Shauntae and Candy laughed. "Shut up, Sherice. Why you gotta always be so crazy?" Candy said.

Sherice had her own parting words. "You got this, Shauntae. Keep doing what you doing. You'll be married with a car and a credit card in no time. Remember, I want to be the first one you take for a spin in the new Lex or Mercedes."

"You know I'll be there. First stop, Candler Road."

"A'ight den. We out." Sherice marched herself to the car. Candy gave Shauntae one more hug and left.

When she went into the house, Shauntae instantly felt the difference. She was back in the high life again. She left her suitcases in the foyer for Gary to take upstairs when he got home.

She wandered around the house, trying to figure out what to do with herself. She wasn't sleepy and didn't feel like watching television. She ended up in the kitchen, looking in the refrigerator and pantry to see what she could cook.

It looked like Gary had gone and gotten groceries while she was gone. She found some chicken breasts and fresh vegetables. She found some asparagus and decided she wanted to try to cook it. She went into Gary's office and got on his computer. After browsing a couple of YouTube videos, she decided to roast it and the other vegetables with olive oil and herbs.

For the next few hours, she went back and forth between the kitchen and the computer. She called Candy a few times when she didn't have an ingredient and Candy helped her pick out a good substitute of something she did have.

The whole time she was cooking, Shauntae was thinking about the stuff she had seen on the relationship videos. Thinking about how Gary wanted a good family and that they couldn't have one if it was based on lies. Thinking about the way Bobby looked at Candy and how she wanted Gary to look at her like that because she was real and not a pretender.

She decided she was gon' tell him everything. She would feed him a gourmet meal and then they would sit on the couch in the family room and she would tell him the whole truth. She'd leave her bags packed in the foyer, and if he wanted her to leave, she'd call Sherice to come get her. She'd persuade Sherice to let her stay for the weekend and then she'd go back to Candy's house. She'd figure out the rest from there.

She tried to find a YouTube video to help her, but what was she gon' put in the search engine? I lied to my baby daddy about not having children but I really have a child who I lost because I almost killed her and if I go near her I'll get arrested? That was one thing YouTube wasn't gon' be able to tell her how to do.

After the meal was ready, Shauntae picked up the phone to call Gary. When he answered, she said, "Baby, I wanted to let you know. I'm home."

Thirty

It wasn't even an hour before Shauntae heard the chime on the garage door. She had gone upstairs and changed out of her cooking clothes into a black knit dress. Most of her jeans didn't fit anymore.

"Shauntae, I'm home." Gary's thick bass boomed from downstairs.

Shauntae hadn't expected to feel that shivery feeling when she heard his voice. She smoothed her hair down and walked down the steps. Before she got to the bottom, she was in Gary's arms. She had forgotten how it felt when he completely swallowed her up in manliness.

"Baby, you're home." Gary kissed her until she had to make him stop. "What's wrong?" He looked worried.

"Nothing. Just—"

He kissed her again. And again and again until next thing she knew, he had scooped her up and carried her upstairs to his bed. He kept telling her how much he loved her and how much he missed her and how happy he was she was home.

He kept talking and kissing her until Shauntae felt like she was drinking strong wine too fast on a empty stomach. All her plans about telling him the truth got cloudier and cloudier, like her brain got when she drank too much wine. By the time they finished making love, the thoughts was completely gone.

All she could think of was the look in Gary's eyes when he looked at her. The sound of his voice when he said he loved her. The smells of his sweat and cologne mixed together in a sexy blend. How comfortable the bed was in this big, glorious house that could be hers, all hers, if she kept doing what she was doing.

"Baby, I'm sorry. I couldn't help myself. I was so happy for you to be home. And besides, we're getting married. First thing Monday morning. It would have been first thing tomorrow if it weren't Saturday." He leaned down to kiss her belly. "Is the baby okay? I wasn't even thinking. You feel okay?"

"I'm fine and the baby is fine." First thing Monday morning they were getting married? She should feel excited. Instead she felt confused.

Gary sat up in bed and sniffed. "What is that smell? Something smells really good."

"I made dinner."

"You cooked?"

"Yeah, why you say it like that?"

"I didn't realize you could cook. You hadn't since you been here so I figured . . ."

"Like I said, there's a lot you don't know about me." The sex afterglow was wearing off and Shauntae was ready to confess again. She wanted to have all her cards on the table before they said "I do."

She sat up on the side of the bed. "Gary, we should talk."

Gary kissed her on the neck. "I know. We will. But not now. For now, I want to enjoy you. And I'm hungry." He got up from the bed and walked into his closet to change clothes. "What did you cook?" he called out.

"Roasted chicken, roasted vegetables, and candied, smashed sweet potatoes. I made strawberry shortcake for dessert. There's no whipped cream, though."

He came out of the closet looking surprised. "You cooked all that?"

Shauntae smiled and nodded.

"Well, let's eat then."

Shauntae went into her bathroom to take a splash bath and put her dress back on. When she got to the kitchen, Gary had one plate in the microwave and the other steaming on the kitchen counter. She sat down at the table and he brought both plates over. "I had no idea you could cook like this."

He gave her a big smile. "I'm looking forward to getting to know everything about you. I finished my deal and I'm gonna take a few days off. We can get married on Monday and then go anywhere you want. We could drive down to the Sea Islands for a little honeymoon, except it might be too cold. We could go up to the mountains or head over to Asheville. Anywhere you want to go. Somewhere quiet and relaxed where we can talk."

"What about the girls?"

"I've already talked to them. They know Daddy is gonna be out of town for a few days."

"We should talk before we go. Before we get married. That way you can be sure about us. About me."

"I've told you. I'm already sure. There's nothing you can say that would make me stop loving you."

"That's because you don't know what I'm going to say. I'm trying to tell you—"

Gary leaned over and stopped her words with a kiss. "Baby, please, not tonight. This has been a hard week. I haven't slept the whole time, worrying about you and the baby. It was a push to get the business deal through, and then the talk at the hospital with Darla and the girls was hard. Please, honey. Can we just be together tonight? I promise tomorrow I'll listen to whatever it is that you have to say that you think is so bad. Tonight, let's just love each other."

Shauntae let out a deep breath. "Okay."

He kissed her on the nose and went back to eating. "This food is so good. I can't believe my baby can cook like this. Beautiful, a good, loving, sweet, Christian woman, and can cook. I hit the jackpot."

It was more than Shauntae could take. She got up.

"What's wrong?"

"Gotta go to the bathroom. The baby is getting bigger and I'm going more often."

She sat on the toilet seat for a while with her head in her hands. Here she was, finally trying to do right, and he wouldn't let her. And she was going back and forth between whether she wanted to. Maybe Gary was right. She should enjoy the evening, the whole weekend. She would have a good time until Monday morning before it was time to go to the justice of the peace.

Then she would tell him everything.

Thirty-one

If Gary's loving made Shauntae feel like she was drinking wine, then the next two days was like smoking crack. When Gary said he planned to "make it up to her," he meant it. He woke up late, so he took her out to brunch at a fancy restaurant not too far from the house. Shauntae looked at all the dishes on the menu and wrote some down so she could look them up on YouTube.

When he saw how excited she was about cooking some of the dishes, he took her to the grocery store and told her to get whatever she wanted. She called Candy four times asking for advice on what to buy until Candy finally stayed on the phone with her until she finished shopping.

After they brought the groceries home, Gary took her shopping for some new clothes. They went to a fancy maternity shop at the mall—Perimeter Mall, nothing like the ghettofabulous South Dekalb Mall. Shauntae tried on a whole bunch of outfits. They had so much cute stuff, she couldn't decide what to get. Gary told her not to decide and pulled out his credit card and paid for all of it.

After that, they browsed in a baby shop for more than an hour. They picked out some things, but decided to come back and buy them when they knew the baby's sex.

After all the shopping, he took her to another fancy restaurant for dinner. On the way home, he turned into a Toyota dealership. He leaned over and kissed her on the nose, "What's your favorite color, baby?"

Shauntae was so shocked, she could barely talk. "I don't even know."

About an hour later, she was driving off the lot in her new vehicle. She could imagine the ragging she would get when she pulled up at Sherice's house in a minivan. Gary had said it was best because to squeeze the girls and a car seat in the back of a regular car wouldn't work. And, it would be great for when they had the next baby.

Shauntae was too happy to care what Sherice would think. She had never had a new vehicle in her whole life. That new-car smell had her high as a kite.

When they got home, Shauntae started to take her new clothes to the guest room, but Gary stopped her. "Why don't you hang them in your closet in our bedroom, honey? Then you won't have to move them later."

When she came out the closet, Gary said, "We'll have to get you a new dresser, too. Want to go furniture shopping tomorrow? I'm thinking there might be other new stuff you want to get to make this your home. This is all stuff me and Darla bought together and I thought you might want to make some changes."

The next day, Gary slept late again, so they skipped church. After Sunday brunch, they went to a bunch of furniture stores. Shauntae didn't want to buy anything, yet. She wanted to YouTube some interior decorating stuff first. It was fun just looking, though. It was crazy knowing she could pick out anything she wanted and she could bring it home simply by saying, "I like that one." She didn't know she could ever feel like that in her life.

She could hear Sherice's and her mama's voices, *You'd be crazy to mess this up. Don't tell that man nothing. He don't need to know the truth.*

Each time Gary pulled out his credit card, Shauntae agreed with them a little bit more. What was she thinking? Wasn't this the life she always dreamed about, but never thought she could have?

That night, after another one of Shauntae's gourmet dinners, they made love again. Neither of them felt too bad about it since they were getting married the next morning. Gary had made her an appointment at Dr. Murray's office, and then they were going straight to the justice of the peace from there. Then they were leaving for a few days in Asheville. Shauntae had never been nowhere but Atlanta and California so she was looking forward to it.

Gary was real tired and was knocked out by ten o'clock. Shauntae slipped out of the bed and went downstairs with her cell phone. She wanted to tell her girls everything that was going on.

She decided to call Candy first. She wasn't ready for Sherice to diss her minivan. Candy answered on the first ring. She whispered, "Wassup, girl?"

"Why you whispering?"

"Hold on a second." Candy was quiet for a minute. "Bobby is still here. He's staying the night again. Girl, you was right. It was wonderful. I ain't got no words to describe it. You were right about the difference between having sex and making love. And you was right again; he told me he loved me. He said he want us to be together. I can't believe this is happening to me."

"Wow, Candy, wow! He said he loved you?"

"Yeah. He want me to be his woman. He said he gon' buy me a new bed because he can't be sleeping in this old, knotty bed my grandmother used to sleep in. I got a man."

Shauntae was real happy for her girl, but in the back of her mind she was thinking that if she told Gary everything, she wouldn't be able to stay at Candy's if he put her out.

"How are things with Gary since you been back?"

"Oh, it's been good. Got a doctor's appointment and we'll see the sex of the baby in the morning."

"Make sure you call me and tell me what you having. I gotta go. Bobby is calling me."

"A'ight. I'm real happy for you. Y'all have a good time."

Shauntae called Sherice next.

"What's up, heffa? How you living?"

Shauntae had to laugh at Sherice's crazy behind. "I'm good. Back in there with my man."

"How back in there? You in the pockets yet? I need a little money. My rent is due and I been low on sponsors lately. Can you help me out?"

"I just got back. I ain't got no credit card yet. And if I did, could I even put your rent on a credit card?"

"You can't get no access to cash?"

"What I'm s'posed to say? 'Gary, can you pay my girl's rent?' That ain't gon' work. You gotta give me more time, Sherice."

"I ain't got no time. This fool talking 'bout putting me out in the next couple of days."

"Dang. I wish I could help you. All I got is fifty-nine dollars."

"What I'm s'posed to do with fifty-nine dollars? Never mind. I gotta make some phone calls. I'll talk to you later." Sherice hung up the phone.

Shauntae was glad she didn't tell Sherice about her new clothes and her minivan. Knowing Sherice, she'd want her to try to sell something to pay her rent.

It was a good thing she didn't tell Gary the truth. If he put her out, she wouldn't have nowhere to go. And her little fifty-nine dollars wouldn't take her very far.

It looked like she was getting married in the morning.

Thirty-two

The next week was like a fairy tale. Shauntae felt like she was in the movie *Pretty Woman* and that she had been rescued by her knight on a white horse.

The ultrasound was a emotional experience. She had got two ultrasounds with Brianna, but this was different. Unlike Devon, who sat with the ultrasound person and asked questions like Shauntae wasn't even in the room, Gary sat next to her and held her hand. He kept kissing her face. They talked about the blobs they were seeing on the screen and laughed together when it seemed like the baby was waving at them.

When the ultrasound person pointed to a blob that showed that Shauntae was right about the baby being a boy, Gary kissed her and then he started crying and talking about how happy he was that she was giving him a son. Shauntae couldn't believe how happy he was about everything. And it made her happy about everything. She was actually starting to get happy about having this baby. She planned to watch all the YouTube videos she could so she could be the best mother possible.

Dr. Murray said everything looked great with the baby. She said that Shauntae was twenty-two weeks pregnant and that her due date was around July third.

Shauntae looked sharp at the justice of the peace in the beautiful, cream-colored maternity suit Gary had bought her. They said their "I do's" real quick and then got in the car to head to Asheville for their honeymoon.

When they got to the five-star hotel, Shauntae wondered how much money Gary had. She had never seen nothing like it before. It was fancy and rich feeling, like Gary's house and the restaurants and stores he had been taking her to. Shauntae was getting a little bit more comfortable with that fancy-feeling stuff.

The suite he got was more like a well-decorated apartment than a hotel room. It had a dining table and couches and chairs and a bed so comfortable Shauntae wanted to spend the whole honeymoon there. The hotel had a bunch of different restaurants that served fancy food. Instead of turning her nose up at it, Shauntae wanted to taste everything and then learn how to make the stuff she liked.

Every morning, after wonderful nights of lovemaking, or snuggling in the bed together, they had a fancy breakfast, and then Shauntae went to the spa while Gary played golf. She didn't even know he played golf.

The spa had a special massage for pregnant women. And then they had a massage where they used some hot rocks and rubbed them all over her body. And then there was another where they used these special oils with different smells that left Shauntae feeling high.

One day, she and Gary got a couple's massage. He said he'd rather play golf than lie on a table with somebody rubbing him, but he had wanted to try it since Shauntae was hyping it up every day.

A couple of days, they went into Asheville and there were cute stores everywhere. Gary kept buying her nice things that cost ridiculous prices. People with money lived in a whole different world. There were a couple of times that Shauntae told Gary that what he was buying for her wasn't worth the ridiculous sky-high price he was paying, but he told her nothing was too good for her.

They went to this special garden that was specially grown for people to come and see how pretty the flowers was. At first, Shauntae couldn't understand what the big deal was about going to see some flowers. When she got there, she understood. She had never seen anything so beautiful in all her life. Gary kept talking about how much of an artist God is and Shauntae had to agree. The whole place looked like God had picked up a paintbrush and made something beautiful for His children to enjoy.

The whole thing was too good to be true. Even though she felt bad, Shauntae was glad she hadn't told Gary the truth. It was the best week of her whole life and no matter what happened, she had enjoyed it. People like her never even dreamed about stuff like that, let alone got to live it.

Even with all the spa treatments, fancy meals, expensive gifts, and everything, what Shauntae loved the most was being in the bed with Gary every night. It was the best sex—or best lovemaking—she ever had. But it was even better snuggling with him every night. His body was warm and felt strong and manly. A couple of times, she woke up in the middle of the night. When she felt the heat coming off his body and heard his breathing and felt the weight of his arm over her, she knew she was somebody's wife—a feeling she thought she'd never have.

On Friday evening when they got in bed, Gary said, "Maybe we'll go home tomorrow. We haven't been to church in forever. Wouldn't that be the perfect end to our honeymoon week? To go worship the Lord together?"

Shauntae tried to keep the panic out of her eyes. "Aw, honey. You're not supposed to go to church while you celebrating your honeymoon. How 'bout we stay and have our own little personal church service right here?" She kissed him real deep, knowing it wouldn't take much to change his mind.

"Okay, baby. We'll stay until Sunday night. But we have to go to church next Sunday. I don't think I've ever been away from church this long."

"Okay. Next Sunday for sure."

They usually fell asleep together after some good loving, Gary's body wrapped around hers, his hands holding on to her belly. That night, after his breathing changed, Shauntae was awake all by herself, trying to figure out what to do about church. She couldn't risk running into Devon, Cassandra, and Brianna. Devon hadn't called her back to say nothing about lifting the warrant.

Gary rubbed his hands over her belly and kissed her in his sleep. Shauntae decided to go ahead and enjoy what little bit of her honeymoon she had left. She'd deal with Devon when she got back home.

Thirty-three

Shauntae and Gary got home late Sunday afternoon after spending their last luxurious day at the Grove Park Inn. After Gary left for work Monday morning, Shauntae stayed in the big king-sized bed in what was now their bedroom.

She watched movies and lounged in bed half the day and then got up and cooked before Gary got home. She was happy to be in the kitchen again.

The next day, she picked up Candy and brought her to the house. They spent the whole day in the kitchen cooking and talking. Even though Shauntae had called Candy from Asheville, Candy couldn't believe Shauntae had got a new car, got married, and gone on a honeymoon since they last saw each other. Shauntae shared every detail of the whole trip.

Candy had news of her own. Bobby was talking about their future together. They were deciding if she was gonna move in his house with him and his sons or if they was getting a new house. He wanted to fix up her grandmother's house to rent out.

Candy and Shauntae had the best time talking about their men and their plans and everything that was making them happy. The whole day, they kept saying, "Don't tell Sherice." Neither one of them felt like hearing her mouth or dealing with her rent situation.

Shauntae didn't talk to Sherice the whole week she was gone. No telling what she had done to pay her rent.

Shauntae would tell her she was married and had gotten the car, but she didn't want Sherice to know nothing about the shopping or her honeymoon. She was sure Sherice wouldn't be happy for her like Candy was. Especially since she didn't have nothing good going for herself.

The Wednesday after they got back, Shauntae knew she needed to call Devon. Sunday was getting closer and closer and she had to figure out what to do about church. She practiced her most perfect English for about an hour before she finally called him.

He sounded irritated when he picked up the phone. "Hello?"

"Hey, Devon, it's Shauntae."

"I know who it is. What do you want?"

"I'm sorry. I know you're at work; did I catch you at a bad time?"

He let out a deep breath and then made his voice a little bit nicer. "No, it's not a bad time. What do you want?"

"Devon, I know that with our past and stuff, seeing my name on the phone probably doesn't make you happy. I want to apologize for everything I ever did to make your life difficult and Brianna's life difficult. I'm sorry. If I could go back and change everything, I would. But I can't. All I can do is say I'm sorry and hope that you'll forgive me."

"If you're saying all this so I can lift the warrant—"

"I'm not saying this so you'll lift the warrant. I can understand why you would think that because I've done some really shady stuff in the past. I don't expect you to believe that I changed overnight. I'm asking for a chance to prove that I'm different. Would you give me that chance?"

There was a long silence on Devon's end.

Shauntae filled it by saying, "And you can please apologize to Cassandra for me for how I disrespected her every time I saw her? She seems like she's real nice and she's been good to my daughter even when . . . well, especially when I wasn't there for her. Could you thank her for me? I would do it myself but I think she'd be more upset to hear from me than you are."

Devon was still silent.

"Devon?"

"I'm listening. Thinking. I still want to know why I should believe you're going to be different."

"I got married this week. I'm having a baby in a few months. Devon, I messed things up so bad with Brianna. I gotta get it right this time. I can't be treacherous and triflin' all my life, can I?"

Devon chuckled and it gave Shauntae some hope. "Yeah, I know I was treacherous and triflin'. And I'm sorry. So sorry. You have to believe me. And I'm not calling about the warrant. You said you would call me when you decided and I respect that. I need to ask you about something else."

"Here we go."

"Come on, you're supposed to be giving me a chance." She wanted to tell him about her honeymoon and her new car and new clothes and how rich Gary was so he wouldn't have to worry about her wanting to get in his pockets. But then he would think she was still up to her old tricks. "The thing is . . . me and my husband go to the same church as you. Can you believe that? What are the chances, as big as Atlanta is? And, well, the first Sunday I came, I saw you, Brianna, and Cassandra and it scared me. I haven't been back to church since. But I need to go back. I want to go back."

"Need to go back for him or for you?"

"Both. For him, because it's important that we go to church as a family. And for me, because I'm trying to figure God out. I can't say I'm a Christian yet, but I want to be a better person and I know He's my best chance at that."

After a pause, Devon said, "I understand not becoming a Christian right away and taking time to figure that out. I've done the same thing since me and Cassandra have been together."

Shauntae bit her lip. She was getting more hopeful.

"But how will that work? Brianna goes to church there. If you saw her last time you came, you could see her again. I'm not sure she's ready for that. I'm not sure I'm ready for that."

It was Shauntae's turn to be silent. She finally said, "I understand. I don't want to cause her any more pain than I already have. Thanks for listening. And once again, I'm sorry to you, Cassandra, and especially Brianna for all the pain I caused you all. Maybe not now, but hopefully one day, you'll be able to forgive me. You take care, okay?"

Devon chuckled. "That's it? You're not gonna cuss me out or scream and yell or tell me I'm ruining your life?"

Shauntae laughed a little bit. "Like I told you, I'm different. When you give Brianna a hug tonight, sneak her one from me, okay? Take good care of her." Shauntae hung up the phone.

What was she gonna do? There was no way Gary was gonna not go to church this Sunday or any other Sunday. And there was no way she could explain why she couldn't go without telling all her dirty secrets.

She decided to pray. "God, me and you been doing real good lately. I know I ain't done this completely right because I haven't told him the truth. But I tried, God! You was there! You heard me trying to tell him and he wouldn't let me. And, God, you know this was the best week of my whole miserable life. I want to keep this life. I feel like you gave it to me. It ain't like the devil would do nothing this nice for me."

Shauntae didn't know if she was praying right. She didn't sound holy and spiritual like Gary. All she could do was talk to God. "I need you to help me out, okay? I don't know how to fix all this. If you help me, I promise, I'm going to become the good person I'm pretending to be. Please help me be a good person. And help me figure out how to get me and Gary back to church."

Shauntae thought for a minute and then said, "For real though, God, if you fix it to where I can go to church with my husband, then I'll know that all the good stuff happening to me is from you and not the devil. And then we can talk about whether I could be a Christian or not. Okay, God?"

Shauntae sat there on the couch for a minute. She didn't know if God was supposed to answer her or if there was something else she was supposed to do. A few seconds later, her phone vibrated. It was a text from Devon.

> Me, Cassandra, and Brianna go to the second service. We use the back entrance, where children's church is. If you and your husband go to early service and use the front entrance, and leave right after service, it could work. If you watch carefully, there should be no accidental run-ins. I can't believe I'm agreeing to this so please don't make me regret giving you a chance.

Shauntae screamed and dropped the phone. God answered her. She couldn't believe He was actually listening to her and had answered her right away. So it was Him that was making all this good stuff happen in her life. Shauntae screamed again. So did that mean that God really loved her like everybody kept saying?

The baby started turning flips in her stomach. Shauntae rubbed the spot where she felt him. "Sorry, li'l baby. Mama's okay. She just excited."

What if it was a coincidence? What if it really wasn't God, but Devon being his usual nice self? "God, how do I know that was you? I ain't trying to get on your nerves. You know I'm new with all this stuff."

A few seconds later, her cell phone vibrated again. Shauntae picked it up off the floor and saw a new message from Devon.

I'll talk to Cassandra later about lifting the warrant. I swear if you do anything to hurt Brianna, you won't have to worry about jail. I'll kill you myself. You asked for a chance and I'm giving it to you. Please don't make me regret it.

She screamed and dropped the phone again. "God, it is you! It is you! You love me." And then them durn pregnancy hormones took over and Shauntae started crying. "Thank you, God. I'm sorry for everything bad I ever did. Please forgive me. Thank you for everything you done for me. You gave me this whole new life and I don't even deserve it. I promise, I'm gonna do my best to be a good person. I need you to help me though. I want to be a good person, a good wife, and a good mama. Can you help me with that? Thank you, God."

Shauntae waited to see if something else was gonna happen. No more text messages came through and nothing felt different. She sat there for a second waiting for another sign that God had heard her and that He was gonna make her a better person.

Then she figured maybe God didn't give a sign every time He heard a prayer and answered it. But then, how would she know if He heard her or not? And then she felt it. She felt the baby kick. Not the fluttering, but a real kick. God was answering her.

So God was gonna make her a better person. She was gonna be a good wife and mother. She rubbed her belly.

"Hear that, li'l baby? I'm gonna be a good mama. I'm gonna love you so much."

She thought about everything God had done for her just that day. She was gonna get to go to church with her husband. Most likely Devon was going to lift the warrant. And she was gonna be a for real good person and not a pretend good person. And so if God was helping her, maybe He was okay with her not telling Gary the truth. Right? If He wasn't okay, then He wouldn't have helped her.

So it was settled. She wasn't going to tell Gary about Brianna and everything else and God was okay with it. But did that mean that God was going to keep Gary from finding out?

Thirty-four

For the next few weeks, things went real smooth. It wasn't hard to persuade Gary to go to first service. Since her miraculous recovery, Darla was back at church and was taking the girls to second service. He felt like it was better if they didn't all go to church at the same time. "At least for now," he said.

He and Shauntae went to eight o'clock service, out for Sunday brunch, and then they spent some time together at home. Gary went to see the girls in the evening. He went to visit them often. Gary never said anything about bringing the girls home after that time she messed up. Shauntae hadn't brought it up, but it bothered her. If he didn't think she was a good enough mother to be around her girls, did he think she would be a good mother to their son?

Maybe he wanted to keep the peace with Darla. She had finished rehab and was home with therapy people coming three times a week. Gary said she was still acting nice. She had even bought them a wedding gift. Maybe Gary was afraid that if he started bringing the girls over, Darla wouldn't be so friendly. Shauntae wasn't as scared anymore, since Devon had called her and told her that he and Cassandra decided to lift the arrest warrant.

Shauntae really liked church, too. She loved the music. The pastor always preached a good sermon that was just for her. It was like God would go into her head and read her thoughts and then tell them to the pastor and then he would make a sermon that would give her all the answers she needed.

Every time he talked, the pastor made God seem like He was a real nice, cool, sweet Daddy who loved her very much. He wanted her to do right because He wanted the best for her and not because He was mean or didn't like her to have fun and enjoy herself. It was like she had learned on one of the YouTube videos on parenting: good parents set boundaries and say no to stuff that would hurt their kids. They want the best for their kids and sometimes they make rules to keep them safe. Everything she was learning about being a good parent was teaching her how God wanted to be a good parent to her.

Sometimes it was hard to believe God was that nice and good because everything she had ever heard about Him made Him seem mean and hard to please. She liked this new God much better than the old One.

One Sunday when they were leaving church, Gary and Shauntae ran into Dr. Murray and her husband and two kids. Shauntae was excited to see her. She didn't know they went to the same church. They stood there talking for a while, but then Shauntae realized they needed to hurry up and leave before it was time for Devon, Cassandra, and Brianna to get there. It had been three weeks and they hadn't had any accidental meetings so far.

As they were saying good-bye, Dr. Murray put a brochure in her hand. She said she was involved in the Christian education department at the church and thought there might be some nice classes Shauntae might want to take.

On the way to brunch, Shauntae looked through the brochure and saw some stuff that was perfect for her. There was a "Parenting God's Way" class and a "Being a Godly Wife" class she wanted to take. She remembered her prayer about wanting to become a good wife and mother and knew God had picked those classes just for her.

Shauntae scanned the brochure and saw a class Dr. Murray taught called "Becoming God's Woman" that would help women feel better about themselves so they could be the best person they could be. The brochure said the class helped to get rid of hurts and pains from the past so a person could have a healthy present and future. Shauntae thought about all the times she heard her mother's voice in her head saying all kinds of bad stuff. She wondered if that class could get rid of Mama's voice.

She decided to take all three. She knew God was helping her, but she had heard a scripture that God helps those who help themselves. So even though He was helping her, she was gon' do her part.

Gary put a hand on her knee. "What's that you're reading?"

Shauntae closed the brochure and slipped it in her purse. "Dr. Murray told me about some classes at the church. One on being a good wife and another on being the best I can be." Shauntae paused for a second before telling him about the last one. "There's a parenting class I want to take, too."

"Sounds good, baby. Glad you're taking advantage of what the church has to offer. They have a lot of resources."

Shauntae worked up the courage to ask, "So, when I finish the parenting class, do you think you'll feel comfortable bringing the girls to the house again?"

Gary turned around to look at her as they pulled up to a red light. "What?"

"The last time you brought the girls over the house was when I messed up by telling them about the baby and us getting married. Remember? We had that argument about me not being a good mother. You haven't brought them over since."

Gary frowned. "Is that what you think? That the girls haven't been to the house because I don't think you'd be a good mother?"

Shauntae nodded slowly.

The light changed and Gary took off slowly. "Baby, that's not it at all. You know Darla had the accident and her mother came and I've been trying to keep their life as close to normal as possible."

"But remember, you had planned for me to be a part of the whole thing. You were going to show me their school and soccer schedule and their uniforms and all that stuff. That was before I messed up. Afterward, you never said a word and haven't let me anywhere near them."

Gary shook his head. "Shauntae, that's not why the girls haven't been over. It's because—"

"You don't have to explain. I understand. I've been doing a lot of studying online about parenting and I've learned so much. Being a parent isn't easy and there's so much stuff to know. And you can really mess up a child's life if you don't do things right."

"I don't think you're going to mess up the girls' lives by not doing something right."

Shauntae was silent for a second as Gary wheeled his car into a parking space at Ray's on the River. It had become their favorite place for Sunday brunch. He turned off the car.

"Can I tell you something?" Shauntae asked.

Gary nodded.

"You know how you had a wonderful childhood and your mother and father loved you and treated you well?"

Gary nodded again.

"Well, I didn't have that. My father left when I was little and later my stepfather . . . let's just say he was a bad man and treated me very badly. And my mama wasn't a good mother. She said all kinds of bad things to me and yelled and screamed and beat me. She put me out of the house when I was seventeen."

Gary reached out and took Shauntae's hand.

"Because of how I grew up, I learned a lot of bad habits and had a whole bunch of messed-up thoughts. I made a lot of mistakes in my life and bad decisions that hurt people really bad. I've lost a very special person because of it." Shauntae hung her head when she thought about Brianna. "So yes, it would be possible for me to mess up the girls' lives by making some crazy mistake or saying the wrong thing to them."

Gary squeezed her hand tight.

"I'm trying to learn better. I'm learning a lot from church and from the videos about parenting. And now I want to take these classes. I want to be the best mom I can be. Not only for our son but for your daughters, too."

Gary reached over and kissed Shauntae. "Thanks for sharing that with me. I didn't know that stuff about your family." He frowned and said, "With all that we've talked about concerning family, I'm surprised it never came up before."

Shauntae hung her head. "I think I was afraid to tell you. You talked about your family and it made me . . . ashamed of how I grew up. I thought if you knew, you wouldn't want to marry me anymore." Shauntae held up a hand to stop Gary from interrupting. "I know better than that now. I'm sorry I didn't tell you earlier, okay?"

"Okay, honey." Gary looked at her like he was seeing her for the first time.

"What?" Shauntae asked.

Gary shook his head. "Nothing. I'm happy you shared that with me. And happy that you're doing everything you can to be the best person you can be."

Shauntae let out a deep breath. Somehow, telling Gary about her childhood made her feel better. It made her feel closer to him and it made her feel good that he knew some bad stuff and still loved her. "Thanks, baby. I love you."

"I love you too." Gary leaned in to kiss her, but at that moment her stomach growled really loud. They both laughed. Gary put his hand on the car door. "Guess I better take you inside and feed you, huh?"

Later that evening while Gary was visiting the girls, Shauntae pulled out her cell phone. She wanted to let Devon know about the classes she would be taking in case he, Cassandra, or Brianna had stuff going on at the church at the same time. She thought about how sour his voice sounded the last time she'd called and decided to text him. It was a detailed text, telling him she planned on taking some classes at the church because she wanted to keep growing. She named the classes and the times. She ended by saying she wanted to check to make sure those weren't times any of them were at church and if so, how could they plan to not run into each other.

After she sent it, she sat and waited. She hoped she didn't have to give up any of the classes. All three of them were important to her. Devon's answer came back quick.

> We're taking a premarital class on the same night as your parenting class but Brianna isn't with us so everything should be fine. Glad to hear that you're taking the classes and trying to grow. Wish you the best. God bless.

Shauntae didn't know why the message touched her like it did. Maybe because it meant Devon was starting to believe she could change. She was also glad to know Devon and Cassandra were getting married. It made her happy that Brianna would grow up in a good family with a good mother and father.

Thinking about it made her cry. And then for some reason, she felt sad.

Shauntae got up and went in the kitchen and started pulling stuff out of the refrigerator to cook. Cooking had become one of the things that made her feel happy no matter what was going on.

Like the last couple of times when she had talked to Sherice. Sherice was mad because Shauntae had waited so long to tell her about the wedding and the new car and everything. She got even madder when Shauntae let it slip that Candy had come to the house to visit her. She accused Shauntae of becoming like Keosha and dissing her and not coming to pick her up in the car to take her shopping like she had said. Shauntae hadn't exactly made a promise about shopping but Sherice was already cussing and screaming so Shauntae didn't bother to correct her.

The next time they talked, Sherice accused her of ignoring her so she wouldn't have to help out with her bills. She said Shauntae had used her to catch Gary, but now that she was in his pockets, she had gone ghost. Every time they talked, Shauntae tried to explain, but Sherice ended up cussing and screaming. And every time they hung up, Shauntae ended up in the kitchen making some gourmet meal or baking some wonderful dessert.

She was in the middle of making a pot roast and homemade yeast rolls when Gary came home. He had barely gotten in the kitchen good when he grabbed her and scooped her up in his arms.

Shauntae squealed and asked, "Baby, what has gotten into you?"

He put her down. "Guess what?" He looked like an excited little boy.

"What?"

"I talked to Darla tonight. She's okay with the girls coming over to visit on the weekends. Or if you want to keep our weekend time, we can get them during the week. It's a little more disruptive to interrupt their school week by switching houses, but the point is she's okay with the girls spending time here every week."

"That's great news. Wow." She wasn't as excited as she knew he wanted her to be.

Gary looked at her closely. "You okay with this?"

Shauntae nodded and bit her lip.

Gary took her in his arms. "What's wrong, honey?"

Shauntae shook her head.

"Something's wrong. Tell me."

Shauntae shrugged. She couldn't quite figure out why she was feeling some kinda way.

Gary asked, "You scared?"

Shauntae thought about it. "Yeah, maybe a little." Was that what she was feeling?

"What are you afraid of?"

Shauntae squinted her eyes, thinking. All this relationship and communication and feelings stuff she was learning was hard work. "I think I'm afraid of messing up. Of making another big mistake that proves I'm not a good mother to your girls." Shauntae thought for another second. "And that would mean that I'm not a good enough mother for our son." Shauntae rubbed her belly. "Yeah, I'm real scared of not being a good mother to our son."

"Why are you so scared of that? You made one mistake with the girls and now you're afraid that you're not going to be a good mother?"

Shauntae pulled herself out of Gary's arms. After flipping the oven light on and peeking in, she grabbed some mitts and took out the yeast rolls. They were fluffy and perfectly brown. She took the butter out the refrigerator and rubbed it on top of each one.

"Smells wonderful." Gary reached for one, but Shauntae popped his hand.

"They're still hot. Give them a minute."

Gary watched as she buttered the rolls. "Baby, talk to me. One mistake doesn't make you a bad mother."

Tears started rolling down Shauntae's face. "It wasn't one mistake. It was a whole lot of mistakes. I told you the other day, my mama really messed me up and I've made a lot of bad mistakes. If you knew what kind of person I used to be, you would never let me around your girls. Never." Shauntae started crying for real.

Gary pulled her into his chest. "Used to be, honey, used to be. Remember what Pastor preached on Sunday? You can't let your past control your future. You're not the same person you used to be. Remember, that's what the blood of Jesus is about—transforming us into a new person. You're a new creature. Don't be afraid of who you used to be. Be confident in who you are right now."

Shauntae said, "But you don't know what I've done. How can you say that when you don't know what I've done?"

Gary answered, "It's not about what you've done. It's about what Jesus did. On the cross He got rid of everything you've ever done. Leave it there. Okay?"

Shauntae nodded without lifting her head. She sniffled. "What if . . . What happens if—"

"Please stop worrying. I promise you're going to be okay." Gary lifted Shauntae's chin. "You're gonna be a good mother to the girls and to our son. I want you to believe that, okay?"

Shauntae nodded. "I don't think Daphne likes me."

Gary chuckled. "Yeah, Daphne can be a tough one. Don't worry. You'll find a way to win her heart. Like you won mine."

Shauntae smiled. "You're so sweet to me. Thanks for loving me the way you do."

Gary kissed her on the nose. "How could I not?"

Shauntae was going to amp up her YouTube videos that week. Her first parenting class was on Wednesday. Maybe she could stay after and ask the teacher a bunch of questions. She would do whatever she had to do. She was going to prove to everybody—Gary, Darla, Daphne, Devon and Cassandra, her mama—everybody that she could be a good mama.

Most of all, she was gonna prove it to herself.

Thirty-five

Shauntae spent the whole week watching parenting videos on YouTube. Her parenting class on Wednesday was good, but she was upset that they only covered one topic each week. She guessed it didn't make sense to expect them to teach everything about being a good mama in one night.

On Friday morning, Shauntae asked Gary a whole bunch of questions about what the girls liked to eat. She made a list and went shopping so she could spend the whole day cooking. Gary was picking the girls up from afterschool and bringing them home.

Shauntae was glad she could do her favorite thing all day. When she finished dinner, she tried to sit down and relax but she was too nervous. She got up and made a chocolate cake from scratch and then a little later some oatmeal cookies. Finally it was time for them to come home. Shauntae changed out of her cooking clothes into a pink jumpsuit and sat on a kitchen stool, waiting to hear the garage door open.

Daphne came in the door first. She barely glanced at Shauntae when she walked by, headed toward the stairs.

Morgan came in next. She stood and stared at Shauntae without saying something. Shauntae remembered how sweet Morgan was to her before she found out that she was pregnant and marrying her father. She stood staring at Shauntae for a second.

"Hi, Morgan. How are you? It's good to see you."

"Hi," Morgan said, softly. She looked toward the stairs to see if Daphne was gone already. Shauntae wondered if Daphne had told Morgan not to talk to her.

"How was school?" Shauntae wanted to reach out for her, but she was scared of chasing her away.

"Good." Morgan stuck a finger in her mouth.

Gary finally came in the door, carrying two small suitcases. "Hey, honey. How was your day?"

Shauntae stood up to greet him. She usually met him at the door with a hug and a kiss but she didn't think it was a good idea to do that in front of Morgan.

When Shauntae stood up, Morgan's eyes got real big. Shauntae wondered if it was too much for Morgan to see her pregnant belly. At seven months, there was no way she could hide it.

Morgan's eyes never left Shauntae's belly. "You have a baby in there, huh?"

Shauntae nodded.

"Does it hurt?"

Shauntae smiled. "No, it doesn't hurt. Well, sometimes my back hurts, but no, my belly doesn't hurt."

Morgan frowned. "How did the baby get in there?"

Both Gary and Shauntae laughed. Gary put a hand on Morgan's shoulder. "How about we talk about that later?"

Morgan scrunched up her face like she didn't understand why they were laughing and why they wouldn't answer her question. "How's the baby going to get out?"

Gary shook his head. "Guess I should have been ready for this, huh?"

Shauntae hadn't even thought to look on YouTube for videos to help with this conversation. "I think that's something else that you and your daddy can talk about later."

Morgan folded her arms and pouted. Gary laughed and leaned over and tickled her. He looked around. "Where's Daphne?"

"She went upstairs," Morgan answered. "She didn't even say hello to Miss Shauntae."

Gary frowned and then called out. "Daphne? Come back downstairs."

Shauntae said, "Don't make her speak to me. It'll only make things worse. Let's just give it time."

"She knows better than to be rude."

"Baby, it's okay," Shauntae said.

Daphne came into the kitchen. "Yes, Daddy?"

"Did you say hello to Miss Shauntae when you came in?"

Daphne nodded.

"No, you didn't," Morgan said. "I saw you. You came in, looked at her without saying anything, and went straight upstairs. You told a lie. We're not supposed to tell lies. It's a sin. I learned that in Miss Cassandra's class."

Shauntae's breath caught. "Miss Cassandra?"

"The infamous Miss Cassandra," Gary said. "Morgan's children's church teacher. She's all we ever hear about." Gary turned toward his daughter. "Daphne, you know I don't tolerate rude behavior."

Shauntae remembered when Brianna started going to children's church and Cassandra's art class. Whenever she came over, all Brianna ever talked about was Miss Cassandra. She never thought about Morgan and Brianna, being close in age, having the same teacher in children's church.

"Shauntae?" Gary said.

"Huh?" Shauntae shook herself out of her thoughts.

"Daphne said hello to you."

Shauntae looked down to find Daphne staring at her with her mother's evil eyes full of hate. "I'm sorry, Daphne. Hi, how was your day at school?"

"Fine." Her mouth was so tight Shauntae didn't even know how that word got out.

Shauntae looked at her and Morgan. “Would you guys like an afternoon snack? I have vegetable sticks or some fresh oatmeal cookies. I baked them today.”

Daphne curled up her nose. “You baked? No, thank you.”

“Daphne . . .” Gary’s voice had a warning tone to it. Like Daphne had one more smart thing to say and then she was gonna get it.

Shauntae wondered what “getting it” looked like in this house. She was sure it wasn’t a beating. It was probably a timeout like she had learned from the videos.

Morgan said, “Mommy doesn’t let us eat cookies after school. Too much sugar.”

“I thought about that,” Shauntae said. “That’s why I made them with applesauce and bananas. There’s hardly any sugar at all. Think of it as oatmeal and fruit.” Why was she begging them to eat her cookies?

“Sounds good. I think Mommy would approve,” Gary said.

“Yaaaay, I want cookies.” Morgan sat herself down at the table.

Daphne turned up her nose. “No, thanks. I’ll find something else.” She walked to the pantry and looked inside. “Daddy, you don’t have any of our favorite snacks.”

“I’m sorry, honey,” Gary said. “Miss Shauntae has been doing the shopping.”

Daphne turned and rolled her eyes.

Shauntae put a small plate with two large cookies on it in front of Morgan.

“Yum,” she said in appreciation. Her eyes looked all happy and Shauntae knew it wouldn’t take much to win Morgan over again.

Shauntae said to Daphne, “If you tell me what your favorite snacks are, I’ll make sure to buy them and have them here whenever you guys come.”

"No, thank you."

Shauntae shrugged and turned to Morgan. "You want milk with your cookies?"

Morgan nodded. "These are umm, umm good," she said, her mouth stuffed with cookies. "Dappy, you should try them."

Daphne glared at Morgan like she had sold her out.

"Thanks, Moogie. I'm glad you like them," Shauntae said, remembering the nickname Daphne had used last time the girls were there.

Daphne glared at Shauntae. "You don't get to call her that. Only family members get to call her that." Her voice got loud. "And you're not a family member, so don't ever call her that again. Her name is Morgan."

Gary stepped up next to Daphne and started to say something but Shauntae held up her hand. She said, as calmly as she could, "Daphne, I apologize for using Morgan's nickname. I didn't realize it would bother you so much and I'm sorry. But it is not appropriate for you to yell at me. I'm an adult and you're a child and you should never yell at any adult. I know your mother and your father have taught you that. The way you're behaving does not represent the little girl I'm sure they've raised you to be."

Shauntae waited for Daphne to say something, but she just stood there looking mad.

Shauntae continued, "You don't have to like me, but you do have to respect me. I'm married to your father now, so somehow we have to learn to be family. Family is important to me and especially to your father, so we need to find a way to make this work."

Daphne crossed her arms and made a nasty, rude face.

Gary said, "Perhaps you need to go to your room to think about what Miss Shauntae said."

Daphne stood there.

Gary's voice was firmer. "That was not a request."

Even the way Daphne turned to go upstairs had attitude.

Gary put a hand on Shauntae's shoulder. "You okay?"

Shauntae nodded.

"You handled that well, honey." He planted a quick kiss on her forehead. "Proud of you."

Shauntae sat down at the table across from Morgan. Her hands were shaking a little.

Morgan looked up at her. "Sorry about that. I don't know why Dappy is so mad. These cookies are really good. Thanks for making them."

"You're welcome, Morgan."

Morgan took a big swallow of milk that left her a milk moustache. "You can call me Moogie."

Shauntae smiled. Inside, she felt like she could cry. "Thank you, Moogie. But how about I call you Moogie in private and not in front of Daphne. Just until she's not mad anymore, okay?"

Morgan smiled real big and nodded. "Can I have another cookie?"

Shauntae gave her a little frown. "I don't want you to spoil your appetite. We're having something special for dinner."

"What is it?"

"It's a surprise." Shauntae took Morgan's plate and cup to the sink.

Morgan hopped up from the table. "Daddy, it's a no homework day. Can I go next door and see if Tiffany can come out and play? We'll stay in the backyard."

"Yes, dear. Make sure you stay where Daddy can see you."

Morgan went running toward the front door. When the door closed, Gary took her in his arms. Shauntae melted into him. She had been waiting for that hug all day. She spoke into his chest. "I told you Daphne hates me."

Gary rubbed her back. "She doesn't hate you. This all happened so fast. She'll come around. Give her time. But I liked the way you handled her. See, I told you you'd be a good mother."

Shauntae was happy for him to say that. But she wouldn't be completely happy until Daphne liked her.

Later at the dinner table, Morgan cheered when she saw the meatloaf and mashed potatoes Shauntae had made. "That's my favorite."

"That's why I made it." Shauntae dished up a kid-sized portion for Morgan. She reached out for Daphne to pass her plate, but Daphne ignored her. Shauntae shrugged and served her and Gary's plates. Little Miss Attitude could starve if she wanted to. If she said one wrong thing, Shauntae would be the one to send her to her room this time.

"It's Dappy's favorite too." Morgan gave Daphne a mean stare, like she wanted her sister to straighten up and act right.

Daphne sat there, staring at the table.

After a few bites, Morgan looked up from her plate. "Miss Shauntae, this is sooooooo good. Thank you for cooking for us. The nanny's mommy got sick so the nanny had to get on a plane to go see her and she's been gone for a long time and Grandma can't cook a lot because of her arthritis so we've been eating a lot of food from restaurants and stuff. Mommy can't cook again yet. She never cooked much anyway. She was at work all the time. But she says now she's gonna cook more when she gets all better and the doctor said she was gonna be all better really soon. But Mommy really doesn't like to cook at all. I think she's gonna wait for the nanny to come back. Hey, I thought you couldn't cook? Remember before when you made pancakes but they weren't really pancakes? They were big, lumpy, black things."

Shauntae laughed.

Morgan shoveled a big mouthful of mashed potatoes into her mouth. "Can you teach me how to cook?"

"I'd love to teach you how to cook. I tell you what. We can pick some of your favorite foods and some of your mama's favorite foods and then we can cook a bunch of stuff and put it in Tupperware and put it in the freezer and then you guys will have home-cooked meals at your house. We can go grocery shopping in the morning and cook all day if you want to."

Morgan clapped her hands together. "That would be fun. I get to cook for Mommy. She'll be so happy. Can Dappy help?"

Shauntae looked at Daphne, who was still sulking. "If she'd like to, I'd love for Daphne to cook with us."

Daphne didn't say anything. After a few more minutes of watching everybody eat, Daphne lifted her plate in Shauntae's direction.

Shauntae raised an eyebrow and looked at Daphne and waited.

Through poked out lips, Daphne finally said, "Miss Shauntae, may I have some food?"

"Of course, Daphne." Shauntae took the plate, put a medium-sized amount of food on it and passed it back to Daphne.

They all sat listening to Morgan chat on and on about her day at school, playing with her friends and what she wanted to cook with Miss Shauntae. The more she talked, the more she reminded Shauntae of Brianna. But instead of being irritated like she used to be when Brianna talked on and on, Morgan made Shauntae smile. It was like she had learned on the video. Kids' minds are simple and pure and it's cool to see the world the way they do.

After about ten minutes, Daphne scraped her plate. She looked up at Shauntae and her face wasn't looking so mad. "Uh, the food was really good, Miss Shauntae. May I please have some more?"

"Of course." Shauntae tried not to smile when she filled Daphne's plate again. "Save room for dessert, though."

Morgan's eyes lit up. "What is it?"

Shauntae smiled at her.

"I know. It's a surprise." Morgan sat there for a second and then asked, "I know Daddy said he would talk to me later, but is it a secret about the baby, if it's a girl or a boy?"

Shauntae looked at Gary and frowned. He didn't tell them about the baby? Did he not want her to talk about it?

Gary said, "I thought we would tell them together."

Shauntae smiled and looked back at Morgan. "It's a boy. You're gonna have a baby brother."

"A brother?" Morgan frowned. "How is the baby gonna be my brother if . . ."

"He's not gonna be your brother," Daphne said. "He's gonna be your half brother. Because he's from your dad, but he has a different mother, he's not your whole brother like I'm your whole sister. It's what happens when parents get divorced and they marry other people and have children. And then like if Miss Shauntae already had another kid with a different daddy not the same as our daddy, that would be our stepbrother or stepsister." The whole time she was talking, Daphne was giving Gary an evil stare, like he messed up her whole life or something.

"I don't understand." Morgan's voice was a little sad. "So he's not going to be my baby brother?"

"No—"

"Yes," Gary cut Daphne off before she could say anything else. "Yes, Moogie, the baby will be your little brother. What Daphne said is kinda true, but I would prefer if we not use words like 'half' or 'step.' We're one happy family."

"Happy family?" Daphne's voice got loud again. "We had a happy family and you and Mommy ruined it and now you've ruined it even worse by marrying another woman and having a baby. Now our family is gonna be all messed up and all confused like some of my friends at school."

"Daphne . . ." Gary's voice was firm and warning, but Shauntae knew him well enough to know that what Daphne said had hurt his heart. He felt guilty enough about how everything had happened and how it affected them.

Shauntae reached out to take his hand. She knew it was probably gonna make Daphne even madder, but she wanted to try to say something. "Daphne, I know this isn't the happy family you wanted. Sometimes things don't happen the perfect way we want them to in life. And you get to decide—do I want to be mad and angry and mean and blame everybody else for the way things are? Or do I decide to be happy no matter how my life looks?

"I spent a lot of years being angry and hurting people's feelings and making bad decisions because of bad things that happened in my life, but then one day, I decided to be happy no matter what and made some changes in my life. And if we believe God is a good Father that takes good care of us, then we believe that things are gonna turn out okay, no matter how bad they look."

Daphne crossed her arms and tears fell down her face.

Shauntae continued, "You can say that your family is all messed up and confused. Or you can say, 'I have a mommy and a daddy who really love me. I have a stepmommy who would love me if I gave her a chance. And I have a great little sister and soon I'm gonna have a little brother.' If you think about it, that's a whole lot of love, isn't it?"

Daphne turned to her father and said, "May I be excused?"

Gary let out a frustrated breath. "No, you may not. Miss Shauntae made dessert."

"I'm not hungry anymore."

"You know nobody leaves the table until everyone is finished eating."

"I thought that rule was just for family."

Gary stared at her hard. "Daphne, I know you're not happy with all of this. But you need to make some choices about your attitude. Your behavior is unacceptable, so you need to make some choices about changing it. I'd hate to see you spend all our father-daughter time in your room."

"Why can't we spend it at Mom's house like we have been?"

"Because that's Mom's house and this is my house. And the truth is, that's how things are now. We can either make the best of it or we can make the worst of it. Your choice."

"Maybe I need to stay at Mom's house, then."

Gary's face fell. Shauntae wanted to hug him, but she knew it would only make things worse. He finally said, "You know how much I love you and want to spend time with you. I won't force you to come see me, but . . ." Gary shrugged.

"Stop being mean, Dappy. You're making Daddy sad." Morgan looked like she wanted to stab her sister with her fork.

"Daddy made us sad, didn't he?" Daphne yelled at her little sister.

"You're not supposed to get people back. You're supposed to forgive. Miss Cassandra says—"

"Ugh, Moogie, don't you think people get tired of hearing about what Miss Cassandra says? Why don't you shut up!"

"Daphne, that's enough." Gary's voice boomed so loud that everybody at the table jumped. "You will sit there until we all finish eating and you can either choose to speak to people nicely or you cannot speak at all. But if you say another rude, loud, or disrespectful thing, I promise you will regret it. You know I don't like to, but I will use the rod if you continue this behavior."

At the mention of "the rod" both Daphne and Morgan froze. So they do get a beating if they acted up real bad. Well, probably a spanking instead of a beating.

Gary had scared both the girls into silence to the point where Shauntae felt sorry for them. She wanted to lighten things up. "Morgan, are you ready for dessert?"

Morgan nodded, but still was quiet.

Shauntae went to the refrigerator and took out the fresh fruit salad and whipped cream she had made and brought it to the table.

Morgan's eyes went big. "Look, Dappy, it has all your favorite fruits."

It was still early May, but Shauntae had been able to find all the fruits Gary had said were Daphne's favorites.

Daphne didn't say a word.

Shauntae spooned some fruit into a dessert cup and topped it with whipped cream and passed it to Morgan and then served Gary. Her appetite was gone so she didn't take any for herself.

"Oh, look at the shapes," Morgan squealed.

Shauntae had spent all afternoon cutting some of the fruit into circles, butterflies, and hearts with small cookie cutters she had found.

"Butterflies are my favorite. Thanks, Miss Shauntae."

"You're welcome, Morgan."

The fruit salad got Morgan talking again. This time she really reminded Shauntae of Brianna because she kept talking about Miss Cassandra, like Brianna used to.

"Maybe one day you can meet her, Miss Shauntae. She's real nice, like you. She's my favorite teacher in the whole world. And my best friend in the whole world is in her class, too. Miss Cassandra is her godmommy and when her daddy marries Miss Cassandra, then she gets to be her real mommy. I guess it's kinda like Daphne was saying. Brianna's family is all mixed up too. Her first mommy ran away and left her and went to California. So she really doesn't have two mommies. She just has Miss Cassandra. But Miss Cassandra is the best mommy in the whole world, so Brianna isn't too sad about it. Well, sometimes she gets real sad about it. She wishes she could talk to her first mommy and she hopes she's okay. Sometimes she's scared that something bad happened to her, but then she says she prays for her every night so she knows God must be taking care of her."

Shauntae couldn't move or breathe. She stared at Morgan's lips moving, but she couldn't hear what she was saying anymore. That chirpy little voice kept going, without realizing it had just ripped Shauntae's heart out.

Brianna talked about her? Brianna thought about her? Brianna got sad about her? Brianna prayed for her?

"Huh, Miss Shauntae?" Morgan was waiting for Shauntae to answer whatever question she had asked.

"I'm sorry, Morgan. What did you say?" Shauntae made herself ask, even though everything in her wanted to scream and cry.

"I said if Miss Cassandra is Brianna's godmommy and she's gonna be her real mommy soon, but me and Dappy still have our first mommy and she's our real mommy and we have a godmommy, then what are you?"

"She's not anything," Daphne shouted. "She's not anything to us, Moogie. Stop asking stupid questions!"

Shauntae stood up from the table and mumbled, "Excuse me." She stumbled over to the back stairs and started up toward her and Gary's bedroom. She heard Gary's voice behind her booming, "Daphne, go to your room." Then he called after her, "Shauntae, wait."

Shauntae fell onto the bed. She couldn't stop herself from shaking and then started crying.

Brianna got scared that something bad had happened to her? Devon didn't tell Brianna that her mother was okay? Did he even mention that he heard from her? Thoughts about her daughter were messing up Shauntae's heart.

And then something else started bothering her and Shauntae didn't know which was worse.

With Morgan and Brianna being friends, how long was it before Brianna said her mother's name or showed her a picture? How long would it be before Morgan figured out that Brianna's first mother was her stepmother?

Thirty-six

That night, Shauntae couldn't stop crying, no matter what Gary said. He kept apologizing, but she couldn't stop. She felt bad because Gary thought she was hurt behind what Daphne had said. He didn't realize it was really Morgan's words that had messed her up.

The next morning, Gary asked her if she felt okay enough to spend the day with Morgan. He wanted to take Daphne to Darla's house so they could talk to her and figure out what to do with her. Shauntae knew she should've been glad that Gary felt okay leaving Morgan with her alone. It meant he really thought she could be a good mama.

But she couldn't stop feeling sad about Brianna. When she had left Brianna, she had told her that she was going away for a long time and that she would maybe come see her when she grew up. She had thought Brianna would forget all about her. Or that she would hate her so much for how bad she treated her that she wouldn't care about her no more.

But Brianna didn't forget. And she did care about her.

Not long after Shauntae heard Gary and Daphne leave, she lay in bed trying to make herself get up and go check on Morgan. A few minutes later, she heard footsteps coming into the room. A few seconds later, Morgan crawled up into the bed and snuggled herself into Shauntae's body.

"Miss Shauntae, are you 'sleep?"

Shauntae didn't say anything. She knew if she said something, she might start crying again. She kept her eyes closed. A few seconds later, she felt Morgan's hands on her belly.

"Hi, baby brother. I'm your big sister, Morgan. I don't know how you're gonna get out of there, but I'll be waiting for you when you're ready to come out."

Shauntae wanted to laugh. But then she wanted to cry. A part of her wished it was Brianna curled up in the bed with her, talking to her little brother. She had never cuddled or snuggled with Brianna before. If she ever got the chance, she would do it.

Shauntae opened her eyes. "Good morning, Moogie. You sleep okay?"

Morgan nodded.

Shauntae brushed Morgan's hair back. "You ready to go shopping?"

Morgan nodded.

"Okay, go wash your face and brush your teeth and put some clothes on."

After Morgan went running to her room, Shauntae dragged herself out of the bed. She looked at her puffy eyes in the mirror and wanted to start crying again. All she could do was say, "God, help me fix this, okay?" She thought about it for a second and said, "Or could you just fix it for me?"

She wasn't sure if it was right to ask God to fix her mess, but really, she didn't know how to. This was something only He could fix.

By the time Gary came back to get Morgan to take her home, Shauntae was tired. They had made four dishes and more oatmeal cookies to send home with Morgan. Morgan talked the whole day. And sometimes she played and turned in circles when she was supposed to be helping. And even though she didn't sing her words and dance all her movements like Brianna did, the more time Shauntae spent with her, the more Morgan reminded her of Brianna. Which made her want to see Brianna.

By the time Gary got home from dropping her off, Shauntae was in the bed asleep. Probably from being tired after cooking all day with a six-year-old girl and probably from being sad that it wasn't her own little girl.

She woke up at about four in the morning since she went to bed so early. She lay there listening to Gary breathe, feeling the warmth of his body, and wishing it could make the sadness in her heart go away. She thought of waking him up to make love, but she knew all the drama from the weekend had worn him out too.

She decided to talk to God. She talked to Him about Brianna, about the new baby, about Morgan, about Daphne learning to like her, about all the stuff she was doing to be a better person. Mostly she talked about Brianna. At the end she said, "God, I know I was a terrible mother. I know I don't deserve it. But could you give me another chance? Could you fix it so somehow, so I could at least see my little girl again?"

After praying that prayer, Shauntae fell back asleep. She felt better inside and slept until it was time for her and Gary to go to church in the morning.

On the way to church, Gary's cell phone rang. He talked for a few minutes and then passed the phone to Shauntae. "It's Darla."

Shauntae froze. Darla wanted to talk to her? "Hello?"

"Shauntae, good morning. How are you?"

"Fine. Um, how are you? I hear that you're recovering well from the accident."

"I am, thank you. I won't keep you long. I know Gary relayed my message, but I wanted to speak to you personally to apologize for how I treated you when I first met you. It was rude and completely uncalled for."

"Oh . . . it's okay." Shauntae felt uncomfortable and wished Darla had left it at Gary giving her the message.

"I also wanted to thank you for sending the food. It was such an unexpected . . . blessing and I really appreciate your thoughtfulness."

"Oh, you're welcome."

"And thanks for spending time with Morgan yesterday. She can't stop talking about you and how much fun she had. I really appreciate you taking care of her while me and Gary spent some time with Daphne. I'm sorry for the way she spoke to you yesterday. I don't know whether Gary told you, but we're planning on having her start seeing a child therapist again. Both she and Morgan went when we first separated and we think Daphne can benefit from going back. I hope you'll be patient with her as we trust things to get better."

"Of course. I can understand why she's having such a hard time with everything. The way things have happened isn't the best for a child of her age and her behavior is actually expected." Shauntae remembered some stuff she had seen on a YouTube video.

"Yes, I guess it is." Darla sounded like she was impressed. "Anyway, thanks for understanding. I really appreciate it. I'm hoping that we can have an amicable relationship. I think it's best for the girls, and for everyone involved."

"Yes, of course." Shauntae wasn't sure what an amicable relationship was, but she figured it meant they should all get along. "Thanks so much for calling, Darla. I'll be praying that you continue to get better."

"Thanks and God bless."

Shauntae hung up the phone and passed it back to Gary. "Wow, I wasn't expecting that. She really has changed."

"Yeah, it's pretty amazing, huh?" Gary turned to look at her. "Baby, are you okay? You seem a little, I don't know, tired or sad or something. I hope Morgan wasn't too much for you yesterday."

"No, she was fine. We had a good day." Shauntae changed the subject before she started crying. "Glad to hear that Daphne will be going to a therapist. I really hope it helps."

"Me too, honey." Gary let out a deep breath. "I'm sure it will. God is going to take care of everything. She'll be fine."

Shauntae hoped so. She took Darla's phone call as a sign that God had heard her prayers and that He was gonna fix everything for her.

Church had Shauntae all emotional. She cried through the whole service. The music touched her, the dancers danced, and the pastor preached another one of his sermons on how much God loved her. This time she really believed it. When they did the altar call, Shauntae got up out of her seat and went to the front and got herself saved. She had kinda felt like she was already saved since she was talking to God and He was in His God kinda way talking to her, but she wanted to make it official and real.

When she got back to her seat, Gary held her and she cried for a long time. Luckily, when they was giving the altar call, they had called out a whole bunch of different stuff like people who wanted to go to a new level in God's love, or people who wanted to give their lives back to God, or people who wanted a new anointing. Maybe Gary thought she had gone up to get more of God's love in her heart. It didn't matter. If he asked her, she was ready to tell him. Everything. She felt brand new in God's love, like her past was wiped away. It was like the pastor said—she was a new creature in Christ.

After Shauntae stopped crying and got herself together, she looked down at her watch. It was time for second service. They needed to get out of there.

On their way out of the sanctuary, a tall, thin brown brother walked up to Gary. They slapped hands and exchanged man hugs. Gary introduced her, but Shauntae barely paid attention because she was worried about leaving before Devon, Cassandra, and Brianna got there. Gary kept talking and finally Shauntae tugged his arm. She raised an eyebrow and rubbed her belly.

"Man, let me get my wife out of here. We gotta feed the baby. Let me call you when I get in the car and we'll finish this up."

"A'ight, man. That's cool," the guy said. He reached out to shake Shauntae's hand and said, "Nice to meet you."

Shauntae shook it real quick, then pulled Gary toward the door. She hoped she wasn't too rude, but then again pregnant women could get away with almost anything.

As they were driving out of the parking lot, Shauntae spotted Devon's car. It was headed straight for them. As their cars passed each other, Shauntae covered her face, but looked through her hands and saw Brianna in the back seat. Her mouth was moving a mile a minute and in her head, Shauntae could hear her daughter's singsong voice. Brianna was so busy talking that Shauntae was sure she didn't see her. But Cassandra did. They looked each other straight in the eyes for a second as their cars passed.

At first she got scared. But then Shauntae remembered the peace she felt at the altar after that woman had helped her accept Jesus into her heart. The woman had put her hands on her and prayed about a whole lot of stuff. She prayed for her marriage and for the baby. She prayed that everything in Shauntae's life would work out for good and that God would let some things happen that convinced her of His love for her. She prayed that Shauntae would know the love of the Father like never before.

So instead of being scared, Shauntae took it as a sign. God was showing her that He would fix things so Devon and Cassandra would let her see Brianna and she would get to be in her little girl's life again. He would fix it so that she could tell Gary the whole truth about Brianna and then all of them—Darla, Daphne, Morgan, Gary, Shauntae, Devon, Cassandra, and Brianna—could all get along somehow as some kinda weird, mixed-up family.

A few minutes later, her cell phone went off. She looked down at the text.

That was too close! What happened?

Shauntae wrote back:

I got saved today. Ended up staying too long. Sorry. Shauntae thought about it for a minute and then added, I would like to meet with you and Cassandra to talk about something very important. Thank you for believing in me so far. Please can we meet sometime soon?

Gary was still talking to his friend on the phone and didn't notice that Shauntae had closed her eyes and was praying. After a few moments, her cell phone vibrated again.

Congratulations on getting saved. Glad to see that God is doing good things in your life. Me and Cassandra will look at our schedules for the week and I'll text you later to let you know when we can meet.

Shauntae closed her eyes and whispered, “Thank you, God.” She knew it was only a matter of time before she could see her little girl.

Thirty-seven

Later that evening, after they had stuffed themselves on leftovers and taken a long nap, Gary and Shauntae were snuggled up on the couch. Gary was watching CNN and Shauntae was thinking. After talking to Darla and then hearing the pastor talk about God's love and forgiveness and thinking about stuff Gary had been saying to her, something was bothering her. She couldn't get the thoughts out of her head, so she finally asked Gary, "Honey, can I ask you something?"

Gary nodded without taking his eyes off the news.

"It's kinda important. Well, it's real important."

Gary looked down at her and then looked back up at the television. "Sure, baby." He lifted the remote and clicked the television off.

"You know how the pastor always talks about God's love and how much God forgives us and how nothing we do can ever make Him stop loving us?"

Gary nodded.

"Well, when you hug me and love on me and tell me that nothing I can ever do can make you stop loving me, it makes me feel the same way. Like you love me like God loves me."

Gary kissed her nose. "That's sweet, baby. I can only hope that I could love you as much as God loves you. I mean, a man is supposed to love his wife like Christ loved the church."

"Right. But . . ." Shauntae stopped to think of how to ask what she wanted to ask. "When I talked to Darla this morning, she sounded like she was a real nice person. And you said when she woke up from the coma that that's how she used to be when you guys first got together, back when you loved her."

Gary nodded, frowning like he was trying to figure out where she was going.

"So what happened to you and Darla? If you loved her like that and nothing she could do could make you stop loving her, what happened? Why did you stop loving her?"

Gary blew out a long breath of air. He took his arm from around Shauntae and leaned forward on the couch. He sat there for a few minutes rubbing his hands together. "I guess this is something we should have talked about before."

Shauntae sat and waited.

"I didn't always think that way and I wasn't always the man I am now. In fact, the way I am now is because of things that happened between me and Darla. I've always loved family and it's always been important, but it's more important to me now because of what happened. Sometimes you don't realize how important something is until you lose it."

Gary sat back against the couch. "When me and Darla got married, we had big dreams for what we wanted our lives to be. She was going to become partner at a top-tier law firm, and I was going to run my own million-dollar company. We were going to have four kids, a big house, and an amazing life.

"When Daphne was born, I was the happiest man on the planet. I couldn't wait to have another child, but Darla kept putting it off. She said she never imagined how much work a child was and how much it took away from the career she was trying to build. She changed up the plan and said she only wanted to have one child."

Gary shook his head slowly. "I waited for her to change her mind, but she kept putting in more hours at the law firm, leaving me and Daphne at home in the evenings. My business grew and it seemed like the more successful I was, the harder she worked. I don't know how, but somehow between her long work hours and her birth control, she got pregnant with Morgan. I was happy, but she was angry, sad, and out-of-control emotional. She even talked about aborting our child. Can you believe it? She wanted to get rid of our baby so she could stay on course with making partner." Gary seemed like he was getting mad all over again, just talking about it. Shauntae wondered if that's why he was so upset when he found out about her abortions.

"I reminded her that we were Christians and that we couldn't do that. I don't really think she would have done it, but the fact that she thought about it was unbelievable to me. Anyway, we had Morgan and I fell in love with my second daughter. I still wanted more children, but Darla wasn't hearing it. After she gave birth to Morgan, she had her tubes tied without telling me."

Gary sat there for a second and then he reached over and rubbed Shauntae's belly. "For her to do that meant she didn't care about me and what was important to me. I could understand if she had told me from the beginning that she didn't want children, but we had agreed that we both wanted four children. For her to tie her tubes without telling me was unforgivable."

Unforgivable. Shauntae didn't think that was a word in Gary's dictionary. What would he do if he found out about Brianna? Was that unforgivable too?

"Our marriage went from bad to worse. Me and the nanny basically took care of the girls while Darla worked.

She went back to work almost immediately after Morgan was born. Between running my business and then coming home to spend time with the girls, I barely slept. Can you believe that it was me who got up in the middle of the night to feed Morgan? Darla slept through her crying. What kind of mother does that?"

Shauntae remembered Devon waking her up some nights to feed Brianna and wondered what Gary would think about her if he knew.

"And so me and the girls got closer and closer and Darla got further and further from all of us. I couldn't forgive her and I started to hate her."

Shauntae wondered if the same thing would happen once Gary found out about her.

"And then one week, Darla was out of town doing research for a case. The girls were tucked in and the nanny was live-in at the time because my work schedule was hectic and I needed the extra help. One night, I needed to get out of the house and . . . breathe. Even though I loved my girls and my favorite thing was spending time with them, the house was so full of tension and hatred that sometimes I couldn't stand it here. So I went out for a drink. Not a smart thing to do when you're angry and tired and your wife hasn't had sex with you in months."

Gary rubbed his hands together. "Next thing I knew, I ended up in the bed of a woman I met that night. This time it was me who did something unforgivable." Gary looked at her like he was trying to figure out what she was thinking—like he was afraid she thought bad about him.

He didn't have to worry about that. That night, Gary had gotten messed up with somebody just like her. Who was she to judge?

"I couldn't believe I did something like that. I met with the men's pastor, Mark, the guy I introduced you to today. We talked a lot and I realized it was my unforgiveness that made me commit adultery. Maybe if I had forgiven Darla, things wouldn't have been so bad between us. But me not forgiving her caused me to end up committing a sin as bad as hers. My wife lied to me and betrayed me and I cheated on her.

"I confessed to Darla what had happened and she left me and the girls. She came back a few weeks later, but her heart was stone cold. I persuaded her to go to counseling with me and we both admitted our faults, but she couldn't forgive me. So for both of us, unforgiveness killed the marriage. That's why I swore never to let unforgiveness live in my heart again. Never. If Jesus could forgive us for anything and everything we ever did, how can we consider anything someone does to us unforgivable?"

Gary took Shauntae's hand and squeezed. "I guess I should have told you that sooner. I cheated on my wife. It's not something I'm proud of and it's not anything I ever plan to do again. I hope you understand I'm not that kind of person. It was the state of my heart at the time. Unforgiveness leads to bitterness, which leads to sin. I never want to find myself in that place again."

"Thanks for sharing that with me, baby. I do understand." Shauntae felt like it was time. Maybe God had let Gary tell her all that so she would know that it was okay for her to tell him the truth about everything. She lay back in his arms for a second, wondering where to start. What would he think when he found out that she was ten times worse as a mother than Darla ever was? Would he still say that nothing was unforgivable?

Shauntae let out a deep breath. All she could do was try.

She was about to open her mouth when her cell phone vibrated. There was a text from Devon.

Sorry to take so long to get back to you. Me and Cassandra's schedules are crazy and we won't be able to meet for the next couple of weeks. Unless you're able to meet this evening. We have some time while Brianna is at her grandparents. Let me know as soon as you can.

Shauntae jumped up off the couch. "Baby, I hate to leave suddenly, but there's something real important I need to take care of."

"Now?" Gary stood up to follow her. "Where are you going? Is something wrong?"

"No, I'm hoping that something is very right. Please, let me do this. I promise I'll explain everything when I get back."

And Shauntae meant everything.

Thirty-eight

Thirty minutes later, Shauntae was sitting in Starbucks, waiting for Devon and Cassandra to show up. She chose a private table near the back so they could have a conversation without people hearing them. She didn't know whether it was the strong smell of brewing coffee or her nerves that was bothering her stomach.

After she waited ten minutes, shaking her leg and biting her fingers, she saw them come in the front door. Devon was looking good in a pair of jeans and a T-shirt and Cassandra was looking sharp and sassy in a short, cute pink dress. They looked like the perfect couple. Shauntae knew people thought the same thing when they saw her and Gary together.

When they saw her, Shauntae stood up. She didn't know what to do with herself. She made herself smile. When they got to the table, she put out her hand. "Hi, thanks for coming. I appreciate you guys agreeing to meet me." She shook Devon's hand and then shook Cassandra's hand and said, "Nice to see you again, Cassandra."

As Shauntae sat down, she noticed a look between them kinda like they thought she was suspect and kinda like they couldn't wait to hear what she had to say.

Shauntae had tried to practice her speech for them on her way there, but stuff kept coming out wrong. Finally, she told God He had gotten things this far so He had to help her say the right thing.

They all sat in a weird, crazy kinda silence for a moment until Devon said, "Wow, you're really pregnant. When are you due?"

Shauntae rubbed her belly. "July third but I'm getting so huge and July is so hot, I hope it's sooner." That didn't sound right so she said, "I mean, I don't want to have the baby premature or nothing and I want him to be healthy and everything, but you know . . ." She gave a little laugh, but noticed that Cassandra was giving her the side eye.

She decided to go ahead and start talking. "I have a lot to say to you guys, and I hope you'll listen and give me a chance before you make any decisions."

Devon raised an eyebrow and Cassandra tightened her lips.

"I know it sounds crazy, but since the last time you guys saw me, a lot has changed in my life. I got pregnant, I got married, and I'm a different person now. Today at church, I got saved and it was for real. Like me and God are for real."

Shauntae tried to see in their faces what they thought but their faces didn't change. "I know I did some real bad stuff in the past. Devon, I gave you hell from the first time you met me. Cassandra, I treated you rude and evil every time we were in the same room. I was a horrible mother and did stuff to Brianna that was . . . unforgivable." There was that ugly word. "Completely unforgivable. And yet, here I am, asking both of you to forgive me.

"That's what made me finally decide I wanted to get saved. I came to understand that nothing is unforgivable—that no matter what I've done, no matter how bad a person I was, God still loves me and forgives me. Isn't that crazy? That He could love us that much?"

Shauntae paused until the loud espresso machine got quiet.

"And so I've been really working hard at becoming a better person. I study a lot on how to be a good parent and I'm even taking a parenting class at the church."

Shauntae took a deep breath. "I want to be a part of Brianna's life again."

She held up a hand when they both put their lips like they was about to say something. "I'm not talking about custody or about going to court and I'm definitely not talking about a check. I just want to be able to . . . see her. I want to hug her and tell her I'm sorry and that I love her. I want her to know I'm okay."

Shauntae was talking faster and faster and she knew she was sounding desperate. "I know you guys think it's best if she forgets about me, but she hasn't forgotten about me. She still cares about me."

Shauntae turned to Cassandra. "There's a little girl in your children's church class, Morgan, Brianna's best friend?"

Cassandra frowned and nodded.

"Morgan is my husband's daughter. She says Brianna talks about me all the time and prays for me. She prays for me." A tear slid down Shauntae's cheek. "She told Morgan that sometimes she worries about whether I'm okay. Can't I . . . can't I just see her? Can't she just see me so she'll know her mama is okay and is sorry and loves her?"

Shauntae wiped the tears running down her face. Cassandra dug around in the huge purse she was carrying and handed her a tissue. She and Devon sat there looking at each other and it was like they were talking to each other with their eyes.

Shauntae made one last plea. "Can't you guys forgive me and believe that I've changed?"

Cassandra put a hand on Shauntae's arm. "It's not that we don't forgive you or we don't believe that you've changed. It's just . . ." Cassandra looked at Devon.

He said, "It's just that we want what's best for Brianna. This has only ever been about her. We don't want her hurt."

"I don't want her hurt, either. All I want is a chance to love her and make things right."

Cassandra and Devon looked at each other and talked with their eyes again. Shauntae wished they would say whatever they were thinking out loud.

Devon shook his head. "I knew this was coming when you texted me about the parenting classes." He didn't say anything else and sat there pulling on his goatee and staring at the floor.

Shauntae asked, "Don't you think Brianna should get to meet her baby brother? Don't you think they should know each other? They're brother and sister."

Cassandra and Devon looked at each other again. Devon finally spoke, "What are we talking about here? You said no custody, but what exactly is it that you want?"

Shauntae shrugged. "I haven't got that far yet. I was just hoping to see her." She thought for a second. "I would like to see her on a regular. I don't want to have to rush out of church anymore. I'd love to be able to say hi to her on Sunday mornings. And maybe sometimes she can come over to the house and spend the night with Morgan." Shauntae thought a little longer. "And then maybe sometimes me and her can go somewhere and spend some time together. I'm not saying a whole lot. But enough for her to know that I'm her mother and I'm here and I love her."

Devon took a deep breath and held it. Cassandra put a hand on his knee and they looked at each other. Then she nodded. He raised an eyebrow and she nodded again.

Devon finally looked at Shauntae. "Okay."

Shauntae's eyes bugged open. "Okay?"

He nodded. "Yes, okay. You can see Brianna. But I swear, if—"

Cassandra squeezed Devon's knee and he stopped talking. She said, "Give us time to get used to the idea and then we'll figure out some sort of schedule?"

"Yes, please, yes, thank you, yes." Shauntae could hardly talk. She was going to get to see her daughter. God was answering her prayer.

They sat for a few minutes and came up with a time for Shauntae to see Brianna for the first time and then left. Shauntae practically ran to the car.

Cassandra and Devon had agreed that she could see Brianna on Saturday. Shauntae couldn't believe it. She put the minivan in drive and headed home.

Now all she had to do was tell Gary.

Thirty-nine

Shauntae didn't know what she was expecting when she told Gary the truth about everything. Maybe she was expecting him to say, "I forgive you, honey," and then take her in his arms and carry her upstairs and make love to her. Or maybe she expected him to get really angry and yell and scream and shout, but then say, "I forgive you, honey," and then maybe make love to her right there in the living room. Or maybe she had expected him to be so hurt that he started crying and asking her why and how could she do that to him, but then after he thought about it, he would say, "I forgive you, honey," and then they would make love in the kitchen.

She wasn't sure what she thought he would do, but she had expected, "I forgive you, honey," to be a part of it.

Instead, when she finished talking, his face got tight, his eyes got angry, he stood up without saying a word, and left. Slammed the garage door and left without saying anything.

That was two days ago. Shauntae hadn't heard a word from Gary since. She had called his phone hundreds of times. She had sent more text messages than she could count. She wanted to call Darla to see if she knew where he was, but she didn't want her to know they were having problems.

Shauntae paced, prayed, cooked, and still nothing from Gary. The third day, she woke up calling him and went to sleep texting him. The fourth day, she stayed in the bed praying almost all day.

At first, she got mad at God because she had done the right thing and it had ended up so wrong. But she couldn't blame Him. This was all her fault. She could only hope God would help Gary forgive her and bring him back to her.

She kept thinking, would things have been different if she had told him sooner? Should she have told him about Brianna without telling him about her past? Should she have waited longer before she told him, maybe after giving birth to his son? She kept going over it in her mind but no matter what it came down to, she needed to tell him the whole truth.

And then she thought all kinds of bad thoughts. Where was he staying? Was he so upset that he was in a bar drinking? If he did get drunk in a bar, would he end up in some strange woman's bed? He had said that he would never let unforgiveness make him end up in another woman's bed, but what if that was all talk? What if he got some woman pregnant? Would he kick Shauntae out and bring his next baby mama home?

What if he was over at Darla's house spending time with her? And since she was back to acting like she did when they first met, what if he was falling in love with her all over again? Was she about to lose her husband to his first wife? Darla wanted him back. What if the only thing blocking them from getting back together was her and the baby, and now that he didn't want her anymore, he could go back and marry the mother of his daughters? The two of them had enough money to hire some serious lawyers. What if they decided to sue her for full custody of her child and dragged in her whole history with Brianna and all her lies?

All day, her mind was full of all the awful things that could happen. She called Candy, but she couldn't help much. The situation was jacked up, so what advice could she give?

Shauntae didn't think about calling Sherice. Sherice blamed Shauntae for her losing her apartment since she never gave her any money. The few times Shauntae had tried to call her, she had cussed and screamed and called her all kinds of names so finally Shauntae stopped calling.

On Friday afternoon, Shauntae had a doctor's appointment. She texted Gary to remind him about it. He didn't answer. The whole time she was in Dr. Murray's office, she kept waiting for him to walk in the door. Maybe he was mad at her, but at least he would want to check on their child. At the end of the visit, Dr. Murray asked about Gary and Shauntae burst into tears.

Dr. Murray gave her tissue and told her that she had one more patient waiting before her lunch break but if she would wait for her, she'd be back so they could talk. The two of them had gotten to know each other a little from Shauntae being in the class at the church.

When Dr. Murray came back about twenty minutes later, Shauntae poured out her heart and told her everything. Dr. Murray sat there for a while not saying anything, which made Shauntae worry.

She finally said, "You know you did the right thing, albeit a little late. But better late than never, right?"

Shauntae nodded and wiped her nose. She had cried more in the last four months than she had in her entire life. "What should I do?"

"There's nothing you can do, my dear. All you can do is what you have been doing. Wait, hope, and pray. I'm proud of you for all the changes you've made and that you decided to tell him the truth. Now you can only wait and see how he decides to respond. And take care of yourself and the baby. And get yourself ready to go see your little girl tomorrow. That's gonna be a really big day. Can I pray for you?"

Shauntae nodded.

Dr. Murray took both Shauntae's hands in hers. "Father, we thank you for everything you've done in Shauntae's life. Thanks for your love transforming her very nature and character. Thank you that no matter what, she is your daughter who you love very much. Help her to rest in your love for her. God, we ask that you give Gary grace to forgive and that you let there be healing between the two of them. Bless Shauntae's meeting with Brianna and help them to rebuild their relationship. And we entrust this new baby to you, God. Keep him safe and healthy and let him be a great blessing. We pray in Jesus' name, amen."

Dr. Murray took a business card from her drawer and wrote on the back of it. "This is my cell number. Call me if you need anything, any time."

"Thanks so much for everything." Shauntae tucked the card into her wallet.

When Shauntae got home, Gary's car was sitting in the driveway. Shauntae's heart started racing. Had God answered Dr. Murray's prayers already?

Her hands were shaking as she walked from the garage into the kitchen. She didn't see Gary anywhere. She walked up the back steps to their bedroom. She found him there sitting on the bed. He must have heard her come in, but he didn't look up and didn't say anything.

Shauntae wasn't sure what to do. From his face, it didn't look like he came back to make up. She stood there in the doorway waiting for him to say something.

When he finally said, "How's the baby?" Shauntae barely recognized his voice. He sounded hard and cold, like he sounded when he talked to Darla that first day she came over.

Shauntae's heart dropped to her knees. He hated her. She had committed the unforgivable sin. "Dr. Murray says the baby looks fine. He's growing and his heartbeat sounds good. I put on a little more weight than she expected. Probably from all the cooking." Shauntae hoped that would make him at least smile. Last week, he had stood in the mirror looking at the small bike-sized tire growing around his middle and had complained that Shauntae was fattening him up. Shauntae had offered to stop cooking, but he had refused. He said she'd have to love him with a little extra around the waist.

"Good. When is your next appointment?"

"Two weeks. On Friday at eleven-thirty. Do you want to come?"

Gary didn't say anything. It was then that Shauntae saw his two bags sitting in the doorway of the bathroom. Her breath caught in her chest. "You're leaving again?"

"What did you think I would do?"

"I thought you would forgive me, like you said. I thought nothing I could do was unforgivable. I thought you would love me like God loves me and do what you said."

"Do you realize that our entire relationship is built on a lie? No, on a bunch of lies. In fact, the whole relationship itself is a lie. What did you expect? For me to say, 'I forgive you, honey,' and then pretend the whole thing never happened?"

It almost made Shauntae laugh when he said that. But it wasn't funny. It was stupid for her to believe that he could forgive her.

"We've been living a lie. You played me for a fool. I'm supposed to get over that?"

Shauntae shrugged and shook her head.

"Not only did you play me for a fool and use me, you put my daughters at risk. What if Darla had never had the accident and had done the background check? She could have gotten the girls and made it to where I could never see them again. You put me at risk of losing my daughters. Did you even think about that?"

"I did think about it. I thought about it a lot."

"And?"

"And none of that happened. God was taking care of—"

"Don't even bring God into this. Do you even know God?"

Gary's words cut Shauntae to her heart. "Of course I know God. I'm saved, Gary. I told you that all of this is Him. It's been Him. Changing me and transforming me. I'm not the person I was when I met you. Everything about me is different. Because you loved me. And you showed me that God loved me."

Gary sat there for a second not saying anything. Shauntae prayed silently that her words would get through to him.

"How can you have a daughter you haven't seen or so much as mentioned the whole time we've been together? What kind of mother does that?"

"I'm not that kind of mother anymore. I realize how horrible I was and I've done everything I can to change. I'm going to see her tomorrow. And me and her father are going to make arrangements for me to be in her life."

"If I were him, I wouldn't let you anywhere near her." The look in Gary's eyes and the anger in his voice made Shauntae want to cry.

"They're letting me see her because they see how much I've changed. They know the person I was before and they see the person I am now and they think it's okay. They forgave me, like you said you would."

"Don't try to throw my words up in my face. When I said that, I was talking to somebody else." Gary was yelling now. He stood up. "I was talking to my wife, the good little Christian girl who loves family and loves Jesus. Not some gold-digging, baby-aborting, child-abusing, lying, scheming whore!"

It felt like Gary had knocked all the air out of her chest. He picked up his bags and walked down the back stairs to the family room. Shauntae knew he was headed toward the garage door.

Something rose up in her and she ran after him. She caught up to him in the kitchen and yelled, "You don't get to call me that. Jesus forgave me and it's gone forever. Even if you don't forgive me, He has. So you don't get to call me what I used to be. I'm not that woman anymore!"

He stared at her with an evil look in his eye, but he didn't say anything.

Shauntae said more softly this time. "I'm not all those things you said. I'm a good person. And I'm going to be a good mother—a very good mother. And I'm saved now. I'm God's daughter. So you don't get to call me any of that."

Shauntae knew by the look in his eyes that things were over with Gary. She said, "Sorry for everything. Sorry for lying and misleading you. Sorry that I couldn't be the woman you wanted me to be. Sorry for hurting you. You don't have to leave. This is your house. I'll pack my stuff and go."

Gary answered, "You can stay here until you have the baby. I have somewhere to go. I'm pretty sure you don't. I want to know that my child is in a safe place until he's born."

"And after that?"

"After that, we'll go to court."

Shauntae burst into tears. "You can't take my baby away from me. I won't let you. Dr. Murray will testify for me. My parenting class mentors will testify for me. All the women in all my classes at church will testify for me. They'll say that I'm a good person and a good mother. You can't take my baby away from me."

"And you'd better not leave, either. There's nowhere that you can take my child and hide from me, Shauntae. I will find you."

"Do you know how many times I could have left? I didn't leave. I won't leave. I don't care if you believe me. I'm not that person anymore. I'm a good person. I'm a good mother." Shauntae sank to the floor, crying.

Gary threw a debit card onto her lap. "You no longer have access to our joint account or any of the credit cards. This account will have enough money for you to take care of yourself and the baby unless you spend foolishly. You need to eat and take care of yourself so the baby will be okay. If you have another ultrasound, I'd like to be there; otherwise, text me after your doctor visits to let me know everything's okay with the baby. Call me when you go into labor. I'd like to be there for the birth of my child."

Shauntae couldn't stop crying. A few seconds later she heard the door slam and Gary was gone for good.

Forty

Shauntae was up crying most of the night. She finally fell asleep at about two in the morning. She called Dr. Murray at around one and explained to her what had happened. Dr. Murray talked to her until she felt a little bit better, prayed with her, and told her to take some Benadryl so she could sleep. She told her to focus on Brianna and nothing else.

Shauntae tried to follow her advice, but there were too many thoughts in her head. Like how she was going to afford a lawyer to be able to keep her baby? How was she going to live after Gary threw her out of the house? Would Devon let her still be in Brianna's life when he found out that she was broke and desperate again? She kept telling herself that God was going to work everything out for her good. If He loved her and forgave her, surely He was gonna take care of her, right?

She finally drifted off to sleep. It seemed like only a few minutes later when she woke up, but it was actually nine in the morning. She made herself eat some breakfast since she hadn't eaten anything since lunch the day before.

And then she waited for time to pass. She was supposed to see Brianna when she finished Cassandra's art class that afternoon. Maybe she could do something nice for Brianna. She wasn't sure what. She needed to be real tight with money. She didn't know how much Gary had put in the account he had opened for her and she didn't want to buy an expensive present.

She wanted to cook something, but then remembered Brianna's diabetes. She went to get online to look for a diabetic recipe but Gary had taken his computer. She called Candy to ask her to look up something for her. While Candy was looking, Shauntae told her everything Gary had said.

Candy was real quiet.

Shauntae asked, "You ain't got nothing to say?"

"I wish I knew what to say, but you probably want some good, Christian advice and you know I ain't got none of that to give."

Shauntae smiled a little. "What would be your non-Christian advice?"

Candy laughed. "Girl, I don't even know. The whole situation was messed up from the beginning. We all thought you would ride it as long as you could. We didn't think you was gon' fall in love and get married and want to live happily ever after."

A tear slid down Shauntae's cheek. "Yeah, I don't know what I was thinking. I guess I'm crazy and stupid."

"Don't say that, Shauntae. Ain't nothing crazy and stupid about love. Next time, you just need to do it right."

"Next time? I ain't never doing nothing like this again. It hurts too much."

"It ain't got to hurt next time. You'll do it right if you ever do it again."

Shauntae didn't want to think about ever doing it again. "Whatever. You find me a recipe?"

"Yeah, you got a pen?"

Candy gave her a recipe for diabetic peanut butter cookies. Shauntae remembered how much Brianna liked peanut butter.

When they were about to hang up, Candy said, "I know this is bad timing with everything you got going on, but I need a big favor."

"What you need? Anything." Shauntae remembered their motto that no matter what happened with a man, they always had each other's backs. Even though it looked like they had lost Sherice, Shauntae knew she and Candy would stick together.

"Well, Bobby got me a catering gig for next weekend. One of his clients is getting married and asked if he knew anybody that could do a good wedding cake. Bobby got to running his mouth and got me a job doing the cake and the whole wedding dinner. I know it's a whole lot to ask with you all pregnant and heartbroken and stuff, but can you use your van to help me get groceries and then to take the stuff to the wedding?"

"Only if you let me help you cook everything."

"Are you serious?"

"What else I'm gon' do? Lie around the house and cry and be depressed? I got you. Let me know when and I'll be there."

"A'ight. I'll call you next week. Thanks, girl."

"You my girl foreva." Shauntae hung up the phone. At least she had something to look forward to next weekend. For now, she was ready to bake some cookies and go see Brianna.

When Shauntae rang Devon's doorbell, there was a scary feeling in her stomach. Would Brianna even want to see her? What if she acted like Daphne and said she wasn't her mother no more and told her to go away and never come back?

Devon let her in and told her to have a seat. "She's in the back with Cassandra. I'll get her."

A few minutes later, Shauntae heard those dancing, running feet and then that singsong voice. "Mama, you're here. Daddy told me you were coming but I didn't believe him." Brianna ran right up to Shauntae and then stopped.

"Brianna, look at you. You're so big and pretty." Shauntae held out her arms. Brianna slowly walked into them. Shauntae knew Brianna's hesitation was her fault. She was hardly ever affectionate with Brianna before. "You grew up so big. What in the world have you been eating?"

Brianna said, "Spaghetti and pizza and pancakes and waffles and Grandma's cooking and Miss Cassandra's cooking." She pulled up her shirt and pointed to her belly. "Daddy says if I keep eating so much, my belly is gonna explode."

Shauntae laughed and poked Brianna's little fat belly.

Brianna's eyes fell on Shauntae's belly and got real big. "Oh boy, Mama. Looks like you been eating too much too."

Everybody laughed except Brianna, who looked confused.

"Mama hasn't been eating too much. Mama's gonna have a baby." She moved over on the couch and patted for Brianna to sit down next to her. "In about two months, I'm gonna have you a baby brother."

Brianna's eyes got big and round. "A baby brother?" She clapped her hands and asked, "What's his name?"

"I don't know, yet. You want to help me name him?"

"I get to name him?"

"You can help. I'm sure you can come up with some really good names."

Brianna scrunched her face up. "I can't think of anything right now."

Shauntae laughed. "You don't have to think of anything right now. In the next few days, if you think of any names, write them down and then we can look at them the next time you see me."

Brianna's eyes got big again. "The next time? I get to see you again?"

Shauntae nodded. Brianna turned to look at Cassandra and Devon and they nodded too. She turned back around and threw her arms around Shauntae. “Yaaaaay!”

Shauntae wrapped her arms around Brianna and held on tight. She kissed Brianna on the cheek. A tear slipped down her face.

Brianna reached up to wipe it away. “Mama, why are you crying?”

Shauntae wiped her face. “I’m happy to see you, Bree. I wasn’t sure I’d get to see you again.”

“Me too. You said you weren’t going to see me again until I was big, like grownup big, but I’m only seven and you’re here.”

“I know, Bree. Mama is so sorry about that.” Shauntae put an arm around Brianna’s shoulder and pulled her close. “Mama is so sorry about so many things. Bad things I did to you before. I’m so sorry that—”

“It’s okay. I forgive you. I’m glad you’re back.”

Fresh tears rolled down Shauntae’s cheeks. Those words were music to her ears. “Thank you, sweetie. Thank you so much.”

“Mama, you look different and you talk different. You look fancy and you talk fancy. Did you turn into a different person when you went to California?”

Shauntae laughed a little through her tears. “No, I turned into a different person when I came back to Atlanta.”

“What happened?”

Shauntae thought for a moment before she said anything. “A lot happened, Bree. I guess I should say, Jesus came into my heart and showed me how much He loved me and it changed me into a different person.”

Brianna’s mouth fell open. “You know Jesus?”

Shauntae laughed and nodded. “Yep. He lives right here.” Shauntae pointed to her heart.

Brianna pointed to hers. "He lives right here too. Wow, Mama. Maybe you can go to church with me sometimes. You can't come to children's church, though. You have to go to big people's church with Daddy."

All the adults laughed.

Shauntae felt the baby move. She reached for Brianna's hand. "Let me show you something." She put Brianna's hand on her stomach. A few seconds later, he kicked again and then rolled his butt up against Brianna's hand.

Brianna pulled her hand back and squealed. "Oh my goodness."

"That's your baby brother."

Brianna put both hands on her belly and leaned down to talk to it. "Hi, baby brother. I'm your big sister, Brianna. I don't know how you're gonna get out of there, but when you do, we can play."

Brianna's words made Shauntae cry again. She was happy that it was Brianna saying almost the same exact thing Morgan had said. She had wished at that moment that it was Brianna and now it was. But now she was thinking about Morgan and realized Morgan would probably never put her hands on her pregnant belly again. Gary would probably never even let her near her.

"Mama, why do you keep crying?"

"I'm happy to see you, Bree. You've made me very happy today."

"You made me happy too." Brianna put her arms around Shauntae again and held on tight.

Shauntae couldn't believe her evil tail had given birth to such a sweet child. She couldn't believe there was a time that she looked forward to her shutting up and going to sleep. She couldn't believe how much she used to look forward to Devon picking her up to get her off her hands. She couldn't believe that she had ever left her and planned to never see her again. She gave Brianna a squeeze.

"Brianna, I brought you something." Shauntae had almost forgotten. "I learned how to cook. I made you some peanut butter cookies."

Brianna frowned. "Did you forget about my diabetes? I can't eat cookies." She leaned in closer to Shauntae and said in a whisper loud enough for everyone in the room to hear, "Remember what happened last time? If you make me sick by giving me cookies, I might not get to see you anymore."

Shauntae laughed. "They're diabetic cookies, silly girl. I got a special recipe to make special cookies that were safe for my special girl. I promise I'll never make you sick again."

Shauntae held out the Tupperware container to Devon. "I put the recipe on top. And the carb counts are there, too. She can have two at a time and it's about the same carb count as fruit juice."

Cassandra took the container. Shauntae could tell by the looks on both their faces that they were impressed.

"Thanks, Mama." She grabbed Shauntae's hand and started pulling her off the couch. "You wanna see my room? I have a princess room. Come see it."

Shauntae stood so Brianna wouldn't pull her arm off. She looked at Devon. He nodded that it was okay and she followed Brianna toward the hallway. As she was passing by, Shauntae mouthed the words "thank you" to Devon and Cassandra. Devon nodded and Cassandra smiled.

Shauntae spent the next few hours playing dolls with Brianna and then Brianna showed her some of her dances and songs from Cassandra's art class. Shauntae spent the whole time laughing and enjoying her. She even let Brianna teach her one of the dances. She had a late afternoon snack with Brianna and finally Devon said it was time for her to take a nap. Brianna started crying.

Shauntae told her, "Your daddy said it's time for a nap. You're crying 'cause you're tired, so I'm pretty sure you need one. How about I tuck you in?"

"Will you stay with me while I fall asleep?"

"If your daddy says it's okay. But you can't talk to me or you won't fall asleep."

"Will you sing to me?"

Shauntae laughed. "Your mama singing won't put you to sleep. It'll make you go screaming and running to get away from my voice."

Brianna giggled. "Okay. Can you tell me a story?"

Shauntae didn't know any bedtime stories but she figured she could try. She watched Brianna's long lashes get heavier and heavier while she rambled on and on about a little girl with magic powers who could wave a magic wand and make bad people good. The magic wand had love dust in it that could change even the meanest, baddest person. When Brianna's breathing got slow and heavy, Shauntae gave her a soft kiss on the cheek and tiptoed out of the room.

Devon and Cassandra were sitting in the living room, but stood when she came out.

"Thanks again for letting me see her. That meant the world to me."

Devon and Cassandra were both looking at her kind of funny.

"What's wrong?" Shauntae asked.

"Nothing's wrong," Devon said. "It was good seeing you with Brianna today. I'm glad you came."

"Me too." Shauntae felt weird and uncomfortable so she shook both of their hands. "I hope I'll get to see her again soon? And regular?" She was moving toward the front door.

Devon nodded. "We'll work out a schedule."

Shauntae practically skipped out to her minivan. She had a happy feeling in her heart until she got home. When she pulled into the garage, a heavy, sad feeling sat down in her chest. She didn't feel like going into that big, empty house alone and sleeping in that big, lonely bed.

She pulled out her cell phone and called Candy. "Girl, what you doin'?"

"Trying to figure out how to go run some errands. Bobby drove down to Florida for a hair show. Can you come get me?"

"Can I bring some clothes and stay?"

"Yeah, girl. We can practice cooking some stuff for next weekend."

"I'll be there real soon."

Forty-one

For the next few weeks, Shauntae kept herself busy. Candy's first catering job turned out real good. They passed out business cards and Candy got a bunch of calls to cater other stuff. Everybody said her food was gourmet, but her prices were lower than most people who served food so good. Candy laughed and told them all to enjoy her introductory prices. She intended to get them hooked to the point where they'd pay whatever she asked.

After a couple of gigs, Candy got Bobby's graphic artist to design her a logo. Shauntae almost cried when she saw it. Candy's business card read TWO SISTAS IN THE KITCHEN and had two brown female stick figures with an arm around each other wearing chef's hats and aprons. Candy told her, "I know you gonna have to support yourself real soon, so we gon' make this bidness work."

Candy paid her well for all the gigs they did and they planned to sit down with Bobby to talk about how to make it a real partnership. Shauntae planned to work real hard and save everything she could so she could have a few weeks off after the baby was born. Then she'd bring him with her to Candy's and keep working hard.

She had seen Brianna every Saturday for the past three weeks. Last Saturday, Devon let her take Brianna out to lunch and to the movies. He said they could talk about her spending the night soon.

Dr. Murray kept talking to her and praying with her on every doctor's visit and after class. At her thirty-week visit, Dr. Murray asked her if she had heard from Gary.

"Not a word. I don't expect to. I have to start making plans to move out and find a way to get a lawyer. I can't lose my baby." The baby gave her a big kick right under her ribs and Shauntae smiled and rubbed her belly. "I don't know what I'm gonna do, but God is gonna take care of me."

Dr. Murray finished jotting a note. "I wanted to talk to you about that. My mother lives by herself not too far from here. My father passed away a year and a half ago and she's all by herself. I get over there as often as I can but I would feel a lot better if there was someone there more consistently. The house has a really cute basement apartment. Would you like to take a look at it and consider moving in? She also has a car that she can't really drive much anymore. You could use it and maybe take her out a few times a week."

Shauntae almost fell off the exam table. "Really? But I can't afford to pay her rent yet."

Dr. Murray shook her head. "No rent in exchange for you shopping and cooking for her and checking in on her twice a day. She's a diabetic though, so you'd have to make diabetic meals and maybe help keep track of her sugars."

Shauntae smiled. "I can do that."

Shauntae thanked God all the way home. He had her back and was really looking out for her. She had a place to stay and a way to earn money so she could take care of herself and her baby. She would have something to drive and she'd have somewhere nice to bring Brianna when Devon was ready for her to spend the night. God had worked things out for her and she was gonna make it.

When she got home, she sent Gary a text.

Doctor's visit went well today. The baby is growing well and everything looks fine. Thanks for letting me stay here but I've found my own place. It's nice so you don't have to worry about the baby. He'll be well taken care of. Thanks for everything you've done for me. Knowing you has changed everything about my life and I'm grateful. Sorry things didn't work out between us but I'm glad to be the person I am now and more than anything, I'm glad to know God. Hope you and the girls are okay.

She wanted to add "I miss you and I love you" at the end, but she knew it would probably make him mad.

Instead she put, Take care, and pushed send. She went straight upstairs and pulled her suitcases out to start packing. The sooner she got out of this big, lonely house that reminded her of everything she had done wrong, the better. Dr. Murray had talked to her mom and she was ready for Shauntae to move in as soon as possible. Shauntae figured she'd start taking things over in the morning.

She felt bad packing up all the stuff Gary had bought her. She wanted to leave it and the van and everything of his behind so he didn't think she had done everything she did to use him.

But she was pregnant and her maternity clothes were tight, so she surely couldn't wear her regular clothes. She'd either bring the clothes back after she had the baby or sell them and send him the money. She knew they had special shops that took pregnant women's clothes.

She had been in the closet packing and crying for almost an hour when she decided to take a break. She walked out into the bedroom and almost jumped out her skin. Gary was sitting on the bed.

She put her hand over her chest like she could slow her heart down. "You scared me."

"Sorry about that."

"What are you doing here? Oh, I guess you got my text. I guess I should have told you, I'm leaving tomorrow. If you don't mind, I'd like to stay here one more night. I can sleep in the guest room."

"You don't have to stay in the guest room."

"Oh. Okay. So you came to get more stuff?" His closet was only half empty. "You don't need to take anything else. I'll be out tomorrow."

"I came to talk." Shauntae noticed that the anger and hate she saw in Gary's eyes the last time he was there had disappeared.

"Oh. Okay." She stood there and waited.

"Can you sit down?"

Shauntae walked over to the couch in the sitting room.

"You can come over here. I promise I won't bite."

Shauntae slowly walked over to the bed and sat a safe distance from Gary.

"I've been thinking a lot since I left here. And praying. And talking to my men's pastor. I'm sorry for what I said when we last talked. That was harsh and mean and uncalled for."

"Gary, you don't have to apologize to me. After everything I did, you had every right to be mad at me."

Gary nodded. "Yeah, but still, you were right. I can't talk to you or treat you in any way that God wouldn't treat you or talk to. And like you said, He forgives you so . . . I forgive you too."

"Thank you. I appreciate that." Shauntae's eyes were already red and puffy from crying in the closet and she knew if he kept talking, she would start crying again. "I appreciate you apologizing to me."

They sat there quiet for a minute until he said, "Can I ask you a question?"

Shauntae nodded.

"Was any of that real? Did you ever really . . . love me?"

The tears started falling. "Gary, I ain't never loved anybody until I met you. You taught me everything I know about love. I loved you so bad it hurt."

Gary nodded.

Shauntae wiped the tears from her face. “I wish I had gotten saved and learned how to be a good person sooner so . . . Well, anyway. I’m sorry for everything.” Shauntae got up to walk back into the closet, but Gary grabbed her arm.

“Wait, I’m not finished.”

Shauntae sat back down on the bed.

“We both made a lot of mistakes and did everything wrong. I can’t lay all the blame on you. I didn’t take the time to get to know you and we rushed into things. I’m sorry too.”

“Thanks for saying that.” Shauntae was ready for this conversation to end. She wanted to sleep her last night in this house and then wake up and start her new life that was unfolding. She wished he would leave. He had apologized, so what else was there to talk about?

“Morgan told me you saw your daughter.”

Shauntae looked up at him. “She did?”

Gary nodded. “You’re all she talks about now. She’s very happy to have you back in her life. I didn’t tell Morgan it was you. She says now they both have to figure out what to call their first mommies and second mommies.”

“You didn’t tell Morgan that she doesn’t have a second mommy anymore?”

Gary shook his head. “I couldn’t tell her. You know everything they’ve been through the last year or so.”

“You’re going to have to tell her eventually. You might as well get it over with. I’m sure Daphne will be happy. Maybe you and Darla will make things work.”

“I couldn’t marry Darla again. I’m comfortable with the way things are and I’m glad we’re getting along because of the girls but . . .” He shook his head. “That season of my life is over.”

Shauntae was tired. "Well, thanks for apologizing. I need to finish packing up my stuff." She stood up and started toward the closet.

Gary grabbed her arm again. "Wait, I'm not finished."

Shauntae threw her arms up. "What is it? What do you want?" Didn't he know it was painful to be in this same room with him, knowing she might never experience love again like she had experienced here with him?

"Where are you going and what are you going to do?"

"Gary, I told you I'm staying someplace safe. The baby will be safe and well cared for. I'll call you when I go into labor and you can be there."

"But how will you take care of yourself?"

Funny how Gary's need to save a damsel in distress was once her ticket to the life she thought she wanted. Now it was getting on her nerves. She figured she'd help him rest his mind. Shauntae told him about Dr. Murray's mom's house and the car she'd have access to. She pulled one of her and Candy's business cards out of her wallet and told him about the business.

"Don't worry. I'm not going to be an irresponsible mother with this child like I was with Brianna. I've made plans to take care of him. And God is taking real good care of both of us. You don't have to worry."

"Wow. That's really good. I'm happy for you and your business partner. Proud of you. I know how much you love cooking so . . . it's good to do something you love."

Shauntae got up again to go to the closet. Gary grabbed her arm again. "Please wait. Please let me finish talking."

Shauntae looked up at the ceiling. "Gary, this is painful enough. What do you want?"

He let go of her wrist and clasped his hands together. "This is all so messy. Two divorces and three children. I never thought my life would look like this."

Shauntae understood that he was looking at his life and trying to figure everything out because she had been doing the same thing. She wished he would do that with his men's pastor instead of her.

"Do you think we should try to make this work?"

Shauntae frowned. Did he just say what she thought he said? "Make what work?"

"This marriage. I mean, I rushed into this so quick because I wanted to do things God's way. Getting a divorce isn't God's way, either. So I've been thinking—"

Shauntae interrupted him. "You know, I never thought I would say nothing like this. All my life, I wanted a man to marry me and take care of me. And you've done that. This was exactly what I always thought I wanted."

Shauntae let out a deep breath. "But that's not what I want anymore. I don't want to stay married because it's God's way or because you don't want another divorce or because you don't want to have children by different women all over the place. You asked me if I ever loved you and I should ask you the same. Did you ever love me? Because if you're real about it, you'd have to admit you only married me because I was pregnant and because it was the right thing to do. Because you love family and you didn't want to have a bunch of baby mamas and no wife. But like you said, we didn't take the time to get to know each other." She held up a hand to keep him from interrupting. "I know it was hard to get to know me when I was pretending to be something I wasn't but now, this is me. The real me. And you're talking about making it work because you don't want your life to be messy."

Shauntae rubbed her belly. "I've learned a lot about marriage and relationships and being a mom. We both know a marriage won't work because you're trying to do the right thing or because you want your life to look a certain way. If there's not real love, then it won't work."

Shauntae walked back into the closet. She started to pick up the one suitcase she had already packed to move it out of the way and then she heard Gary behind her. "Let me get that."

Gary took the suitcase out into the bedroom while Shauntae opened the second one to start putting her clothes in it. She heard Gary's voice behind her.

"You're right that I rushed into it for all the wrong reasons, but that doesn't mean I didn't love you. I did love you. Or I loved who I thought you were. The person you were pretending to be. I don't know who you really are."

Shauntae folded up a pair of maternity jeans. "That's because I'm figuring it out myself." She stood and pulled a bunch of clothes off the hangers and sat down on the floor beside her suitcase with them. "I've learned a lot about myself these last few months. And I'm learning more every day."

"What have you learned?" Gary pulled another bunch of clothes off the hangers and sat on the closet floor near Shauntae.

She smiled a little sad smile as she accepted the clothes he was folding and handing to her. "I've learned that I really love God and every day I realize more and more how much He really loves me."

Shauntae rubbed her stomach where the baby's foot was kicking her right by her belly button. "I've learned that there's nothing more special in life than being able to be somebody's mama. It's precious and important and a gift from God and I want every day to grow more and more into a better mom. I want my kids to grow up knowing they're loved and they're special."

Shauntae folded up the maternity suit she had gotten married in. She laid it in the suitcase and rubbed her hands over the silk fabric. Maybe she wouldn't sell that. Maybe she would keep it as a reminder of what love felt like. She looked up at Gary. "I learned about love. That love is the best feeling in the world. That I want to love for real and be loved for real. By my friends, by my kids, by God, and maybe, if God gives me another chance, maybe one day by a very special man."

Gary frowned, but kept folding clothes and handing them to her.

"I learned that I love to cook and that I'm really good at it. And that I can make money at it. I'm a partner in a business now. Shauntae Randall is a businesswoman. I can't hardly believe it. And soon, I'll be able to take care of myself. For the first time in my life, I'll be taking care of me and not depending on anybody else. I learned that that's a real good feeling."

Gary looked at her with a real proud look in his eyes. "You learned a lot."

Shauntae nodded. "I did. Thank you for that."

"You should thank God."

Shauntae smiled a sad smile. "I do. Every day." She tucked the last few things in the suitcase and zipped it closed. Gary lifted it and carried it into the bedroom.

"I'm sure I have a few things scattered around the house. I'll come back for them tomorrow after I empty these suitcases."

Gary was standing there staring at her.

"What?"

"Remember the last time we talked and you said, 'Sorry I couldn't be the woman you wanted me to be?' The more I thought about it, the more it bothered me. Because you weren't supposed to be trying to be the woman I wanted you to be. You were supposed to just be you."

"I know that now. My whole focus was 'becoming Mrs. Right' so you would marry me and take care of me and the baby."

"But listen to everything you said you learned. You started out pretending, but in the process you started finding out who you really are. You started just being you."

Shauntae scrunched her nose up, thinking about what he was saying. "Yeah. Now, I am being me."

Gary took one of Shauntae's hands in his. "And in just being you, you are becoming the woman I want."

Shauntae frowned. "What are you saying?"

"I'm saying we both got into this the wrong way and for all the wrong reasons. But what if God is turning the mess we made into something good? You said that you loved me and I said that I loved you and we're already married. I'm thinking, shouldn't we try to make this work?"

Shauntae walked over to the bed and sank down on it. She never imagined that the conversation would end up here. "I don't know. I . . ."

"You don't have to decide tonight. In fact, what if we do things right this time? What if we take the time to really talk and really got to know each other and really figure out if the love we were both feeling was real?"

"You mean like date, even though we're already married?"

Gary chuckled. "Yeah, I guess so. And we can take some relationship classes together at the church. Maybe we'll even back things up and take the premarital class. And we can do some counseling, too." Gary sat down on the bed next to her and took both of her hands in his. "I think we should at least try. I don't want to get a divorce and have to share custody of our child without at least trying to make it work."

Shauntae sat there thinking for a second. "Okay." Her hands were soaking up the familiar warmth of his hands. "I still think I should move out. It would be kinda weird living together trying to date and get to know each other. You know?"

Gary nodded. "Okay. I'll help you move tomorrow. And you can keep the van if you want to. Or not. Whatever you're comfortable with."

Shauntae put a hand on Gary's cheek. "Thanks, Gary. You're such a sweet man. Thanks for being so sweet to me all the time." Shauntae ran her hand across his face. "Thanks for everything you've done for me."

Gary closed his hand over hers. They sat there looking at each other for a second and then he said, "You should get some rest. I'll be back in the morning." Gary stood up to leave. "Since there's not much to move, maybe we can spend the afternoon together? Like our first date or something."

"I'm spending time with Brianna after I move. We have a special day planned tomorrow."

"Oh. Okay." Gary's face fell.

"How about brunch after church on Sunday?" Shauntae asked.

Gary smiled. "Ray's on the River?"

Shauntae nodded. "I'll call you and we'll meet in the lobby when service is over."

Gary kissed her cheek. "I'll see you then."

Forty-two

Shauntae stared down at her beautiful baby boy's face. He looked exactly like his father, which didn't seem fair. Brianna looked exactly like Devon. It was like she couldn't make a baby that looked like her.

It didn't matter, though. He was beautiful. And he was hers. She watched his little cheeks sucking on her breast and laughed. "Greedy boy. That's why you're getting so fat." She pinched one of his fat little legs and rubbed his belly. He reached up with his hand that wasn't clutching her breast and she slipped her finger into it. He closed his fingers around hers and held on tight. The feeling of him holding on to her made Shauntae feel happy inside.

She looked around the room at the pale blue walls in his nursery. The room was filled with everything a mother needed to take care of a newborn baby and was decorated with stuff fit for a prince.

Gary popped his head in the door. "You guys ready? Everybody's downstairs waiting."

"You know this little man eats first." Shauntae kissed Gary Jr.'s finger. "He should be done soon. Wait a minute so you can hold him while I change into something more comfortable." A few seconds later, the baby closed his eyes and slipped into his little milk coma. He acted like there were drugs in Shauntae's breast milk. He could barely finish eating and would be knocked out asleep.

Shauntae handed him to Gary. "Don't forget to burp him." She threw a cloth diaper over Gary's shoulder and walked down the hall to the master bedroom. She stepped into her closet and looked around at her clothes.

She had to smile thinking about that day almost five months ago when she sat on the floor of this very closet, packing all her clothes to move out. When she was crying and packing, she never thought she'd be moving back in again.

But she had. She and Gary had "dated" for the last two months of her pregnancy. They had done the premarital class at the church and had done marital counseling with Gary's men's pastor, Mark, and his wife. They went on dates several times a week and then, after a while, Shauntae came over to cook for Gary almost every day. Even though she'd had her own place, they spent most of their time together, falling in love—for real this time.

When she went into labor, they were actually out shopping for the baby. They went straight to the hospital and Gary Jr. was born not even two hours later. Gary insisted that she move back home after the baby was born and she'd been there ever since.

Shauntae slipped out of the fancy white dress she had worn to church that morning. Baby Gary had been christened on his three-month birthday. She put on her favorite comfortable but cute black knit dress, which was still a little snug. She wasn't sure if it was baby weight or weight that she had put on from eating so much of her cooking.

Gary came into the bedroom with the sleeping baby on his shoulder. "Come on, honey. Let's go down and eat. Everybody's waiting."

He followed her down the back stairs to the living room where their whole "family" was waiting for them. They were having a big dinner after the christening.

Candy and their new "Two Sistas in the Kitchen" employee were getting the food ready. Business had been good the last few months. Shauntae had worked right up until the week before she delivered, when Gary had insisted she stop. Candy brought Sylvia on to cover her until she came back to work, but things were going so well that they kept her.

As soon as Gary came downstairs with the baby, Daphne was there to take him and put him in his bassinet. In the last few months, things had gotten better between Shauntae and Daphne, especially after the baby was born. She was a devoted big sister and was a big help to Shauntae when she was there.

Morgan and Brianna were huddled in the corner, giggling and talking. When they found out they were "sisters," they couldn't believe it and became even more inseparable. They had sleepovers almost every weekend for the past few months. And when Devon and Cassandra went on their honeymoon a few weeks ago, Morgan and Brianna stayed at Gary and Shauntae's house for a whole week.

After Gary and Shauntae had decided that they were really going to make their marriage work, they had met with Devon and Cassandra for dinner. By that time, the weird awkwardness between Shauntae, Devon, and Cassandra was gone. By the time Gary entered the picture, the four of them got along real well. Not best friends or anything like that, but cool enough to hang out when their daughters were spending time together.

Shauntae had never thought there would be a day when Devon and Cassandra were in her and Gary's house, but there they were, getting ready to have dinner with everybody else. Darla was there, too, which was surprising because she was busy all the time. After she started back at her law firm, her old workaholic habits picked up again, which meant Daphne and Morgan were spending more time at Gary and Shauntae's house than only the weekends.

Gary's men's pastor, Mark, and his wife were also there to share in their special day. They had walked them through some difficult counseling sessions while they were putting things back together. They couldn't wait to preside over Gary and Shauntae's "official" church wedding that December.

The last guest was Shauntae's favorite—Mama Evelyn, Dr. Murray's mother. In the couple of months that Shauntae was living in her house, the older woman had become like a mother to her and treated her better than Shauntae's own mother ever had. Even though she wasn't living there anymore, Shauntae still went to see her almost every day and still prepared all her meals.

Mama Evelyn had told all her friends about Shauntae and Candy, and now half of their business came from a kind of "gourmet medical Meals On Wheels" program they had developed. They kept getting more and more referrals of older people with special dietary needs who they cooked for and delivered meals to. If that part of their catering business kept growing, Shauntae and Candy would have to hire a couple more employees soon.

"Okay, the food is ready. Everybody come to the table," Candy called out. The adults went into the dining room and the girls stayed at the breakfast table in the kitchen.

After everyone was seated around the huge dining table, Mark had them all join hands while he blessed the food.

After they finished praying, Gary stood to say a few words. "I want to thank all of you for coming to celebrate our dedicating Baby Gary back to God today. For me, I'm also celebrating my marriage and the beautiful wife God has blessed me with. I'm thankful for my daughters, my son, and all of you, our friends." He squeezed Shauntae's hand. "Baby, you want to say anything?"

Shauntae stood up. "I want to thank all of you for being here too." She looked around the table. "I know it might seem kinda strange for us to all be together with the history between some of us and the way everything has happened, but I'm really happy that we're all able to be together the way we are."

She looked at Gary, Devon, and Darla. "We all share four children who have our blood running through them, and I know it's the best blessing for them that we've all found a way to work together. This could be really difficult, but it's not, and I'm grateful for that."

She looked at Cassandra. "I appreciate you being a mother to Brianna when I couldn't, and then being willing to let me be a mother to her again when I could. I'm really happy for you and Devon and I'm glad we all get to share her."

She looked at Darla. "Thanks for sharing your beautiful daughters with me. Even after everything that's happened, you allow me to share being their mother with you. That's a real honor for me.

"Mama Evelyn, it hasn't been that long, but you've become such a sweet mama to me. Your love has healed so many places in my heart and has helped me to become an even better mama to all my kids." The older woman blew her a kiss.

Shauntae said to Candy, who had joined them at the table. "To my girl, Candy. Thanks for being such an amazing friend and for giving me the gift of cooking and letting me be a part of your business. You helped me discover some greatness inside of me and I'm so thankful.

"And to our dear pastors. Thanks for everything that you've walked us through and helped us to become. Me and Gary owe you big."

Shauntae squeezed Gary's hand. "And, finally, to my husband. Thanks for showing me what real love is. Your love completely changed my life. I'm the woman I am today because of your love and God's love. Thank you, baby." Shauntae leaned down to kiss Gary.

As they all ate and talked and laughed and the girls ran in and out of the kitchen and the baby cried and wanted to eat again, Shauntae felt like it was one of the best days ever. She was living a life she had never even dreamed of. She was becoming a successful businesswoman and her business was expanding daily. She had a "mother" who loved her like she was her own. She lived in a beautiful home with an amazing, loving husband. She had four beautiful children, and even though things weren't perfect and they weren't considered a normal family, they had made up their own, new normal and it was working just fine.

But most of all, she had a Father who loved her and who had brought into her life all the love she could ever want. She had forgotten to say it when she was thanking everybody at the dinner table, so while all the loud craziness was going on, she closed her eyes and turned her face upward and said, "Thanks, God. Thanks for my family and thanks for showing me real love."

The End

Readers' Group Questions

1. Shauntae, Sherice, and Candy made a "career" of hustling men. Discuss what led each of them to that choice. In spite of being a hustler, Shauntae seems to have a romantic streak. How does this affect her relationship with Gary?
2. Often, Shauntae can hear her mother's voice in her ear, telling her how stupid she is and berating her about choices she's making. Shauntae wonders who she would have been if she grew up in a house with a "good" mother and father. How much does our upbringing affect who we become?
3. After Shauntae realized she was in danger of going to jail because Darla was going to do a background check, she stayed at Gary's house rather than going to the bus station. Why do you think she stayed?
4. Why do you think Gary wanted to marry Shauntae? How did that affect their relationship initially? How did that affect their relationship after he found out the truth about Shauntae?
5. When Shauntae started to open her heart up to God, she said that she was talking to Him and it seemed like He was trying to talk to her. What are the different ways that God speaks to us? After Shauntae's prayers, she waited for an immediate answer from God. Discuss how God answers prayers.
6. The whole premise of the book is that Shauntae needed to figure out exactly what to do to "become Mrs. Right." What do you think about Sherice's and Mama's advice, Shauntae's studying movie

characters, and all she did to please Gary? What was the difference between her studying the movies at the beginning and her studying the YouTube videos at the end? By the end of the book, what became Shauntae's motivation for wanting to become Mrs. Right?

7. Gary told Shauntae throughout the whole book that there was nothing she could do that he wouldn't forgive. Why did he say this? How did his reaction to her telling him the truth correspond to him saying nothing was unforgivable?
8. Throughout the story, God kept sending Shauntae the message of His love for her and that nothing she could do was unforgivable. Shauntae had trouble believing it and kept wondering whether God could be that good. Why might non-Christians or even Christians have trouble receiving the message of God's love and grace?
9. Discuss the change in Shauntae's character over the course of the book. What motivated her change? What factors caused her to change the most? What were the greatest obstacles to her changing?
10. Even after finding out the truth about Shauntae, Gary takes her back. Why do you think he took her back? Was this a realistic ending?

UC HIS GLORY BOOK CLUB!

www.uchisglorybookclub.net

UC His Glory Book Club is the spirit-inspired brainchild of Joylynn Jossel, Author and Acquisitions Editor of Urban Christian, and Kendra Norman-Bellamy, Author for Urban Christian. This is an online book club that hosts authors of Urban Christian. We welcome as members all men and women who have a passion for reading Christian-based fiction.

UC His Glory Book Club pledges our commitment to provide support, positive feedback, encouragement, and a forum whereby members can openly discuss and review the literary works of Urban Christian authors.

There is no membership fee associated with UC His Glory Book Club; however, we do ask that you support the authors through purchasing, encouraging, providing book reviews, and of course, your prayers. We also ask that you respect our beliefs and follow the guidelines of the book club. We hope to receive your valuable input, opinions, and reviews that build up, rather than tear down our authors.

What We Believe:

—We believe that Jesus is the Christ, Son of the Living God

—We believe the Bible is the true, living Word of God

—We believe all Urban Christian authors should use their God-given writing abilities to honor God and share the message of the written word God has given to each of them uniquely.

—We believe in supporting Urban Christian authors in their literary endeavors by reading, purchasing and sharing their titles with our online community.

—We believe that in everything we do in our literary arena should be done in a manner that will lead to God being glorified and honored.

We look forward to the online fellowship with you. Please visit us often at www.uchisglorybookclub.net.

Many Blessing to You!

Shelia E. Lipsey,
President, UC His Glory Book Club

About the Author

Sherri L. Lewis authored her first book at the age of six. Her family considered her pencil and crayon on brightly colored construction paper creation a masterpiece. She continued to enjoy writing short stories and poems throughout her young adult life.

Her writing was put on hold while she attended Howard University as an undergraduate, then medical school at the University of Pennsylvania School of Medicine. The writing bug bit again a few years ago and pencil, crayon, and construction paper were replaced by laptop and printer.

After working almost fifteen years in the medical field, Sherri recently left her career as a family physician to pursue writing and ministry full time. In September of 2010, she founded the Bethel Cameroon School of Supernatural Ministry in West Africa. Thus far, she has graduated three classes of radical revivalists! Her ministry adventures include travel to Cameroon, Nigeria, Kenya, Honduras, Barbados, and Jamaica.

Sherri's life passion is to express the reality of the Kingdom of God through the arts including music, dance, film and television, and literature; and through sound biblical teaching. Her ministry thrusts include the message of the Kingdom, intimacy with God, intercessory prayer, understanding prophetic ministry, ministering emotional healing, and birthing individuals into their destiny.

Sherri lives between Buea, Cameroon and Atlanta, Georgia.

Notes

Notes

Notes